THE FIFTH AVENUE APARTMENT

PAMELA M. KELLEY

PIPING PLOVER PRESS, INC.

ACKNOWLEDGMENTS

A special thank you to real estate agent, Jennifer Lee, of Serhant, for answering my many questions about real estate sales in Manhattan. Thanks also to Anne Graber of Compass Real Estate for showing us around her open house and our dream apartment at 1025 Fifth Avenue. As always, thank you to my early readers, Taylor and Jane Barbagallo, Amy Petrowich, Cindy Tahse, and Laura Horah.

CHAPTER ONE

Sophie Lawton stepped off the train at Penn Station, followed the herd of people up the stairs, exited onto Seventh Avenue, and the magic of the city enveloped her. It was like this every time she made the trip in from Hudson, which was only two hours north of Manhattan. But it was a world away.

It was over two miles to her aunt's apartment on Fifth Avenue, but it was a beautiful, sunny day and Sophie enjoyed the walk. She soaked in the sights and sounds— the cars honking, people walking by in their suits looking important and in a hurry. The energy of the city always amazed her, it felt full of possibilities.

Sophie still dreamed of living in Manhattan—someday. It was impossibly expensive, and it would be many years before she could afford to live there— even with roommates. She'd visited college friends over the years that lived in Manhattan. They'd had high paying jobs and yet they were crammed into the smallest apartment with bedrooms that barely fit a bed.

None of them lived there anymore, though. They'd all married and settled down in the suburbs, Connecticut mostly. While Sophie was still in Hudson and as of two weeks ago, had moved home with her parents—an absolute last resort. But it couldn't be helped.

She smiled as she reached her aunt's address on Fifth Avenue. Aunt Penny was actually her great-aunt, and she lived in a beautiful building that was near the Metropolitan Museum of Art and overlooked Central Park. Sophie rang the bell and her aunt buzzed her in. She took the elevator to the fourth floor. There were only two apartments on the that floor and they were both massive by New York standards. By any standard, really.

Her aunt's door opened as Sophie reached it and Aunt Penny pulled her in for a hug. She always smelled of vanilla and cinnamon. Sophie was only five foot four, yet always felt like she towered over her tiny aunt who wasn't quite five feet. Aunt Penny had recently turned ninety-two. She looked impeccable, as always, with her snowy hair piled into an elegant bun. And she wore a baby blue sweater suit with a double string of creamy pearls.

"It's so good to see you, dear. Did you have a good trip in?"

"I did. No delays and it was a nice walk over."

Her aunt raised her eyebrows. "You should have taken a cab. That's a very long walk."

"I didn't mind at all," Sophie assured her.

"Well, we'll be taking a cab to the restaurant. Drop your bag in your room and we'll head out."

Sophie did as instructed. She always stayed in the same guest room. It was spacious and had a lovely view of the park. The apartment had four bedrooms, a huge living room, a library with a working fireplace, and a full-sized kitchen, which was unusual. Most Manhattan apartments had tiny galley kitchens. Until a few months ago, her uncle Joe had lived there too. They'd never had children, but somehow the apartment didn't feel so huge with the two of them there. They'd had visitors often, and Aunt Penny always loved to have friends and family stay with them.

A cab pulled up a few minutes after they stepped outside and as usual, they went to Alice's Tea Cup for afternoon tea. They'd been going there since Sophie was eight or nine and it was a special place, full of memories. They ordered their usual, the Mad Hatter, which was tea for two and included tiny sandwiches—they always chose the BLT and curried chicken salad. There were also delicious desserts, and the best scones in the world. Sophie measured all scones against the ones from Alice's Tea Cup —and no others came close. They had tea of course, and as usual, her aunt added a glass of prosecco for each of them.

"To your visit! I'm so happy I have you for a full week, my dear. You know you're always welcome to stay as long as you like." Aunt Penny lifted her glass of prosecco and Sophie did the same. They clinked glasses before taking a sip.

"Thank you. I'm thrilled to be here." It had been a long two weeks since Sophie had moved home. And her mother hadn't exactly approved of the trip into the city.

"Do you really think this is a good idea? You need to find a job, Sophie. How can you do that if you are gallivanting around Manhattan? I know you adore Aunt Penny, but you need to focus."

"It's just a week and I've been checking the job listings and mailing out resumes online. I can still do that from there. I haven't seen her in ages, and I think we both need this visit."

Sophie split a warm scone and spread a generous amount of clotted cream and strawberry jam over it before taking a bite.

"How is it going at home? Is Ethel behaving herself?" Aunt Penny smiled ever so slightly. She knew that Sophie's mother could be difficult.

"She didn't exactly approve of this trip," Sophie admitted. "But I assured her I can still job search from here."

"That's true. You young people can do anything with a computer these days. What kind of job are you hoping for? Do you want to work for another law firm?"

Sophie shuddered at the thought. "I don't think so. I've worked for four now, since graduating college and they're all the same. I don't mind the work itself, but they're all such stressful environments. Lawyers are not happy people and there's always at least one attorney that makes everyone miserable."

And Sophie didn't even mention the support staff—her colleagues—were often just as bad with cattiness and cutthroat behavior. It was exhausting. "I think I might just temp and try out some other industries."

Her aunt nodded. "That's a wonderful idea. You have strong office skills, and it might be fun to see where else you can apply them. Will you stay in Hudson?"

"For now, yes. I don't really have much of a choice. I

lost my job a week before I was due to re-sign my lease and the apartment complex required proof of employment. The move home is just temporary—until I can secure a new job and build up some savings." Sophie was tempted to take on a second job as well so she wouldn't have to spend as much time at home and could move out sooner.

"Well, I have a proposition for you, my dear. What if you just moved here? Now that my Joe is gone, I have more than enough room and I'd love the company." She coughed suddenly, a deep rumbly cough that made Sophie instantly worried.

"Aunt Penny are you okay?"

Her aunt waved her concern away. "It's nothing. Just a little tickle. It comes and goes. My allergies are awful this year. So, what do you think? I know I might not be the most exciting roommate, but maybe it's better than staying in Hudson with Ethel and Tom?" Her eyes twinkled and Sophie laughed out loud.

"That's an understatement. If you're serious I would actually love that."

"You don't have to decide today. Take the week and if you're still inclined to stay, head home and get your things."

Sophie smiled and took her aunt's hand and squeezed it gently. "There's nothing to think about. I would love to stay here with you."

CHAPTER TWO

After a wonderful, relaxing week with Aunt Penny, Sophie was even more sure of her decision to move into the Fifth Avenue apartment. Aunt Penny was easy company and aside from her pesky allergies, she was otherwise very healthy. And her mind was still razor sharp. Sophie was the forgetful one that locked herself out of the apartment one afternoon. Her aunt had laughed.

"Honey, you're just stressed. Once you're settled in here, I bet you'll feel much better, and you'll be able to focus and move forward."

Sophie certainly hoped so. Since being let go—even though it wasn't performance related—the firm was closing her office—she still felt down, especially after moving home. Her mother had a way of making Sophie doubt herself and her decisions.

Although she supposed her mother had a point—at almost thirty, Sophie really shouldn't have allowed herself to get into such a predicament. She should have had more money saved, been further ahead—and while she didn't say it—Sophie knew her mother was also disappointed that she wasn't married or engaged yet.

Sophie hadn't even come close to getting engaged, with anyone. She dated here and there but so far, her longest relationship had been just under a year and that was five years ago. David had been a great guy, but they both knew it wasn't going any further and both were relieved when Sophie suggested maybe they should move on. Her mother had been bitterly disappointed though. She'd been convinced David was the one—just because he'd stuck around the longest.

And Sophie had really tried to get ahead. It would have been easier if she'd had roommates, but she loved having her own place. She'd had roommates for the first few years after college, until she got a raise and saved up enough to get her own, small place. She worked as a legal assistant, often handling paralegal duties as well, but the paralegals had always made sure to point out that she wasn't one of them.

It had irked some of them, that the attorneys Sophie supported preferred for Sophie to handle some of the work that the paralegals would normally do. It created friction that the attorneys were unaware of, but that Sophie had to deal with on a regular basis.

Her mother had suggested that Sophie just get her paralegal certificate as she'd make more money that way.

"They don't necessarily make more than a top legal assistant," Sophie said. "And I don't want to be a paralegal. I like the mix of responsibilities that I handle now." She especially enjoyed interfacing with the clients—answering questions and keeping them updated with the details and progress of their cases.

Salaries for legal assistants and paralegals were not especially high in Hudson, so Sophie had to be careful with her spending. She'd made enough to cover the rent on a small one-bedroom apartment and had a little left over that she tried to save, but it seemed like every time she got ahead, there was always something unexpected that came up, usually car related. Her Honda Civic was reliable, but she'd bought it used and within two years it needed a new timing belt and then all-new tires. She'd bought the tires a week before she was laid off which had wiped out most of her meager savings. Ironically, she wouldn't even need the car when she moved in with Aunt Penny.

But she could sell it. During the week she was with her aunt, Sophie listed the car and all the contents of her self-storage unit—all the furniture she'd had in her small apartment. It didn't make sense to keep paying to store it. Eventually, if she needed to move again, she could just start over.

Her mother thought she was crazy to move to Manhattan.

"Have you really thought this through? You're only thirty. Do you really want to live with your 92-year-old great-aunt?" Sophie had to bite her tongue from responding that she'd much rather live with Aunt Penny than at home.

"It's a great opportunity for me to temp for a while and try out some different industries. There's so much work in

Manhattan and it pays a lot more. I'll be able to build up my savings."

"Hmm, well you do need to do that," her mother agreed. "It just doesn't seem very practical. Aunt Penny's not going to live forever. Then what will you do? You'll never be able to afford to stay in the city."

"I'll cross that bridge when I have to. Until then, I'm excited for this next adventure."

Sophie spent the week getting her car and storage items sold. What didn't sell she donated to a local thrift shop and what they didn't want, she tossed in the trash. She packed up the items she couldn't bear to part with—a few small paintings, some books that she had read more than once and some other odd items. She packed up most of her clothes in boxes, too, and shipped it all to her aunt's address.

So, when she said her goodbyes and set off for the train, she only had an overnight bag, her purse and laptop with her. And for the first time ever, Sophie had over ten thousand dollars in her checking account after selling her car and furniture. The financial stress she'd been feeling was finally gone.

For the next two weeks, Sophie still felt like she was on vacation, just visiting her aunt. Aunt Penny loved to go out to dinner several times a week and they went to all her favorite local restaurants. Sophie met with two temp agencies that had good ratings online and told them she was flexible and would consider anything administrative as long as it wasn't legal. She was open on the length of the assignment but preferred at least a week if possible.

"I'm really curious to see what it's like working in different types of companies and I think it would be hard to know if I'm only there for a day or two," she explained to Kara, one of the recruiters that she met with.

"That's fine, we'll focus on jobs that are for a week or two so you can try a bunch of places. Let us know what you are liking and not liking, and we'll keep it in mind as new things come in." She glanced through the computer at the new openings that had come in that day. This recruiting firm was much bigger than the one Sophie had gone to the day before. That one didn't have anything available but promised to call when something new came in.

"How soon could you start?" Kara asked. "We have something that just came in, and they ideally want someone to start tomorrow."

It was Thursday and Sophie hadn't thought she'd start that soon, but she had no plans.

"I can do that."

Kara smiled. "Excellent. Here's the address. Be there at eight thirty. Madison Financial Services. The dress is pretty conservative there, but you can't go wrong with basic blue or black. What you have on would be perfect, actually." Sophie was wearing navy pants, a crisp white shirt, a string of pearls and a matching blue blazer. It was part of her usual rotation at the law firm.

So, that was good. She didn't have to worry about buying new clothes. Though she was sick of all those stuffy outfits. And she hadn't gone shopping yet since she'd moved there.

She was dying to check out one of the many sample sales that popped up each week. She could treat herself to one new outfit now that she had a little money in the bank. And she was employed! Even if it was just temporary.

"This assignment is for just over a week. Next Friday will be your last day. We'll be in touch mid-week if something new comes in for the following week. Here's my card, call me with any questions. I'll send you an email with instructions on filling out your time sheet."

"Thank you." Sophie took the business card and stood to leave.

"Good luck, Sophie. Madison Financial is one of our best clients. This is a great first assignment for you."

When Sophie got home from the temp agency it was almost five, and Aunt Penny was sitting in her living room, in her favorite oversized armchair, with her feet on a matching ottoman and her enormous cat, Charlie, sprawled across her lap. Charlie was a tuxedo cat, black and white with a mischievous face. He looked up as Sophie walked into the room and as soon as he recognized her, he yawned and settled back down.

Aunt Penny smiled when she saw her. "Would you like a glass of wine? I was just thinking it's about that time."

"Sure, I'll pour us both a glass." Sophie returned a moment later, handed Aunt Penny a glass of chardonnay and settled in the matching chair next to her.

"So, how did you make out this afternoon?" Aunt Penny asked.

Sophie took a quick sip of wine. "Good." She told her about the assignment.

"And you start tomorrow? That's impressive." Her aunt looked deep in thought for a moment. "You know I think I read something about Madison Financial not too long ago. They were one of several companies profiled in an article about high-stress work environments. They are very successful though. After working at a law firm, maybe it won't seem so bad."

Sophie laughed. "That figures. Well, it's just for a week. I doubt it will be as stressful as the law firm, so I'm sure it will be fine."

"So, what do you want to do for supper? I was thinking we could have pizza delivered. There's a great place I think you'll like. They make the best eggplant, feta, and spinach pizza. How does that sound?" Aunt Penny asked.

"It sounds delicious."

CHAPTER THREE

Sophie didn't think it was possible, but Madison Financial was the most stressful environment she'd ever worked in. Her job was answering phones on the trading floor, in a huge open room where people were crowded together. They sat side by side at tiny desks and they literally screamed all day long as they worked.

They screamed when they made their trade and when they didn't get the price they wanted. The support staff looked terrified as traders barked orders at them and they scurried off to do their bidding. The only saving grace was that Sophie knew it was just for a week.

When Friday rolled around, she breathed a sigh of relief that it would be her last day. She hadn't yet heard from the agency, so by three that afternoon, she assumed that she'd have the following Monday off.

But at a quarter to five, her phone rang, and it was Kara from the agency.

"Sophie! We have a new assignment that I think you might love. They want someone to start Monday and be there for two weeks. It's an advertising agency, a fun, creative environment. People kill to work there. What do you think?"

"Sure, that sounds good." All Sophie knew about advertising was from the television show *Mad Men* and it made the world look glamorous and intriguing.

Kara gave her the address. "Oh, the dress there is a bit more creative. You're fine with the black and blue but if you want to mix it up, go for it. Really almost anything goes. Have fun."

The next afternoon, while her aunt was at her weekly hair appointment, Sophie checked out one of the sample sales on Fifth Avenue. It was in a big warehouse type space and the designers changed weekly. She wasn't familiar with the designer, but she grew excited as she looked around. The colors were really pretty with lots of sherbet tones—raspberry and blueberry, lemon and orange. She tried on a sleeveless raspberry-colored dress with a simple scoop neck. It was cocktail length and flattering on. With a sweater or cute jacket, it would work for the ad agency. Or if she ever had a date again, for a night out.

She ended up finding a cute pair of jeans too, and an aqua blazer that would look great with the jeans and a simple white t-shirt. She poked in a few other shops, including Barnes and Noble where she picked up a romantic comedy that caught her eye. On her way home, she stopped into Laduree on Madison Ave to get an assortment of her aunt's favorite macarons as a surprise.

When Sophie walked into the apartment, she was struck by the smell of something delicious. Her aunt rarely cooked but she was in the kitchen wearing a cute, frilly pink apron with her glasses perched on the edge of her nose as she read a recipe from a cookbook. Aunt Penny smiled when she saw Sophie and picked up a bottle of marsala wine. She poured a generous amount into the large saucepan that held a pile of sliced mushrooms and a melting knob of butter. Thinly-sliced chicken breasts sat on a plate next to the stove. They were glistening and golden and Sophie felt her stomach rumble looking at them.

"We're having company tonight, our next-door neighbor, Max. He's around your age, maybe a year or two older. I'm making chicken marsala, my company dish. It's been a while though, so I had to refresh my memory and look up the recipe."

"It smells wonderful. Can I help you do anything?" Sophie offered.

"You could fill that pot with water for the pasta. I thought we'd have it over linguine."

Sophie took the pot to the sink and filled it with water and set it back on the stove. Her aunt had already turned the heat on high. Sophie found the salt and added a few shakes to the water.

"Tell me about Max. I'm surprised he's free on a Saturday night," Sophie asked.

"I ran into him earlier today when I went to get the mail. He looked down and said that his plans fell through. His girlfriend is out of town, and he seemed lonely. He's a nice boy. It would be good for you two to know each other.

He has a key to the apartment, and I have one to his. Just in case one of us gets locked out."

Sophie laughed. "You mean like I did last week!"

"It happens to the best of us. Max has been living here for about two years. He bought his mother's apartment when she decided to spend most of her time in Florida. She comes back occasionally for long weekends and around the holidays. It's worked out well for both of them."

"What time is he coming?"

Aunt Penny glanced at the clock. "In about ten minutes. Looks like that water is ready for the pasta." Sophie added the linguine to the pot and took her bags to her room. She ran a brush through her hair and added a swipe of lipstick. She changed out of her casual sweats and pulled on her favorite jeans and a pink cotton sweater with a scoop neck. That would be fine for dinner with the neighbor.

When she returned to the kitchen to check on the pasta, Aunt Penny walked in at the same moment. She'd taken off her apron and looked lovely in a baby blue cashmere cardigan with her pearls.

"I'll get the pasta." Sophie drained it in the sink and put it back in the pot with a pat of butter that she stirred in so the pasta wouldn't stick and to give it a little richness. That was something Aunt Penny had taught her years ago. The chicken breasts were in the big sauté pan now, smothered with the mushrooms and marsala sauce.

"I'll pour the wine." Aunt Penny pulled a fresh bottle of chardonnay out of her wine cooler and opened it expertly. She poured a glass for herself and for Sophie. There was a knock at the door and Aunt Penny looked up.

"He's right on time. Can you let him in?"

Sophie opened the door and smiled at the man standing there holding a bottle of wine. He was average height, maybe five nine or five ten, with wavy brown hair, brown eyes and ridiculously long lashes. He had pale skin and a dusting of freckles across his nose. Very much a boy-next-door look, until he smiled, and dimples appeared on both sides of his mouth giving him a mischievous and intriguing look.

"You must be Sophie?" He held out his hand and Sophie shook it. His grip was firm, his hands slightly calloused.

"And you're Max?"

He nodded. "I think this is the kind of wine your aunt likes? If not, my mother said it's a good one."

Sophie glanced at the label. It was one she didn't recognize, Flowers. Her aunt's face lit up when she saw it, though. "How thoughtful, Max. This is my absolute favorite. I've just opened another bottle, would you like wine or I also have scotch and bourbon?"

"Wine's fine, thanks." Aunt Penny poured him a glass and then went to plate up their food. They ate in the dining room, which also overlooked the park. Aunt Penny had set the table earlier with a fresh white tablecloth. Two tall, tapered candles glowed softly and the sterling silver candlesticks shimmered. It was a cozy setting and as they ate, Sophie learned more about their neighbor.

"Max is dating someone very famous." Aunt Penny's eyes twinkled as Sophie noticed a faint blush spread across Max's cheeks.

"Oh? Who is that?" Sophie asked.

"Millie Moore!" Aunt Penny announced.

"The model?" Sophie recognized the name instantly. Millie Moore was not just a model, she was a super-model. She was British, impossibly thin and tall of course. She had stick straight, long dark brown hair that was almost black, dark brown eyes, and pouty lips. And she had the kind of figure that made men stop in their tracks—a natural, full chest. The kind that smaller chested women like Sophie envied. Millie was maybe twenty-one or twenty-two, if that. Quite a bit younger than Max.

"Yes, the model. They just celebrated a year together recently," Aunt Penny confirmed.

"How did you meet?" Sophie was curious how a seem-ingly average guy like Max would meet and date a supermodel.

"We met on a photo shoot actually for *Vogue* magazine, a little over a year ago. It was one of their rising stars in the arts issues," Max said.

"Max's an author," Aunt Penny explained.

"Oh? What do you write?" Sophie wondered if she'd read any of his books.

"I write mysteries, my most well known is the Andrew Willard series," Max said.

Sophie's jaw dropped. "You're Max Bennett? I've read that whole series. It's one of my favorites." The series featured a small-town sheriff in a sleepy New England town that had more than the usual share of mysterious murders.

"That's me. Your aunt is a bigger fan of my other books, though." He grinned and Aunt Penny laughed.

"Max also writes romantic comedies under the name Sally Benson."

That shocked Sophie even more. She'd read all of those books too. Sally put out a book every May and it was always one of the big summer books. Sophie knew that he usually put out two Max Bennett books a year, and like many of his readers, Sophie often wished he could write faster.

"It has to stay a secret, though," Max said. "I don't think my mystery readers, many of whom are men, would be too keen about me writing romances."

"So that's why the different name?" Sophie asked. She supposed it made sense.

"My publisher insisted. Something about keeping each brand strong. It's a marketing thing I guess."

"Does Millie travel a lot?" Sophie imagined she must. She wondered how often they actually got to see each other.

He nodded. "She does. She shares an apartment in Manhattan with a few other girls who are also models. They're hardly ever there at the same time because they're all traveling. She's in Spain this week but she'll be back in town end of next week and will be around for a few weeks before she heads out again."

"So, do you just write from home?" Sophie asked. She thought it must be a great job, one you could do from just about anywhere.

"Sometimes. I do better in a coffee shop though. There are a few that I rotate between, depending on how busy they are. I try to write a little when I first get up, and then after lunch, I usually head to a coffee shop for the afternoon. It gets me out of the house and breaks the day up a little."

"Is it hard to concentrate with people talking all around you?" Sophie asked.

"No. It's like white noise. I just tune it out and it sounds like a background hum. If the conversations are interesting, I might eavesdrop for a bit." He grinned. "Sometimes I get good story ideas that way."

"That sounds fun. You probably get asked this a lot, but where do you get your ideas? I'm completely uncreative and totally impressed that anyone can create a story like that."

Max grinned. "That's the number one question that people ask me. I don't know where they come from. They just come...sometimes when I read something in the paper or watch the news on TV or while I'm trying to write a different book. That's often when another idea tries to get my attention. And in the shower or on a drive. Something about being relaxed and thinking about nothing at all seems to attract the best ideas."

"That's so interesting." Maybe because she didn't have a creative bone in her body, Sophie found it fascinating to hear about Max's writing process.

"What do you do?" Max asked.

"I'm sort of in transition. I worked as a legal assistant and decided I want to try a new industry, so I'm doing some temping."

"That's a great idea. Have you liked anything yet?"

Sophie laughed and told him about her experience on the trading floor.

"That sounds rough. Those traders make a lot of money, though."

"Money isn't everything," Aunt Penny said. "I think liking what you do is far more important."

"Oh, I agree, totally. I feel very lucky that I get to make a living doing something I love," Max said.

"Next week I'm going to an advertising agency," Sophie said. "That should be a more creative environment, I think."

"It should be. Might still be a bit stressful though. I have a friend that worked at an ad agency for a few years. The hours were intense. He didn't have to be there until ten, but he worked most nights until ten or eleven. He couldn't take it after a while."

Aunt Penny shook her head. "That's too much. What is he doing now?"

"He's doing marketing for a tech startup with a few friends. They still work long hours sometimes but it's because they want to. They love it."

"The nice thing about the temping is that there's an end date, no longer than two weeks at each assignment," Sophie said.

"That's good. Maybe you'll land at a place you love and want to go permanent. That happened to a friend. He started out temping in the mail room at a financial company and they liked him. Now ten years later he's a senior VP and has a really cushy job. I don't know what he does, something in sales, but it seems like he gets paid to play golf with clients."

Sophie smiled. "Do you golf?"

"Yes, but poorly. Do you?"

"No. Maybe one day I'll try it."

"Oh you should!" Aunt Penny said. "I used to love to golf when I was younger. There are women's leagues and it's a great way to meet people. I met some of my closest friends through playing golf at our country club."

"Where was your country club?" How was it possible that Sophie didn't know that her aunt played golf?

"In the Hamptons of course."

"Oh, okay, that makes sense. You never golfed when we visited, so I didn't know." Every summer growing up, Sophie's parents had taken a two-week-long vacation to the Hamptons to stay at Aunt Penny's summer house there. It was a roomy Cape style house on the beach. Sophie hadn't been there in the past five years though. Aunt Penny hadn't mentioned it at all.

"Do you still have the Hamptons house?"

Aunt Penny nodded. "Of course I do. I'll never sell that house. I don't get there like I used to, but I rent it out now and it's booked solid all summer long. It's a good investment. I still keep one week free for myself though, usually in September when the crowds die down, but the weather is still nice."

The Hamptons were beautiful and in the heat of the summer in the city, many people didn't mind the three hour or so drive to get there. But Sophie understood that her aunt didn't have the energy to make the trip that often anymore.

"This chicken was delicious. Maybe you'll share the recipe so I can impress Millie and try to cook for her." Max took his last bite and leaned back in his chair.

Aunt Penny looked pleased by the compliment. "I'll

take a picture of the recipe and send it to you. It's not difficult. And she will love it."

When they finished eating, Sophie brought their plates into the kitchen and put some of the macarons she'd bought earlier onto a platter and set them down on the table.

"Would either of you like coffee or more wine?" she offered.

"I'd like more wine. Let's open the bottle Max brought for us. I bet it will go well with the macarons," Aunt Penny said.

Sophie opened the wine and filled Aunt Penny's and Max's glasses which were both empty. She took the last sip of her own and then filled it too and sat back down.

"Have either of you seen *Only Murders in the Building?*" Aunt Penny asked. "I saw a preview the other day and it looks good. Maybe we can watch an episode or two?"

"I've heard of it, but haven't seen it yet," Sophie said.

"That's the Steve Martin one, right? I haven't seen it either. Let's watch it." Max stood and they took their wine and moved into the living room. Aunt Penny settled in her favorite armchair, while Max and Sophie sat on the adjacent matching sofa. Charlie sauntered over a moment later and hopped into Aunt Penny's lap.

Aunt Penny found the show and they watched two episodes, stopping after the first one to top off their wine glasses and have a macaron or two. They'd all been too full when Sophie first set them out. And they all agreed that the show was a good one.

"Maybe I'll swing by another night this week and we can watch a few more episodes," Max suggested. "I'm not much of a cook as I mentioned earlier but I can order a good pizza."

"Excellent! We'd love that, wouldn't we, Sophie?"

Sophie smiled. "Yes, definitely. That sounds fun. It was so great to meet you, Max."

His eyes were warm as he returned her smile. "You too. Thanks again Miss Penny for a delicious dinner."

"Goodnight, Max. We'll see you soon," Aunt Penny said.

She closed the door behind him and turned to Sophie, "Well, that went well, didn't it? What do you think of Max?"

"He seems really nice. It's amazing that he's dating Millie Moore and it's already been a year."

Aunt Penny frowned. "A year too long, if you ask me."

"I take it you're not a fan. Have you met her?"

"Once, in the hallway. She's a beautiful girl, but they don't spend enough time together. Maybe that's okay with you young people, but I wouldn't like it. I think he needs a nice, normal girl that is around more."

Aunt Penny glanced Sophie's way and her intentions were clear. She wanted to play matchmaker.

"Aunt Penny, Max dates a super model. I'm pretty sure that I am not his type."

"Hmmm. Well, I'm off to bed my dear. See you in the morning."

CHAPTER FOUR

At first, Sophie thought that the ad agency was a much calmer environment. When she arrived at eight thirty almost no one was there. Brooke, the office manager, buzzed her into the office and showed her to the front desk reception area where she would be spending the next two weeks.

"Everyone has direct dial or uses their cell phones, so most of the calls you will get will be from potential new clients." She demonstrated how the phone console worked and then told Sophie to holler if she ran into any issues. "My office is right around the corner. You can also message me through the internal system." She showed Sophie how to do that, and then headed back to her office.

Sophie got herself a coffee—the kitchen was just down the hallway and she ran down and back. But it was very quiet. The phone didn't even ring until after nine. That's when employees started streaming in. Many didn't arrive until after ten, which Sophie thought was interesting. She was steadily busy by then, between the occasional phone call and with people coming in for meetings. The lobby was full most of the day with people waiting.

Sophie watched the flow of traffic go by her desk—to meeting rooms, the big conference room, back and forth all day. She took a lunch break at noon and was relieved by another admin for an hour. And she took advantage of the time to step out of the office. She grabbed a chicken salad sandwich at a nearby shop and sat on a stool by the window. She watched people walking along the street as she ate her sandwich.

The environment was less stressful than the trading floor but after lunch, the energy level increased along with the call volume and number of people walking through the door. And the overall vibe was very different. The ad agency was more colorful and the people were more diverse—she saw several walk by with pink or turquoise hair, piercings, tattoos and attire was all over the map. The creatives, the art people, were the most casual while the account executives were dressed more conservatively.

There were several visitors that afternoon that looked more like they belonged at the financial company Sophie had just left. They introduced themselves as being from Northern Capital Asset Management and when she called back to Andrew, the account executive that was meeting with them, he and two others, all in similar conservative suits, came into the lobby to welcome them. They walked back to the conference room and a moment later Brooke walked over.

"That is a super important meeting. They are a potentially huge new client. They are visiting our agency and a few others before deciding who to go with. Hold all calls for Andrew and don't let anyone else head to the conference room. They have it booked for the next few hours."

In her down time, between calls and visitors, Sophie glanced at some of the marketing material that was sitting in a binder on the front desk. It was a portfolio of some of their recent client work. She flipped through the pages, at their creative ads for soap, laxatives, insurance and mutual funds. It was hard to make any of those things sound exciting, but the ads tried, proclaiming the products were the best ever. She wondered if they worked with any fun clients, with products that would be interesting to create ads for?

When Brooke stopped by at the end of her shift, to let her know she could go ahead and leave for the day, Sophie asked what kind of clients the agency worked with.

Brooke made a face. "Nothing super exciting I'm afraid. We don't get the fashion brands or hot technology products here. Our focus is on consumer goods and financial as that is where the demand is."

"What time do most people leave?" Sophie asked, thinking of the many who didn't arrive until around ten.

Brooke laughed. "It's all over the map. But a lot of people come in later and quite often they work really late, depending on if they are preparing for a pitch. The workload is pretty intense. But we turn the main phones over to voicemail after five and most visitors come in before that. So, when you come in tomorrow, the first thing you'll do is listen to the general mailbox for any after-hours messages. See you tomorrow!"

Sophie's next two weeks were uneventful. Working at the ad agency was better than the trading floor, but she wasn't sorry when her time there was up. She had a new assignment booked for the next week, another receptionist role at one of the hottest real estate firms in the city, Fulton Real Estate. She looked them up online and their website was impressive. They focused on residential real estate sales in Manhattan and their average listing was over two million dollars. Sophie had always been mildly interested in real estate—she loved watching the television shows where they showed property renovations, and how they could transform a house—so she was curious to experience what it might be like to work in a real estate office.

CHAPTER FIVE

The offices for Fulton Real Estate were impressive. The building itself was four stories high and sat on a corner in one of the best areas of Soho. The ceilings were high and there were floor-length windows that let in tons of light. The walls were bright white with lots of colorful artwork and sculptures scattered throughout the reception area.

Sophie's job for the next three weeks was to fill in at the front desk.

"Our regular girl, Mollie, is out on maternity leave. You're the fifth or maybe the sixth person that has covered, so far. No one has lasted more than two weeks," Andrea, the office manager explained. Andrea had a sleek auburn ponytail and wore an elegant black dress. She was a few years older than Sophie—and she looked like a sophisticated New Yorker.

Sophie immediately felt concern at the thought of so much turnover. And Andrea seemed to immediately regret over-sharing. "It's really not a bad job at all," she said hastily. "Mollie has worked here for several years. It can be fast-paced at times, but nothing out of the ordinary, I don't think."

Sophie hoped not. She'd been hesitant to take on a three-week assignment, but Kara had assured her that it was a beautiful office and she was sure that Sophie would like it.

Andrea showed her how the phones worked and the office intranet so Sophie could easily reach people either by phone or email if they were out of the office.

"Here at Fulton, we are all about luxury. Rick wants everyone that comes through these doors to have the Fulton experience," Andrea explained. "Most of the homes that we represent are over five million, and many are well over ten or twenty million. People expect a different level of service when they are able to spend that much on a property."

She showed Sophie where the Nespresso machine was and the refrigerator that had chilled bottles of imported sparkling water. "Offer all visitors a beverage while they wait," Andrea instructed.

"Oh, and every Monday morning, you'll type up notes from the sales meetings. They're all in the conference room now. Rick always records the meetings, and they quickly go over everything new and pending. Do you know how to transcribe from dictation?"

Sophie nodded. "Yes, I did that at the law firm regularly."

Andrea looked pleased to hear it. "Good! That will give you a leg up on the others. I think the dictation was an issue for some of them. If time permits, we'll have other projects for you as well."

"Great. I'm happy to help however possible." Sophie liked keeping busy. If the phones weren't busy or there wasn't a lot of foot traffic coming through the door, she didn't want to just sit around waiting for something to do.

"The phones probably won't be too hectic as all the agents have direct lines or cell phones. But we do get a fair amount of people responding to ads or just calling in from internet searches and you'll round robin those calls. Here's a list of all the agents, just start at the top. When everyone is in the office, put the person on hold for a moment and check to make sure the agent is free to take the call, then put it through."

"What if they can't take the call?" Sophie asked.

Andrea laughed. "Oh, they almost always will as it could mean a sale for them. But if they are tied up on another call, they will tell you and then just go to the next person in line. Once everyone heads out of the office, those calls will go to the agent on duty for the day."

Once Andrea had walked her through everything, she headed back to her office which was right around the corner. "If you get stuck, just give me a holler," she said.

The reception area was quiet except for some soft jazz playing in the background. Sophie pulled up the office listings and browsed through them. She was impressed by the number of high-end properties and the prices. No wonder the rents in the city were so high—the prices to buy were astronomical. There were some beautiful homes though. And besides the high prices, many also had five figure monthly charges for maintenance or common charges.

Fifteen minutes later, she heard a flurry of activity—voices and footsteps coming down the hall. A tall, striking man with light blond hair was flanked on either side by two attractive women about Sophie's age. One had short caramel brown hair and the other had long blonde wavy hair. The man looked to be in his late thirties. They all stopped at the front desk and the man raised his eyebrow and held out his hand.

"Rick Fulton, you must be our new temp?"

"Yes, Sophie Lawton." She shook his hand. His grip was strong.

"Sophie, these are two of my top agents." He glanced at the blonde woman first, "This is Tessa and Caroline."

Caroline smiled big and held out her hand while Tessa appraised her coolly. "Welcome!" Caroline said.

Tessa finally nodded. "Nice to meet you."

"We're heading out to see a property. We'll be back in an hour or so. If anyone calls, please take a message. I have my phone forwarded to the front desk. If it's something urgent, just text me and I'll call them back," Rick said. He then fished a small recorder out of his pocket and handed it to Sophie. "Here's the recording for this morning's meeting. If you could type it up and email it to me, that would be great."

"Will do," Sophie said as the phone rang. She reached to answer it and watched the three of them walk off.

When they returned an hour later, Rick stopped at the front desk and Sophie handed him a stack of messages. Most of the calls while they'd been out had been for Rick. There were a few ad calls too, which she sent back to the on-duty agent. She'd also typed up the notes from the morning meeting. She had to stop and rewind it a few times because she got so caught up in listening. She found it very interesting to hear about the new listings and deals that were pending. The morning went by quickly and before she knew it Andrea came to the front desk. "Time for your lunch break. See you back here at one."

Sophie hadn't even given lunch a thought when she'd left that morning. She headed out and found a Pret a Manger sandwich shop a block away. She got herself a cup of soup and a crusty roll with butter and sat by the window and people-watched as she ate.

She kept an eye on the time and headed back to the office a few minutes early. Andrea stood as soon as Sophie walked through the door.

"It's all yours. I'm right down the hall if you need anything." Andrea headed off to her office and Sophie settled back at the front desk.

The rest of the day flew by, and it was a nice mix of calls and people coming in. When her shift was over and she was shutting down for the day, she noticed the two agents she'd met earlier heading toward the front desk. She guessed they were done for the day as well, but they stopped for a moment to chat.

"How did your first day go?" Caroline asked with a friendly smile. Sophie liked her right away.

"It was good. You have some really beautiful listings. I looked them over in between calls," Sophie said.

Tessa narrowed her eyes a bit. "Are you looking to be a realtor?"

The question took Sophie by surprise. "Not at all. I'm really not sure what I want to do, that's why I'm temping."

Tessa nodded. "That's fine. We've just had a lot of turnover in this role recently. And as far as I know, we're not looking to hire more agents. We have plenty."

"Well, so far, it's more interesting than the last few places I've temped at," Sophie said with a smile.

"Good! Hopefully you'll like it here. It's really a great company," Caroline said.

"Don't get too comfortable though. Mollie is coming back soon," Tessa said. She was a beautiful girl, but so prickly. Sophie wondered what she was like with her clients. Based on what she'd seen so far, she'd much rather work with Caroline than grumpy Tessa.

"Right. Andrea said she's on maternity leave," Sophie said.

"There's always a chance she might not come back," Caroline said. "Sometimes people don't once the baby comes."

"I'm sure Mollie will be back. She loves it here," Tessa said.

Sophie wasn't quite sure how to take Tessa. She wasn't welcoming at all.

"Well, I'm glad you like it so far. We'll see you tomorrow, Sophie," Caroline said.

By the end of her first week, Sophie decided that she really liked the real estate industry. So far, of the temp assignments she'd had, this was her favorite. It was busy but not too crazy and there was enough downtime for her to work on interesting projects like the weekly meeting notes and pulling together new listing brochures. The agents entered all the information and Sophie pulled it into a template with photographs and the graphics program created an elegant online brochure they could email or print out.

Just in the week she'd been there, she'd already learned what some of the more popular areas of the city were and which features of the homes were most popular. She'd also chatted with some of the buyers that came into the office.

"Rick will be out in just a minute. He's just finishing up a call," she told the stylish woman that had arrived a few minutes early to see him. "Would you like one of our fluffy coffees or a sparkling water?" she offered.

The woman, who Sophie guessed was close to her own age, looked amused. "What is a fluffy coffee?"

Sophie smiled. "It's just what I call them. The Nespresso machine makes a foam on top that is just coffee. It's addicting."

"Sure, I'll try one."

Sophie returned a few minutes later with the coffee. The woman took a sip and nodded. "This is really good. So, has anything exciting come in this week?"

Sophie thought for a moment. "Quite a few new things actually. Where are you looking?"

"Well, I told Rick I wanted to be on the Upper East Side but I had lunch yesterday in Soho and I really like the vibe here. So, I guess I'm open to different areas."

"Oh, we just got a really stunning new listing in yesterday. It's a penthouse in Soho. Three bedrooms and a gorgeous kitchen. It also has a pretty den that could be an office or a library. It's elegant but cozy, too." Sophie realized as she raved on about it that she didn't know what price range the woman was looking at and this unit was one of their higher end listings, at just over ten million.

"It sounds lovely. I'll definitely ask Rick about it."

"What will you ask Rick about?" He'd walked up to the front desk and was all smiles.

"Sophie was just telling me about a fabulous new listing you have. A penthouse in Soho. I'd love to learn more about it."

Rick looked surprised. "Of course. I didn't realize you were open to Soho. It just came in and it's a beauty. Let's head back to my office."

They disappeared and Sophie turned her attention to her ringing phone.

Twenty minutes later, Rick and the woman headed out and Rick told Sophie to take messages while he was gone. He returned ninety minutes later and was smiling as he walked in the door.

"Sophie, great job today. My client loved that Soho apartment and put an offer in. I'm pretty sure that it will be accepted." He looked at her curiously. "How did you know to mention the Soho listing? She hadn't been looking in that area."

Sophie smiled. "She asked what was new and mentioned she'd had lunch in Soho recently and loved the feel of the area. I remembered seeing that listing and thinking it was so amazing, and that it seemed like a fit for her. Of course, I didn't know her budget, so maybe I shouldn't have said anything?"

Rick laughed. "No, definitely say something. That woman can buy whatever she wants, and she loved that property. Keep up the good work!"

Kara called later that day to check in and see how Sophie was liking the assignment.

"I love it. It's my favorite so far."

Kara laughed. "Good. I had a feeling you'd like it. When this one ends, I'll keep an eye out for other assignments with real estate firms. They come up fairly regularly."

"Great." Sophie's first week had flown by, and she was looking forward to the next two weeks. It was nice to finally have a job that she liked for a change.

CHAPTER SIX

S ophie enjoyed her second week at Fulton even more than her first. She felt comfortable in the role now, and she was fascinated with what she was learning about real estate. She looked forward to typing up the weekly notes from the sales meeting and felt like she was there as she listened to the agents talk about new listings and sales and various issues they ran into. It was all interesting and she felt like a sponge, absorbing it all.

One night over dinner at her aunt's favorite Italian restaurant, Sophie told her about a new listing that had come into the office that day.

"It's not far from here, a few blocks down, and the building is just gorgeous. The asking price is twelve million, which Rick thinks might be pushing it a little, but it is Fifth Avenue, so he thinks it is possible."

Aunt Penny smiled. "People do fall in love with Fifth Avenue. I know I did, so many years ago."

"This apartment is almost as nice as yours. Not quite but close. It only has three bedrooms and the kitchen is smaller, but it has lovely views of the park and some beautiful custom molding throughout."

"It sounds lovely," Aunt Penny said. She looked thoughtful for a moment before saying, "Have you ever thought of going into real estate sales?"

The question surprised Sophie. "No, never. I don't think I'm the type for sales." When Sophie thought about salespeople she pictured high energy types like Rick or assertive ones like Tessa.

"You're passionate about it and knowledgeable. That enthusiasm is contagious, and it could translate to success with sales. Might be worth considering."

"Hmmm." Sophie wasn't convinced. Real estate sales and working on all commission seemed a bit terrifying to her. How could you plan and pay your bills when your income was so uncertain?

Aunt Penny coughed suddenly a deep faint rumbling that she couldn't seem to shake.

"How are you feeling? Maybe you should see your doctor? That cough has been lingering."

But Aunt Penny shook her head. "It's nothing but a tickle. I'm fine. Would you like a little more wine?" She held the bottle of chianti over Sophie's glass, and she nodded. "Yes, please."

Friday afternoon a little before five, Tessa and Caroline walked up to the reception desk. Sophie assumed they were probably just saying goodbye before heading out for the weekend, but Tessa surprised her.

"We're going for a drink at Champers, do you want to join us?"

Sophie knew the shock of the invitation must have been evident on her face because both Tessa and Caroline laughed. "We would have invited you out sooner, but we wanted to make sure you were going to stick around first," Tessa added.

"Come out with us," Caroline urged. "It's Friday night and we deserve a cocktail."

Sophie laughed. She had no plans. "Sure, I'm just about done here." She turned the phones onto voicemail and shut down her computer. Then she grabbed her purse and they headed out.

Tessa led the way into Champers Social Club, a boutique restaurant that specialized in champagne cocktails. Sophie had never been there before and was impressed as she looked around. It was a beautiful space, small and cozy, decorated in soft pinks and greens with whimsical pale pink chandeliers. The tiny bar had maybe a half dozen or so seats and a framed photo of Sophia Loren above the wine glasses. It was already busy with people stopping in for after-work cocktails. Tessa went straight to the bar and claimed the three seats that had just opened up.

"What do you want?" Tessa asked. "I'm getting the Blackberry and Thyme spritz."

"That sounds good. I'll have that too," Sophie said.

"I'll have the Champagne Shirley," Caroline said. "It's like a grownup Shirley Temple, with champagne," she explained to Sophie.

When the bartender delivered their drinks, Caroline

held hers up and they toasted to the end of the work week. "Cheers!" she said.

Sophie took a sip of her drink. It was bubbly and fragrant, slightly sweet and delicious.

"I'm starving, let's get some snacks," Tessa said. They decided to order pigs in a blanket, hot artichoke dip and a raw vegetable platter. Everything was delicious. As they sat at the bar, Sophie watched the crowd swell as people seemed to pour into the restaurant.

"We got here just in time," Caroline said happily as she dipped a chip into the bubbling dish of artichokes and melted cheese.

A short while later, Sophie was surprised by a familiar voice behind her.

"Hey there! Nice to see you out, Sophie." She looked up to see Max and his supermodel girlfriend, Millie, standing next to them. They were sipping glasses of champagne. Max introduced Sophie, "This is the very cool neighbor I was telling you about. She and her aunt have me over for TV night."

Millie nodded and smiled ever-so-slightly. "Nice to meet you."

Sophie quickly introduced Tessa and Caroline to them. "We work together at Fulton Real Estate.

Max smiled. "Ah so you're going to be a real estate mogul now then?"

Sophie laughed. "I'm answering the phones."

He grinned. "Everyone has to start somewhere." The buzzer in his hand started to flash and vibrate. "Looks like our table is ready. Enjoy your night, ladies."

As soon as Max and Millie were out of earshot, Tessa

turned to Sophie. "Max Bennett is your neighbor? Where do you live?"

Sophie hesitated. "I'm staying with my aunt. She has an apartment on Fifth Avenue."

Tessa and Caroline both looked impressed. "Must be nice," Tessa said. "I'm sharing an apartment with two other girls in Murray Hill, and it's hideously small and ridiculously expensive."

"Same here," Caroline added. "Our lease is up in a little over a month and we're hearing from other residents that the landlord is hiking rents up by an obscene amount. I may need to look for a new place."

"My lease is up soon too, and I'm not sure what I want to do either," Tessa said. "I love being in the city, but the rents are ridiculous."

"How long have you both worked at Fulton?" Sophie asked.

"We started within a week of each other, almost two years ago. It was my first job in real estate. I think Caroline had more experience," Tessa said.

"I did. I worked for my family's real estate office in upstate New York. It was a good way to learn how to sell. I knew I wanted to be in the city though."

"Do you love it?" Sophie asked. "My aunt actually suggested that I consider it, but the thought of sales and working on commission is a little intimidating."

Tessa and Caroline both nodded. "I can't imagine doing anything else," Tessa said. "Sky is the limit on what we make, and I like being in control of that. The harder I work, the better I do. Though it was slow at first for me and it can be a little nerve-racking at times when all your sure thing deals fall through. That's why I still have roommates. I'm building up my savings."

"That happens more often than we'd like," Caroline added. "Deals fall apart at the last minute for all kinds of reasons—they don't get financing, the appraisal doesn't come in high enough, the seller decides not to sell or the co-op board says no. Nothing is a done deal until it actually closes. But I agree with Tessa. I love it, too."

"You make it sound appealing," Sophie said. "I don't think I'm in a financial position to afford to do it, though. I need a guaranteed salary."

Tessa and Caroline exchanged glances. "If you need that, then real estate sales definitely isn't for you," Tessa said.

"You know we do rentals, too," Caroline said. "Those move faster. The money's not as high but it's where I focused when I started out. And when I felt more comfortable, I shifted more energy to straight sales."

"It's still 100% commission, though," Tessa said.

"True."

Sophie smiled. "I'll just cheer you two on. I'm enjoying the front desk for now and it's just for one more week. I'll be on to something new after that." She hoped that Kara might have more assignments with other real estate firms. It would be interesting to see the difference between offices.

CHAPTER SEVEN

"So, Mollie is definitely coming back on Monday," Andrea said. It was Friday afternoon a little before five and Sophie's last day at Fulton. She wouldn't be going out tonight as both Tessa and Caroline had other plans. But they'd gone for drinks the night before and exchanged numbers and promised to keep in touch. Sophie hoped that she'd see the girls again once she left Fulton, as she had no other friends in the city. But realistically, she wasn't counting on it. She knew it was easy to go for drinks with people when they worked in the same office. Once she left, she suspected she'd be out of sight and out of mind. But maybe they would surprise her.

She was happy though that Kara had already lined up her next assignment and it was at another real estate firm, Broadview Partners. It would be another receptionist role, so she was looking forward to it.

"You did a great job for us. We'd love to request you again if we need any coverage. If you are still temping, that is," Andrea said.

"Oh, I'd love that. I should still be available."

Over dinner that night, Aunt Penny delivered some shocking news. They were at a tiny French restaurant, and they'd had a lovely dinner so far. They were on dessert, sharing a big slice of baked Alaska, when Aunt Penny coughed again. The familiar rumbling that always made Sophie nervous.

"So, it's not a big deal, but I probably should let you know that I have a bit of cancer," Aunt Penny said lightly, as if she was commenting on the weather.

"Cancer?!" Sophie was horrified.

Aunt Penny nodded. "I've had a few skin cancers taken off my nose over the years. One of them went deeper and traveled to my neck. It gets in the way at times and that's what causes my coughing."

Sophie frowned. "What will they do for it?" It sounded like it might be treatable.

"Nothing. I'm ninety-two. I'm not up for any of that chemo or radiation nonsense. I'm not in any pain. It's just occasionally uncomfortable. I wouldn't have said anything at all, but I didn't want you to be shocked if I don't get up one day."

Sophie opened her mouth to speak, but no words came. Aunt Penny reached out and grabbed hold of her hand and squeezed it. "Please don't be alarmed, my dear. I have had a wonderful and long life. I intend to enjoy every remaining day that I have. I might have another year or it might be a few weeks or a month." She smiled peacefully. "I'm fine with whatever it is. I'll be seeing my Joe soon."

"Are you sure you're not in any pain?" Sophie asked.

Aunt Penny gave her hand a gentle squeeze. "I'm really not, except for this slightly annoying cough. I feel fine. A bit more tired than usual, but that's okay. This isn't going to happen immediately. I just thought you should know. Please keep it to yourself though. It's no one else's business and I don't want people to fuss."

Sophie knew she mean Sophie's parents, especially her mother, who would have a million questions and probably try to talk Aunt Penny into treatment, which Sophie knew would make her miserable. Sophie didn't blame her. She would probably feel the same if she was her aunt's age and was feeling fine.

"Let's go home and watch some TV, shall we?" Aunt Penny said brightly.

Sophie nodded. "I'd love that."

Max joined them the following Thursday for pizza and a session of watching *Only Murders in the Building*. A new season had just dropped, and they were excited to watch.

"Are you still at that real estate firm? It looked like you were having fun with the girls from the office," Max said as he reached for a slice of pepperoni pizza.

"No, I finished that assignment last week. I started a new one this week, at another real estate firm."

"Does that mean you've found an industry you like?" he asked.

Sophie nodded. "I think so. This office has a different vibe. The agents are older and it's a bit stuffier, but they're nice and the work itself is interesting. I'm learning a lot about the real estate market."

"How is your latest book coming along?" Aunt Penny asked him.

Max frowned. "It's not at the moment. I'm at that awful stage, about a third of the way in where I have no idea what to do with these people and am convinced it's my worst book yet."

Aunt Penny looked sympathetic. "You do know that's not true, though?"

He smiled at her and laughed a little. "I know that now, yes. It happens with every book. I know I just have to keep plugging along."

"That sounds hard," Sophie said. "You're such a talented writer. Do you enjoy it while you are doing it?"

"Oh, I love it. It's just this middle stretch that isn't as fun. Once I get through it, then it's like skiing downhill and I'm all excited again and type as fast as I can to keep up with my thoughts. It's a real rush at that point." Sophie could see how much he loved it. She envied him a little that he got to do what he truly loved for a living.

Later that night before they headed to bed, Aunt Penny was in a contemplative mood. She sipped her chamomile tea and smiled at Sophie.

"It's been really lovely having you here dear. Thanks for keeping an old woman company."

"I've loved being here, Aunt Penny. And you've never seemed like an old woman to me," Sophie assured her.

"You make me feel young again. I think you're close to

finding your passion. Don't be afraid to make the jump and really go for it. Follow your heart, in business, and in life. It goes by too quickly, and you don't want to have any regrets."

It was good advice and Sophie knew it. "I will, I promise. I think I want to explore the real estate industry more. I'm just not sure what my role should be."

"You'll figure it out. I have no doubt. I'm off to bed now, I think."

"Good night. Sleep well."

Aunt Penny smiled again. "I always do."

Aunt Penny was still sleeping when Sophie left the next morning. It wasn't unusual. Her aunt often slept in until nine or so, and Sophie left a little after seven to make sure she was at the office by eight.

Her day went by quickly. Her role was similar to the role at Fulton, answering phones and greeting visitors and helping on various computer projects, mostly for marketing material. Sophie loved pulling the listing materials together, seeing the photographs and the agent notes about the properties. This assignment was only for a week, covering for a vacation and today would be her last day. She didn't have an assignment lined up yet for next week. She expected Kara would call that afternoon with something.

And she did, at four thirty. "Sophie, I have something new to run by you. It's not real estate. It's on the trading floor of a financial services company. Very busy, what do you think?"

Sophie laughed. "I think I'll pass on that one. No more trading floors for me. Too chaotic."

"No problem. I'll be in touch early next week with more ideas. Have a great weekend."

When Sophie finished for the day, she set off to walk home and stopped off for a box of macarons to surprise her aunt. They were her favorite treat and Sophie loved them too.

She stepped into the apartment and was struck by an eerie quiet. There was no sign of her aunt. Maybe she was out or possibly napping. Sophie noticed that her aunt's purse was on the kitchen counter, where she'd left it when she went to bed the night before. So, she wasn't out.

Sophie walked to her aunt's bedroom. The door was ajar. She peeked in and her aunt was in bed with the covers pulled up to her chin. Her cat, Charlie, was curled up next to her. That was odd. Usually if Aunt Penny laid down for an afternoon nap, she never got under the covers. She just laid on the bed itself with a throw blanket over her.

"Aunt Penny, are you not feeling well?" Sophie called softly. There was no response. She opened the door and walked over to her aunt and as soon as she saw her face, Sophie gasped. Her aunt looked at first glance as if she was peacefully sleeping but her mouth was ajar and her skin was slack. Sophie reached out and touched her forehead and it was oddly cool. She picked up her hand and frantically felt for a pulse but couldn't find one.

She dialed 911 immediately and they said they'd come right out. She paced the apartment in a shocked daze until the EMTs arrived. She let them in and led them to her aunt's bedroom.

"I think she might be gone. I just got home from work and found her here. I couldn't find a pulse..." her voice broke as she spoke, and her throat felt thick with unshed tears.

The EMTs checked Aunt Penny over and confirmed that there was no pulse. "I'm very sorry. We can call the funeral home for you. Do you know who your aunt wanted to use?"

Sophie took a deep breath. "I don't know. But she has a folder with important papers. I can check that to see if she has it listed." The first night Sophie had arrived, her aunt had casually mentioned that she had a folder with emergency information in case something ever happened. Sophie had brushed it off as she didn't want to think about anything bad happening. But now it made sense why her aunt had told her that when she did. She knew that she didn't have much time left.

Sophie found the folder on her aunt's roll-top desk and opened it. The first page had the necessary information. *In the event of my death, please contact Bartlett Funeral Home. All arrangements have been made and paid for. You just need to call them.*

Her aunt had thought of everything. She brought the paper to the EMTs and the lead guy nodded and dialed the number. When he ended the call, he handed the paper back to Sophie.

"They will be out shortly. I'm so sorry for your loss."

They left and Sophie was alone in the apartment. Her aunt was there but she was gone, and Sophie felt utterly alone and sadder than she'd ever felt. She walked around the apartment, looking out the windows as the tears fell and turned into full body-heaving sobs. She curled up on her aunt's favorite armchair and pulled her cozy fleece throw over her. It smelled faintly of her aunt—the familiar scent of cinnamon and vanilla. She already missed her.

Her aunt had such a lively spirit. Sophie had thought she'd be around for several more years at least. And when Aunt Penny told her about the cancer she seemed so unworried that Sophie was sure she had more time. But in retrospect, she understood that her aunt knew the time was closer. And she probably waited as long as she could before saying something. Sophie knew that Aunt Penny had enjoyed their time together, too.

A short while later, two black-suited men came from the funeral home. They were polite and respectful as they told her how sorry they were for her loss and assured her that Aunt Penny would be in good hands. Before they took her, one of them assured Sophie that everything was taken care of.

"Your aunt planned everything, every small detail. It will be a lovely service. If you'd like to call us later today or tomorrow, whenever you are ready, we can discuss the details and choose dates for the wake and service."

Sophie felt a wave of panic. She couldn't do this, she wasn't ready. One of the men smiled kindly. "Why don't you call us tomorrow? When you're feeling more settled. This is a difficult time."

Sophie nodded. "Thank you. I'll do that." After they left, she collapsed on the sofa and the tears fell again. She felt a presence behind her and saw that her aunt's cat,

Charlie, had jumped up onto the back of the sofa and was peering down at her. He let out a mournful cry and she realized he was hurting too. She reached over and petted him, and he settled in beside her on the sofa and she was grateful for his warm presence. "We'll get through this, Charlie." She took a deep breath as the tears came again. She wiped them away and closed her eyes and eventually drifted off to sleep.

CHAPTER EIGHT

W hen Sophie woke the next day, she wondered for a moment if she'd dreamed it all and Aunt Penny would be in the kitchen sipping her rich black coffee and reading the paper. But when she got up and walked to the kitchen, there was nothing but an eerie silence in the apartment. Still half-asleep she peeked into her aunt's bedroom hoping to see her sleeping peacefully. But of course she wasn't there. The bed was still unmade and the image of her aunt's slack face came to her. Sophie pushed it away and went and made the bed quickly. Her aunt always made her bed first thing.

She called the funeral home as soon as they opened a little after nine and spoke to the funeral director. They discussed possible dates and for her to call once she'd talked with her mother and decided what they wanted to do and they'd take care of putting the notices in the papers. Sophie hadn't even thought of that. She realized they needed to write an obituary too.

Sophie spent the morning wandering her aunt's apartment in a state of disbelief. She knew on one level that Aunt Penny was gone, but it just didn't seem real that her bright light had been extinguished. She already missed her terribly. She called her mother, once she gathered the energy to make the call. As expected, her mother was full of questions. Sophie answered them all as best she could.

She spent the rest of the morning working on the obituary and once she was reasonably happy with it, she called her mother and read it to her. Her mother had a few suggestions and Sophie tweaked it and then submitted it to the local papers. They had no idea what to expect for numbers at the wake or service the next day. But Sophie knew that her aunt was well known and had been active in several organizations. She'd been very interested in history and was a member of a historical society and she'd volunteered at an art museum and sat on the board of several other museums. She'd always loved the arts.

"So, you'll be coming home then?" her mother said. "We'll get the apartment on the market. It should sell quickly," her mother said.

Fresh tears fell at the thought of leaving and of her aunt's beloved apartment being sold to strangers. Sophie knew it was what made the most sense though. Her aunt had no doubt left the apartment to Sophie's mother as she had no other family. The thought of moving home was utterly depressing. Maybe there was a way she could stay in the city. She'd saved a little money, enough possibly to rent a room with a few other girls. She wasn't keen on the idea of living with strangers in a tiny apartment. But if it meant staying in the city, it might be worth it.

"I need to stay here for now, at least until after the wake and funeral. I told the funeral people I'd call them as soon as possible to sort out the details."

Her mother agreed that was a good idea since they'd have to come into the city anyway. And Sophie knew her mother was glad for Sophie to take care of it, so she didn't have to. They discussed dates for the wake and funeral. And Sophie told her mother that Aunt Penny had already organized most of it and paid for everything.

"That was a wonderful thing to do," her mother said with appreciation. "It's so hard to know what people would want, and no one really wants to have that conversation."

"That's true. I never wanted to think of Aunt Penny not being here. I miss her so much already," she said.

"Well, she was ninety-two. She had a good run," her mother said. She didn't seem nearly as upset as Sophie was.

"That's what Aunt Penny said too. She had a good run." Sophie's voice broke again as the tears came fast and furious. She'd thought she was all cried out. But evidently not.

Her mother's tone softened. "She loved you dearly. And she really had a long and very happy life. And I'm sure she loved having you stay with her these past few weeks," her mother assured her.

"Thanks. I'm glad I was able to spend the time with her."

They ended the call with her mother saying that she and her father would plan to be in the city by the following Wednesday for a wake that night and funeral service on Thursday.

"We'll have to meet with her attorney, too. For a

reading of her will. I can call and set that up," her mother said.

"Perfect." Sophie was happy to have her mother do that. The thought of her aunt's will was just depressing. It made it all that more official that she was gone.

Sophie ate nothing all day and around five, she decided to wander down to the mailbox and collect her aunt's mail. Maybe she'd order some Chinese food delivered. Or she could just heat up some soup if there was any in the cupboard. She sighed miserably as she walked down the hall. She checked the mail, collecting a stack of catalogs and a few bills and headed up the stairs to her aunt's apartment.

She passed Max along the way, and he stopped short when he saw her face.

"What's wrong?"

Sophie's eyes welled up again and she looked away. It was hard to talk, to say it again. Max put a hand on her shoulder and spoke gently, "Is it your aunt?"

Sophie nodded, unable to say the words. But Max understood. "Is she gone?"

Sophie nodded again and the tears fell. Max pulled her in for a tight hug. "I'm so sorry, Soph. She was a marvelous lady, as you know. I will miss her."

Sophie hiccupped. "Thank you!"

"Do you have any plans tonight? I could come over and keep you company. We could watch TV and toast your aunt."

Sophie loved that idea. She wasn't quite ready to be alone again all night in her aunt's apartment. She'd been dreading it all day. But she also felt bad. It was a Saturday night after all.

"I'd love the company, but don't you have more exciting plans? You should be on a date with your girlfriend," she said.

He grinned. "She's out of the country and I was just planning on a quiet night. How about Chinese? I can pick it up and come around seven if that works?"

"That would be great. Really great. Thank you."

Max knocked on her door at seven sharp, holding a huge bag of Chinese food. "I wasn't sure what to get so I got a little of everything."

Sophie laughed when she saw all the food. He really did get everything it seemed. There were several appetizers, steak teriyaki, chicken fingers, and egg rolls. Spicy chicken lo mein, garlic shrimp with broccoli and house fried rice. She got plates for them both and opened a bottle of Aunt Penny's favorite prosecco. They spread all the food on the coffee table in the living room and settled on the sofa.

Max raised his glass of prosecco and toasted Aunt Penny. "I think she's watching over us now. She'd want us to celebrate her life, not be overly sad. She's with her Joe now."

Sophie nodded. It was hard not to be sad, but Max was right. "I just wish I'd had more time with her," she said.

Max smiled sadly. "It was quality time though. Your aunt went on her own terms."

"She did. She only just told me she was sick less than a week ago. I think she knew it was close. And you're right. She's with Uncle Joe now."

She sipped her prosecco, and they dove into the Chinese food. While they ate, they shared memories of her aunt. Max had known her for several years and long before Sophie had arrived, they'd had the occasional movie night.

"She was a great lady. She really lived life to the fullest," he said in admiration.

"She did. And she was so encouraging." Sophie thought about their conversation the night before. "Aunt Penny told me to follow my passion. To explore real estate if that's what I loved."

Max nodded. "That sounds like good advice. What's next for you?"

Sophie frowned. "I'm not sure. I might have to move home for a while. But it will only be until I find a new place. I didn't think I wanted to live with a bunch of girls in a tiny apartment, but I'd rather do that than live in Hudson. Now that I've been in the city for a few months, I want to stay. Even if it means a bunch of roommates."

"I think you should stay. Who cares if you have a bunch of roommates? It's just a place to sleep." He grinned. "Once you become a real estate mogul, you'll be able to get a better place, a penthouse even!"

Sophie laughed. And was surprised that it was even possible to laugh, given how sad she was. But Max was helping to cheer her up. "I'd settle for a studio of my own," she said.

"You can do it," Max encouraged her.

They stayed up until midnight. Around ten, Sophie opened the box of macarons that she'd bought earlier for her aunt. She handed the box to Max. "They were her favorite. I bought them on my way home from work to surprise her." She felt the sadness sweep over her again as she sat back on the sofa.

Max took one and handed the box to her. "She'd want us to enjoy these." Sophie took a raspberry-filled macaron and popped it in her mouth. She felt the tears threaten to fall again. But a moment later, Max made her laugh and she forgot to cry and reached for another macaron instead.

Finally at a little after midnight, when Sophie had yawned several times, Max stood. "I should probably let you get to bed. Are you okay?" he asked gently.

She nodded gratefully. She was exhausted and ready for bed. "I am, thanks to you. Thanks for keeping me company."

Max pulled her in for a tight hug. His arms wrapped around her and made her instantly relax and feel safe. "It was good for both of us. I miss her too." He pulled back and looked her in the eye. "If you need anything, I'm right down the hall."

"Thanks, Max." She walked him to the door and once he'd gone, she put the half-eaten box of macarons in the kitchen, poured herself a glass of water and headed to bed. Charlie followed her and hopped up on the bed, settling by her feet. As soon as her head hit the pillow, she drifted off to sleep.

.   .   .

Sophie spent the rest of the weekend keeping as busy as possible and was mostly out of the apartment. It was too sad to be there for hours on end by herself. She took her laptop and went to a local coffee shop once she'd showered and changed. While she sipped a coffee and ate a blueberry muffin, she combed the online listings of roommates wanted.

There were quite a few available. Most were three or four to an apartment. Her share of the monthly rent would still be higher than Sophie had paid in Hudson for her own place, but that wasn't a surprise. The temp agency kept her steadily busy and when she crunched the numbers, she could just barely afford to rent one of these places. She hated the idea of roommates that were complete strangers, but she thought of what Max had said —how it was a place to sleep and it kept her in the city. Maybe it wouldn't be too bad.

She emailed several of them to express interest and also looked at the job listings. The only real estate openings she saw were for sales and they were all commission only opportunities. But they all promised unlimited earning potential. But Sophie knew it was risky. Especially now where she'd have to make monthly rent payments, she couldn't take that kind of risk. She needed the security of steady temp work.

She went to a movie that afternoon and she took herself out to dinner at a local restaurant she'd been curious about trying. She sat at the bar and people-watched while she sipped a glass of wine and waited for her order of shrimp scampi to arrive. She chatted with an older couple that sat next to her and they'd recommended the scampi.

When she finally made it home to her aunt's apartment, it was after eight. She watched TV for a while and went to bed early. She did the same thing on Monday, and while she was at the coffee shop, she heard back from two of the places she'd contacted about roommate openings. She made arrangements to visit both the next day. She went to a different restaurant for dinner. She hated to spend the money but she hadn't spent much since she'd been in the city and she just couldn't stay home alone in her aunt's apartment for too long. The hours stretched ahead of her, long and lonely and it helped to get out.

Later that afternoon, Kara called with a new assignment to run by her and Sophie filled her in on what had happened.

"I'm not sure on my timing. I'm looking into new places to stay but it might be a few weeks before I'm available again." They left it that Sophie would call once she was settled.

Tuesday night, she visited two apartments and met with the girls in both. They seemed nice at both places and Sophie told both she was interested. She knew they were talking to lots of others. The apartments were similar, both were three bedrooms and the bedrooms were tiny, barely fitting more than a bed and a chest of drawers. There was also a galley kitchen and a small common area. The ages of the girls ranged from mid-twenties to early-thirties. The thought of moving into one of these apartments was a little depressing and intimidating but also kind of exciting. Sophie realized her emotions were all over the place at the moment. She knew she wanted to stay in the city though. So, if that meant a tiny bedroom and strange roommates, she would do it.

She applied to several more listings that day as one of the girls had told her they were talking to twelve people about the open room. So, she knew she needed to keep applying until she got an offer from one of them.

CHAPTER NINE

Sophie's parents arrived shortly after noon on Wednesday. Her mother swept into her aunt's apartment with her dad following behind quietly. Her mother walked around, looking at all the rooms, pausing only when she stepped into her aunt's bedroom. She shook her head then and Sophie thought she saw a damp sheen across her mother's eyes. But a moment later, it was gone.

"We'll take the back bedroom," her mother announced and her father brought their bags into the room.

Sophie followed her mother's gaze as she walked to the big bay window that looked out over Central Park. "I forgot how lovely this view is." Sophie knew it had been years since her parents had visited the city.

"We can get it listed before we head home," her mother said. "We'll do it after we meet with the attorney on Friday. Maybe he can refer us to a realtor."

Sophie nodded. She found the thought of selling her aunt's apartment horribly depressing.

They held two wakes that day, one from two to four and then again from six to eight. Sophie was amazed at how many people came to pay their respects. Her mother seemed surprised as well. "I didn't expect this, given her age."

Tony and Richard, the owners of her aunt's favorite Italian restaurant were among the first to come, just after two, and sadness was etched on their faces as they spoke to Sophie and her parents.

"Penny was an incredible woman. We've known her for over forty years now. She will be deeply missed."

All the neighbors came. Max had spread the word and he and his mother came together. "Mom flew up from Florida. She loved your aunt," he said.

And there were so many more—people from the museums her aunt had loved so much and been involved with. The lines were long for both sessions. By the time the wake ended a little after eight, Sophie and her parents were exhausted. And starving.

They went to the little Italian restaurant around the corner that her aunt had loved so much. Sophie hadn't wanted to go there by herself, but with her parents it felt appropriate and honored her aunt.

"I'm still in shock that so many came. I didn't realize your aunt knew so many people," her mother said.

"She had a full life here and was involved in the community," Sophie said.

"I'm glad she didn't suffer too much. I didn't realize she had cancer," her mother said.

"I didn't either. She didn't want people to fuss."

Her mother smiled. "That sounds like her."

The funeral the next day was a blur. Sophie always dreaded funerals. She didn't find anything reassuring about them. They were just sad. Overwhelmingly sad. And it was a dark, drizzly day which suited her mood. After the service the burial was held in Brooklyn at the Green-Wood Cemetery. As far as cemeteries go, it was a beautiful spot, but Sophie was glad when it was over and they were on their way to Tony's and Richard's restaurant for the mercy meal.

About thirty came for the after-service meal and they were all her aunt's closest friends. The wine flowed and there were trays of pasta and chicken parmesan, her aunt's favorite dishes. As sad as it was, the mood brightened at the restaurant as her aunt's friends shared their favorite stories about Aunt Penny and how she'd touched their lives.

"I worked with your aunt for many years at the museum. She was so knowledgeable about art and had a child-like wonder at the beauty of it all that was contagious." Linda, a woman in her sixties remembered Aunt Penny fondly.

Sophie enjoyed hearing their stories and by the time everyone left, some of her sadness had lifted too. She knew that Aunt Penny would want them to celebrate her life and to just remember the good times they'd shared.

. . .

They had a quiet evening in the apartment and woke early the next day to meet with Aunt Penny's attorney at nine. Sophie had been dreading the meeting. It was all so depressing. She just wanted to get it over with. She had a few more visits lined up for the next day and had told her parents she'd be home that weekend. She wasn't looking forward to that at all, but her mother wanted to get the apartment listed as soon as possible and said it was best if it was vacant to make it easy to show.

Thomas Windsor, Aunt Penny's attorney, was in his late sixties and had a small but respectable office just a few blocks from the apartment, so they walked over. He led them into his conference room which had soft leather chairs around an oval table with a fireplace in the corner. It was a cozy room. The attorney waited until they were settled and then sat at the head of the table and opened a thick binder.

"First of all, please accept my condolences." He had been at the wake and funeral but still offered them again. "Your aunt was a remarkable woman and a delight to work with. She will be missed." He picked up a piece of paper and glanced around the table.

"As you are aware, she has two main properties, the Fifth Avenue apartment and the Hamptons Estate. She wishes to leave the Hamptons estate to her niece Ethel." He nodded at Sophie's mother who smiled. This was as expected. "She just has one stipulation with the Hamptons Home. She will not allow it to be sold until a year has passed." He looked around the table. "She wants you to use the property before you sell. I think maybe she's hoping you won't want to sell, but after that year has passed, you are free to do whatever you wish with it."

Her mother nodded. "Does she have the same restriction on the Fifth Avenue apartment?"

The lawyer hesitated for a moment. "She does not. But she did indicate that she would like if it wasn't sold immediately but there's no requirement to wait."

"Good, we'll want to put that one on the market immediately. Perhaps you can recommend a realtor?"

Thomas cleared his throat and looked a bit uncomfortable for a moment. "Well, that's actually up to Sophie. Penny has left that property to her, to do whatever she wishes with it. She hopes that she might decide to stay. She has also left Sophie her bank account which has funds to cover the monthly maintenance charges for the apartment for about a year."

Sophie's mother's mouth fell open. "She left it to Sophie? Just to Sophie?"

Thomas nodded. "She was very clear with her wishes. And she made this change several years ago. She knew how much Sophie loved living in the city. And it was her hope that she might want to continue doing so. But she doesn't have to."

"Well, of course she'll want to put it on the market. That's too much money to give up," her mother said. She was clearly put out that Aunt Penny had left the apartment to Sophie. Sophie felt a little uncomfortable with it as well as she'd known her mother was counting on it. But she was also secretly thrilled, too. And her mother had the Hamptons estate which she would no doubt sell as soon as possible. And that was worth just as much as the Fifth Avenue apartment.

"Actually, I don't want to sell. I will be staying in the apartment," Sophie said.

Her mother looked at her in shock. "That's not very practical," she said shortly.

The lawyer smiled slightly. "Your aunt would be very happy to hear that."

CHAPTER TEN

"I still can't believe she left this apartment to you. What was she thinking?" Sophie's mother muttered as they returned to the apartment. Her father had been quiet for the most part but even he was growing frustrated with her mother's complaints.

"Ethel, Penny knew Sophie loved it here and she's always wanted to live in the city. Now she can. And it's not like she left us nothing. The Hamptons estate is quite a property."

"Yes, but we can't do anything with it for a full year," her mother sniffed.

"We can go there and enjoy it. The property will only continue to appreciate in value. We might find that we want to keep it. We could always rent it out for a few weeks each summer. That would likely pay most of the expenses and taxes for the year."

"I don't know about that." Her mother didn't sound keen on the idea of keeping it.

"And Sophie can enjoy it too. It might be nice to get out

of the city now and then when it gets hot in the summer," her father suggested.

"I'd love to do that. I haven't been there in years," Sophie agreed.

"I haven't been there in ages, either," her mother said.

"See, it will be nice. The whole family can enjoy it and then we'll see what we want to do," her father said.

"Yes, well, we should get on the road so we can get home before dark," her mother said. Their bags were all packed and all they had to do was wheel them out of the apartment and get a cab to the train station. Sophie hugged her parents goodbye and walked them out to the street. Once they were in a cab and on their way, she turned to look back at her aunt's apartment which was now hers. It seemed completely surreal.

She went back inside and walked around the apartment, taking everything in with new eyes. She still couldn't believe that Aunt Penny had left it all to her. Sophie had never dreamed she would do that. She'd assumed it would all go to her mother and would be up for sale immediately. It was both a relief and bittersweet that she didn't have to leave—that this apartment was now her home. Charlie walked over and rubbed against her legs, and she reached down to pet him. She'd now inherited her cat, too, and was glad for his company.

When Sophie reached her aunt's bedroom, tears threatened to come again. She closed the door to the room. Eventually, she might make some changes, or at least change the sheets. But for now, she didn't want to touch anything. There were three other bedrooms, she didn't need to worry about using Aunt Penny's room any time soon.

She went to the kitchen and made herself a cup of cinnamon tea and settled at the island with her laptop. She checked her email. She'd heard back from a few more apartments she'd applied to with invitations to go and meet her potential roommates. So far, there had been no offers. She was grateful to Aunt Penny and relieved that she didn't have to deal with living with complete strangers.

It did seem a little strange to have this huge place all to herself, though. It felt vast and empty and without Aunt Penny's sweet energy, it felt lonely, too. But Sophie told herself she'd get used to it soon enough. After all, Aunt Penny hadn't minded living her by herself.

She needed to keep busy though. She looked up Kara's number at the agency and called to let her know she was available to work again.

"Oh, that's great news!" Kara sounded excited to hear from her. Though to be fair, Kara was high energy and always sounded excited—every assignment that she told Sophie about was always 'an awesome opportunity and a great company'. Sophie smiled as Kara said she had something new and amazing that had just come in.

"I thought of you immediately for it since you've already worked there. It's for Fulton Real Estate. Their receptionist that was on maternity leave, came back and only lasted a week. She was miserable and her husband wants her to stay home with their baby. So, they are on the hunt for a new receptionist. And they are open to temp-to-perm. They asked if you might be available. I said I'd check but I wasn't sure if the timing would work for you as they need someone for Monday."

"I can do it!" Sophie felt a rush of excitement. It felt meant to be.

Kara laughed. "Excellent. I'll let them know. Do you think you might be interested in temp-to-perm? If not, they'll probably want to start interviewing for people that want the role permanently."

"I am very interested in that," Sophie said.

"Fantastic. How are you doing Sophie? I know it's been a hard week." Kara sounded so sympathetic that Sophie felt her eyes grow damp again. She'd thought she was done crying. She took a deep breath.

"I'm good. Thanks for asking. It's sad and I miss her, but I'll be okay."

"I'm so sorry for your loss. Take good care of yourself, Sophie."

"I will. Thanks so much, Kara."

CHAPTER ELEVEN

Sophie passed Max and his girlfriend coming into the building on Saturday as she was heading to the coffee shop. They exchanged hellos and Millie offered her condolences. "Max told me about your aunt passing. I'm so sorry for your loss."

"Thank you."

They looked like they'd just come from having breakfast somewhere. Max was holding a newspaper and Millie had a to-go box. Sophie was just trying to get through the weekend. She was anxious to start working on Monday, to keep busy and get into a routine. She wouldn't feel as sad if she kept busy. It was the weekends that stretched out long and empty when time seemed to stand still. She didn't have any friends in the city yet to hang out with.

She thought about calling Caroline or Tessa, but she didn't want to bother them and wasn't ready to talk about her aunt passing yet, either. She hadn't really expected to keep in touch with them after she left the temp job. But now that she was going back, maybe they would be her first real friends in the city.

And now that she was staying here, she could get more involved and meet people. Her aunt had volunteered every other weekend at the Met for years and loved it. Sophie went online to see if there were any volunteer opportunities and there was a weekend opening. The Met was right on Fifth Avenue and would be an easy walk. Sophie filled out an application online and clicked submit. She had no idea if she'd be chosen, but at least she felt like she was doing something.

She went grocery shopping that afternoon at Whole Foods and stocked up on fresh fruits, veggies and chicken. She cooked the chicken when she got home and sliced it up to use in salads that she would bring into work. As she was thinking about what to do for dinner, she got a text message from Max.

"You in tonight? Up for *Murders* and pizza?"

She smiled and texted back. "Definitely."

"Great, how's seven and pepperoni and mushroom?"

"Perfect. See you then."

They'd started watching *Only Murders in the Building* with Aunt Penny and had just started the second season.

Max knocked on the door at seven sharp and walked in with his arms full. He handed Sophie the pizza box, which smelled heavenly. He set his other bag down on the kitchen counter. "I got us salad too, with Italian dressing. So, we can feel a little healthier."

Sophie laughed as she got paper plates and utensils. "Wine or water?" she offered.

Max grinned. "Wine of course."

Sophie opened a bottle of merlot and poured two glasses. They loaded their plates with pizza and salad and settled on the living room sofa.

"So, how are you doing? Your parents have gone home?" Max asked.

She nodded. "They left the day after the funeral, after we met with the attorney about the will."

"Any surprises there?" Max asked casually.

"Yes, actually. My mother was shocked that Aunt Penny left this apartment to me. I was shocked too. I never expected that."

Max smiled. "Well, that's great news."

Sophie looked at him curiously. "You don't seem surprised. Did you know her plans?"

"She may have mentioned to me a few months back that she was leaving it to you. She swore me to secrecy." He grinned. "I think she knew you'd love it as much as she did. Your mother would have just sold it probably?"

Sophie sighed. "Yes, she was planning on listing it before they headed home."

"They got the Hamptons house though, right?"

"They did. My father was more than fine with it. I think my mother's nose was just a little out of joint."

"She'll get over it," Max said as he reached for his pizza.

"It feels so strange to be here without Aunt Penny." Sophie looked around the room. "I feel honored that she left it to me. I won't ever sell it," she said fiercely.

"And that's why she left it to you. She knew what she was doing," Max said.

"I applied for a volunteer job at the Met today. I want to put down some roots now and get to know more people."

"That's a great idea. I volunteer once a month at a food pantry. They're always looking for more people, too. If you're interested, you can come along with me next time I go."

Sophie was intrigued. "What do you do there?"

"I help with the deliveries that come in once a month. We unload boxes of food off the truck and put it on the shelves or in the freezers. It only takes an hour or so. And every Thanksgiving, I help put together the baskets that they give out to needy families."

Sophie smiled. "That sounds fun."

"We make it fun. We order pizza and children from the church come and help."

"I'd love to help with any of that," Sophie said.

"Great, I'll keep you posted."

"Does Millie volunteer with you?" Sophie asked.

Max stayed quiet for a moment and took another bite of pizza before answering. "No, I mentioned it a few times, but she always says it never works with her schedule. She travels a lot. She left for Paris this afternoon and has a job there for the next week and then she's on to Greece."

"That is a lot. Will she come home in between?"

"I doubt it. She says it's easier to just go right on to Greece. The shoots are back to back, with only a day off in between."

Sophie grabbed another slice of pizza. "I like to travel a little, but I don't think I'd like to do that much."

"No, neither would I."

They turned on the show and watched two episodes.

Max headed home around nine and Sophie insisted that he take the leftover pizza with him.

"I'll keep the salad," she said.

"All right, then. If you're around this weekend, I think some of us are going for dinner and drinks on Saturday. It's a fun group. Might be good for you to meet some people now that you're staying."

"I'd love that." Sophie felt the sadness finally start to lift a little. She looked forward to meeting some of Max's friends and getting back to the real estate office.

CHAPTER TWELVE

It felt good to be back at Fulton Real Estate. Everyone seemed happy to see Sophie again, especially Andrea, who greeted her warmly when she arrived Monday morning. "Kara told me that you're interested in this as a temp-to-perm opportunity? We'd love that and I wouldn't have to interview anyone else."

Sophie smiled and assured her that she was definitely interested.

Rick gave her a high-five when he saw her and then immediately handed her the morning's tape to type up. "Glad to have you back, Sophie."

Sophie spent the morning getting up to speed on the new listings that had come in since she'd been gone. She started with typing up the notes of the morning meeting which had all the newest listings and updates. And then in between calls, she studied the list of new properties and read through the descriptions. She also took note of the sales board and which properties had closed since she'd been gone. She was happy to see that the Soho property she'd suggested to Rick's client had just closed a few days ago.

Caroline and Tessa stopped by to chat on their way out to preview a new listing.

"We'll have to definitely get drinks later this week," Caroline suggested, and Sophie happily agreed. Aside from Saturday night with Max and his friends, she had no plans at all.

She brought her lunch in each day and went outside and to a small park area nearby to sit in the sun and eat her salad. The days went by quickly and by the time she got home at night, she was tired but in a good way. She went for long walks along Fifth Avenue after supper and then curled up and read for a bit or watched a little television with Charlie by her side, before heading to bed around ten. She was settling into a routine and while she still had many sad moments, when she wanted to tell Aunt Penny about something that had happened at work and realized she couldn't do that anymore. But the moments passed quickly and by the end of the week, she was looking forward to having drinks with Caroline and Tessa.

They went to a different place this time. Milady's was a restaurant bar and according to Tessa had the best smash burgers. It was crowded when they arrived at a quarter to six, but after ordering drinks at the bar, some seats opened up ten minutes later and they grabbed them. Tessa went with an Aperol Spritz, which Sophie knew was a hugely popular cocktail, but she'd never cared for the taste. She ordered a classic cosmopolitan and Caroline decided to get the same.

"So, what's new and exciting since we last saw you?" Caroline asked.

Sophie hesitated for a moment. "Well, there is some sad news, my Aunt Penny died. She was the one I was living with."

Tessa and Caroline immediately offered their condolences. "Does that mean you have to move?" Tessa asked.

Sophie shook her head. "No, actually I'm staying. My aunt left the apartment to me."

Tessa and Caroline both looked shocked. "She left you the apartment? The one on Fifth Avenue?" Caroline asked.

"She did."

"Well, you'll sell it of course. You can get a lot of money for that property," Tessa said.

"I'm not selling. I wanted to stay in New York and my aunt knew that."

"It's such a huge place though, isn't it? If you sold it, you could get something much smaller, still nicer and put money in the bank," Caroline said practically.

"I could. But I'm not in a hurry to sell it. It's a great location and my aunt loved living there. I think I will, too."

"Well, I have to admit, I'm a little jealous," Tessa said. "I still need to figure out what I'm going to do. Our rent is going way up and I'm not sure I want to stay there."

"I'm in the same situation. But I'll probably re-sign the new lease. It's too hard to find something else and prices are high everywhere," Caroline said.

The conversation shifted to what they were doing for the rest of the weekend. Both Caroline and Tessa had boyfriends and they were seeing them later that evening and had fun plans for the weekend.

"Ed is taking me out on his boat. He lives in Long Island," Caroline said.

"We have tickets to a show tomorrow night, I don't remember which one it is, but Cody is all excited about it," Tessa said.

They decided to order another round of drinks and at Tessa's urging, they all got the smash burger. And it really was good. Sophie wasn't a big red meat eater but occasionally she enjoyed a burger.

And even though they were full, they decided to share a dessert, a chocolate peanut butter blondie with vanilla ice cream.

Sophie was having such a good time, that over dessert she impulsively invited Tessa and Caroline to move in with her.

"I have extra bedrooms and I could use the money to pay the monthly maintenance fees. You could pay me what you're paying now."

Caroline's eyes lit up. "Are you sure? That doesn't seem enough for a Fifth Avenue location."

But Tessa didn't hesitate. "If you're serious, I'm in. I don't even need to see it."

"I'm in too. I would love to see it though, if that's possible, just so I'll know what to bring and what to leave behind," Caroline said.

Sophie felt a rush of happiness. "I'll be around tomorrow afternoon, if you want to come by and see the place."

They both agreed to stop over around two and Tessa insisted on paying the bill instead of splitting it three ways when it came.

"I don't want to take the chance that you might change your mind about us moving in," she teased.

Sophie smiled. "I won't change my mind. I'll see you both tomorrow afternoon."

Caroline and Tessa arrived at two o'clock sharp the next day and they both loved the apartment.

"It's even bigger than I imagined," Caroline said. "Seriously, Sophie, this place is gorgeous. And I wouldn't even have to bring much, mostly just clothing."

Tessa seemed happy with it too. "I didn't like my furniture much anyway. I'll either sell it to my roommates or put an ad online to get rid of it. Do you care which bedroom we take?"

"My aunt's was the front room and I'm leaving that as is. I have the back room and that leaves the other two. They're the same size, so you can decide between yourselves which one you want," Sophie said.

Caroline didn't have a preference and told Tessa she'd be happy with either room.

"So, we'll move in first of the month? November first?" Caroline asked.

Sophie nodded. That was a little over a week away. "That works for me."

Caroline walked through the living room and stood by the large bay window that looked out over Fifth Avenue. "This is such an amazing location. I can't wait to move in."

"It will be fun to have you both here. I could use the company," Sophie admitted.

"It will be fun! I can't wait," Caroline said excitedly.

"It really is a great place," Tessa agreed.

"What are you up to tonight?" Caroline asked.

"Max invited me to go out with him and his friends. We're going to dinner somewhere."

Caroline and Tessa exchanged glances. "Is it a date? Is he no longer with that model?" Tessa asked.

Sophie laughed. "No! Truthfully, I think Max just felt a little sorry for me. I was whining the other night that I didn't have any friends in the city yet."

"Well, you have us," Caroline said with a smile.

Tessa looked thoughtful. "How serious are they? Max is kind of cute. You should go for it," she advised.

"It's not like that. We're just friends. And they seem pretty serious. She just travels a lot."

"Well, have fun. We'll see you at work on Monday," Caroline said. She and Tessa left and after they were gone, Sophie made herself a cup of tea and settled on the sofa to read for a bit before she had to get ready to go out. She was glad that they'd both liked the apartment. Though she couldn't imagine that they wouldn't like it. For them to pay what they were currently paying was a deal—too good for either of them to pass up. Sophie knew she could have charged more, but she didn't want strangers living in her apartment. She felt comfortable with Caroline and Tessa and thought it might be fun to have them as roommates. She looked forward to the company. As much as she loved the apartment, it was big for one person, and she felt a little lonely roaming around it now that her aunt was gone.

Max texted her that they had dinner reservations at seven thirty and that they should leave by seven. He told her the name of the restaurant and it wasn't familiar, so Sophie googled it. It was a trendy Italian place, not overly formal, but not casual either. And this most definitely wasn't a date, so Sophie debated what to wear. She finally settled on a pair of slim black dress pants and a charcoal gray cashmere sweater with a bright pink scarf for a pop of color. She wore her favorite soft leather boots that gave her a little bit of a boost but weren't too high of a heel. And she curled her hair slightly so that it was like a loose, beachy wave. A slick of rosy lipstick, blush and mascara and she was ready.

Max knocked on her door at seven and he whistled softly when he saw her. "You look great. Now this isn't a fixup, but one of the guys coming with us is single. Jared and his girlfriend broke up a little over a month ago and we're just now getting him out there. He's a nice guy, maybe you guys will hit it off. If not, no worries."

Sophie hesitated. "You're sure this isn't a setup?"

Max grinned. "It's totally not. It's just a data point that out of our group going tonight, he's newly single."

It was about a twenty-minute walk to the restaurant, but it was a clear, cool night. Perfect for walking. They arrived a few minutes early and several of the group was already there. The others arrived soon after. Once everyone was there, they went inside and were seated at their reserved table. There were eight of them in total and Max introduced her to everyone. Sophie smiled and nodded and hoped she'd remember their names. There were two couples, Anna and Lori and their boyfriends. The girls worked in publishing and knew Max as he was with the same publisher. His friend Eric, was a long-time friend from college. His girlfriend was working that evening as a bartender at a club nearby and the other guy was the one Max had mentioned earlier, Jared. They had worked together years ago, before Max wrote his first book.

"I was a mutual fund accountant, if you can believe it," Max said. "They had no business hiring me to do anything with numbers. I think I lasted all of six months."

Jared laughed. "It was that last wire transfer that did it."

Max nodded and laughed. "I put an extra zero in and sent a million dollars of the client's money instead of a hundred thousand. They were not happy. Can't say that I blame them."

"They fired you?" Sophie couldn't imagine making such a big mistake.

"They did. They wisely suggested that maybe financial services wasn't a great fit. But at the time, it was the only job I could get."

"What did you do?" Sophie asked.

"I went back to bartending. I'd done that all through college and it was good money. And I'd always liked to stay up late and sleep in. I wrote my book during the day, before I headed into work. Luckily it worked out." He grinned.

"Understatement of the year," Jared said.

"You still work in mutual fund accounting?" Sophie asked.

"I do. I'm an external wholesaler now. I sell insurance products to financial planners and advisors," Jared said.

"Basically, he plays a lot of golf," Max said. "You have to admit it is a cushy job."

Jared grinned. "It doesn't suck."

The other women were friendly and included Sophie in the conversation.

"So, Max says you guys are next door neighbors?" Anna asked.

Sophie explained how Max was neighbors with her aunt and that's how they met.

They both offered their condolences. "It's good that you met Max. It's nice to know your neighbors," Lori said.

"Yeah, Max has been great. It was hard at first to be there without my aunt. I still miss her," Sophie admitted. "I have two friends moving in soon though, so it will be good to have roommates, I think."

Max looked surprised at the news. "I thought you didn't know anyone in the city?"

"It's the two girls from work that I mentioned, Caroline and Tessa. I think you'll like them."

"Hmmm. How well do you really know them, though? What if you don't like them living with you?"

Sophie hadn't thought that far ahead. She felt optimistic though.

"I think it will be fine. We all get along well. And I'll be glad for the company."

"You should have them sign a lease. That way you have an end date in case it doesn't work out. Not trying to be negative, but without a lease, it will be difficult to get someone out if you decide you don't want them there anymore."

Sophie realized that was probably good advice. She nodded. "I'll do that. I'll have them both sign one-year leases."

"Good. I'm happy to read it over if you like. I've signed my share of leases over the years," Max said.

"Great, I'll gladly take you up on that."

The dinner was excellent and the conversation was lively. They went through several bottles of red wine for the table. It was an Italian red blend and it was smooth and delicious. Sophie had chicken marsala with gnocchi and it was so good. She shared a slice of tiramisu with Max for dessert and then the group made their way a few blocks over to the bar where Eric's girlfriend worked.

Her name was Jessica and she waved at them from the bar when they walked in. Sophie had another glass of red wine and they all got their drinks from Jessica and then found seats near the bar. There was a band setting up and once they started to play the bar filled up even more. They played a mix of blues and rock and were really good. It was difficult to talk over the music though, so Sophie finally gave up trying and just enjoyed listening.

They stayed for two sets and then around midnight everyone was ready to head home. It still was nice out, so Max and Sophie decided to walk home. They were a few blocks closer, so it didn't take too long. By the time they reached their building, Sophie was ready to fall into bed. It had been a fun night though.

"Thanks for bringing me out tonight. That was fun. I like your friends," Sophie said.

"It was fun. And I could tell they liked you too." Max grinned. "Especially Jared. He asked me to find out if he could call you. No worries if the answer is no."

Sophie was flattered. But she wasn't sure how she felt about Jared. He seemed like a nice guy, but she hadn't felt any romantic sparks. Still, she knew she tended to be too picky and that sometimes those sparks weren't always there at the beginning. At least that's what her friends said. They'd encouraged her to go out with guys at least a few times before ruling them out. And it's not like she had a long list of men wanting to date her at the moment.

"Sure, feel free to give him my number."

Max looked pleased. "Will do. Sleep well, Sophie."

CHAPTER THIRTEEN

Caroline and Tessa moved in the following weekend. Caroline came first, on Saturday afternoon and Tessa on Sunday morning. That Saturday night, once Caroline was settled in her room, and had unpacked most of her things, she and Sophie walked around the corner and had dinner at her aunt's favorite Italian restaurant. Both Tony and Richard were at the front desk, seating people and checking to make sure everything was going smoothly. They both gave Sophie hugs when they saw her, and she introduced them to Caroline.

"We hope that we will see you often," Tony said.

Richard led them to a great table by the window and sent over a complimentary appetizer, a wedge of creamy burrata cheese with crusty garlic bread on the side. Caroline was impressed.

"Are you a regular here?" she asked.

Sophie smiled. "My aunt was. She came here at least once a week."

They had a lovely meal and a glass of wine each and

then walked home, changed into their pajamas and watched movies in the living room with Charlie curled up between them on the sofa. It was exactly the kind of evening that Sophie had hoped for.

The vibe changed a little though when Tessa arrived the next day around one with her boyfriend, Cody. Tessa introduced him to Sophie, and he seemed like a nice guy. He was average height with muscled arms and short hair. He carried in Tessa's heaviest suitcases. She had a lot of stuff with her—boxes and suitcase—and Sophie and Caroline helped to carry it all into her bedroom, too. Once everything was in, Cody gave her a kiss goodbye and left Tessa to it. She didn't emerge for several hours as she unpacked and put things away. When she did finally join them in the living room, she asked if there was any storage space in the apartment.

Sophie thought for a moment. "Not really, but if it's just a box or two, you could put it in my aunt's room, I suppose."

"Perfect." Tessa went into her room and carried two cardboard boxes into Aunt Penny's bedroom. And then she joined them and flopped on the living room sofa next to Caroline.

"I really hate moving," she said.

"I didn't mind it this time. I was glad to get out of my tiny apartment," Caroline said.

"That's true. Now that I'm here and unpacked, it's all good," Tessa said. She sat up and grinned. "It's almost five o'clock, right?"

Caroline glanced at her watch. "It's a quarter past four."

"Close enough. Who wants a glass of champagne? I brought a bottle for us to crack open tonight to celebrate moving in day."

Sophie went to the kitchen and got some glasses for the champagne. Tessa brought it into the kitchen and twisted it open with a loud pop. She poured glasses for all of them. Sophie found a block of cheddar cheese in the fridge and sliced it up and put it on a tray with some crackers. They returned to their spots in the living room and Sophie set the cheese and crackers on the coffee table.

"Here's to the Fifth Avenue Apartment and a big thank you to Sophie's Aunt Penny," Tessa said.

They all clinked their glasses together and Sophie felt a rush of sadness thinking of Aunt Penny. It was bittersweet that Sophie was living there, enjoying her aunt's apartment. She hoped that it would work out having Caroline and Tessa for roommates. So far, it seemed like they were off to a good start.

The first few weeks with Caroline and Tessa as roommates went better than Sophie expected, much to her relief. Max's comments when they were out to dinner with his friends had planted seeds of doubt. She took his advice and had both girls sign one-year leases and they had no problem with it.

Both had boyfriends and they usually spent one and sometimes both nights with them on the weekends and sometimes a night or two during the week. Sophie went on her first date the weekend after they moved in. Jared had called and invited her to dinner. They went to a cozy

French restaurant, and she had a nice time. Jared was good company and funny. They laughed and the conversation was easy. But there still weren't any sparks. But she'd had fun, so when he suggested they do something the following weekend, she'd agreed. And hoped that some romantic sparks might emerge.

But they didn't. They went out again and had a wonderful time. Sophie insisted on paying but Jared wouldn't hear of it. He was a true gentleman. He seemed to sense the lack of sparks too, and though he suggested going out again, he didn't say when and Sophie just nodded and thanked him again for dinner.

Max came over that Sunday night and had pizza with them. Tessa asked him how things were with his girlfriend.

"We're good. She's in South Africa this week. Her travel schedule is nuts."

Sophie poured cabernet for them and Max took a sip and smiled.

"This one is great. What is it?" he asked.

"It's a new favorite. Austin Hope."

"I'll have to remember that. So, I guess three strikes and Jared is out?"

Sophie was surprised at the comment. "Did he say something to you?"

Max took another sip of his wine. "He said you had a few great dates, but he doesn't think you're into him?"

She sighed. "I tried to be. He's a really nice guy."

"But you're just not feeling it?"

"No. I was hoping the attraction might grow. I've been told I'm too picky," Sophie said with a wry smile.

"I don't believe that. I think attraction can grow sometimes, but there's usually something there to start with," Max said.

"I agree, totally," Tessa said. "Every guy I've had a relationship with, the attraction was there pretty strongly from the beginning."

"There was one time when I wasn't attracted at all to someone. It was a friend that my other friends were trying to push me to be with. I didn't find him attractive, so their pushing actually turned me off. But I got to know him as a friend and a year later, I saw him differently. But by then it was too late, and he was with someone else. I still wonder sometimes if he was the one that got away," Caroline said.

"He wasn't," Tessa said matter-of-factly. "Ed is a great guy. You two are good together."

Caroline took a sip of her wine. "You're right. I know you're right. It's just sometimes after you really get to know someone, they do grow more attractive. It's possible."

"I never thought he was right for Sophie," Max admitted.

"Why did you suggest I go out with him, then?" Sophie asked.

Max shrugged. "He's a nice guy and he was interested. You never know."

CHAPTER FOURTEEN

"Hi, my name is Laura Prescott. I'm hoping you might be able to help me with a rental. I saw one of the office listings. The price was a little higher than I can pay but I'm wondering if you might have anything else? I need a two bedroom and I'm flexible on location as long as it's in Manhattan and not far from public transportation. I work in midtown." It was Monday morning and Sophie had just finished typing up the notes from that morning's sales meeting when the phone rang.

"Let me connect you with one of our realtors, Laura. What is your budget?" Sophie asked. The realtors liked her to collect some basic information before passing the call along.

"I'm really hoping to be under four thousand a month, if possible," she said.

"Hold on a moment, and I'll connect you to one of our realtors."

Sophie checked her list and Caroline was up next. She

buzzed her extension and Caroline picked up immediately.

"Can you take a call for a rental?"

"Sure, what are they looking for?" Caroline asked.

"Two bedrooms, flexible on location, ideally under four thousand."

Caroline sighed. "Ugh, that's going to be tough."

"What about the one Troy mentioned in this morning's meeting? It's on the smaller side but it's in a good neighborhood and they're asking just under four."

"Oh my gosh, you're totally right. Thanks, Sophie, send her over."

Sophie transferred the call and when she turned her attention back to her computer, she saw that Rick Fulton was leaning against the counter, looking at her curiously.

"So, you actually pay attention to what we talk about in the morning meetings. You're not just typing it up. That was a good suggestion for Caroline."

Sophie smiled, pleased by the compliment. "I just finished typing the notes up, so it was fresh in my mind."

"Are you sure you want to stay in the receptionist role? You're doing a great job and we're happy to have you in it. But I can't help but wonder if you might have a knack for the sales side of things."

"I never thought that I wanted sales," Sophie said honestly. "The all-commission thing scares me a little."

Rick shrugged. "It's only scary if you don't sell anything. If you work hard, then the income potential is unlimited. Think about it!"

"I will. Thank you."

And Sophie did think about it. She was comfortable in

the receptionist role. She liked interfacing with clients and the realtors, but she wasn't especially challenged by it. It was a cushy job. Was she ready for something more challenging?

Later that evening when she was watching TV in the apartment with Caroline and Tessa, Sophie told them about her conversation with Rick.

Tessa raised her eyebrows. "When we talked about this before, you were pretty uncomfortable with working on commission only," she said.

"I still am nervous about it. But Rick seems to think I could do it," Sophie said.

"I think you could do it. You instantly thought of that apartment that wasn't even on my radar. I may have been half-asleep during this morning's meeting," Caroline admitted.

"Can you afford to go without any income for a while?" Tessa asked. "Even if you sell something right away, there's an average of three months before you'll see the money."

"It's a little faster with rentals," Caroline said. "But Tessa is right, there is a delay. And there can be ups and downs, especially at first. I used to put all my eggs in one basket once someone made an offer and I'd count on that money."

Tessa nodded. "But you can't do that," she said. "Too many deals fall apart along the way. You need to have lots of balls in the air. I try to plan on half of all my sure things happening. And sometimes they all fall apart. Not to be negative, but it's hard."

"It's a great job, though," Caroline added. "It's just not easy and you do have to work really hard, all the time."

Sophie nodded. "I am in a better position now financially than I was before. I have some money saved and I have a little from Aunt Penny that I can dip into if needed. I'm trying not to touch that if I don't need to, though."

"I really think you might be good at it," Caroline said. "And it is a lot of fun."

"Another downside is that you will often need to work nights and weekends. If that's when your clients want to see properties. Many of them work during the day and don't want to take the time off," Tessa said.

Sophie grinned. "That's not a problem. I am pretty much available anytime."

"Well, maybe you should try it then," Tessa said.

"Maybe I will. I think I want to," Sophie said. "I'll sleep on it and see if I'm still as excited about the idea tomorrow."

CHAPTER FIFTEEN

In the morning, Sophie felt a thrill of excitement. She'd wondered when she went to bed if she was just caught up in the moment—it was flattering that Rick had suggested that she think about moving into sales. But when she woke, she was even more interested. It felt like an opportunity that she should take. She liked the office, and she liked Rick's energy. He was hugely successful and was still young. He'd just turned forty that year and opened his office ten years ago after working as an agent for a few years. Sophie thought that she could learn a lot from him and from the other agents.

She went in an hour early as she knew that Rick was usually the first person in, and he was generally there by seven after going to the gym. She found him in his office at seven thirty and he looked pleased to see her.

"Morning Sophie. You're in bright and early. I like it."

Sophie cleared her throat and took a deep breath. "Can I talk to you for a minute?"

"Sure, come on in. Have a seat."

She sat in the black leather chair that faced Rick's desk. His office was big and looked out on Broadway. It was a bright, colorful office, but was minimally decorated, with a few black and white prints on the walls, a bookcase with a row of motivational business books and his desk itself was almost bare. It was made of sleek, glossy poured concrete and had a phone in one corner, a small lamp, a single manilla folder and a laptop.

"So, what's on your mind?" Rick asked.

Sophie was still staring at his desk, fascinated. It almost looked like no one worked at it. She was used to having stacks of folders and paperwork all over her desk.

"How do you keep your desk so clean?" she asked.

He laughed, a deep rumbly laugh and looked thoroughly amused by the question. "I just process everything as it comes in and either deal with it, or file it away," he said. "But I don't think that's why you wanted to talk to me?"

She smiled. "No, it's not. I thought about what you said yesterday about moving into sales. I talked to Caroline and Tessa about it, and they told me the good and the bad. And I think I want to do it. I mean I know that I do. I'm really interested in real estate."

Rick closed his laptop and gave her his full attention. "I'm very happy to hear that. I'll talk to Andrea and have her call the agency to get a replacement for you ASAP. It might take a day or two, but they're pretty fast."

"Oh, that's fine." Sophie hadn't expected things would move that quickly.

"Since you're here already, why don't you come to the eight o'clock sales meeting. You can record it or take notes, whatever you prefer. But it might be interesting for you to be there in person. We meet every Monday and it usually goes for twenty or thirty minutes.

You'll need to study for the real estate test to get your license. We can send you to a weekend crash course. That's the easiest way to do it—get it over with fast. And until you get your license, I'll have you shadow me and a few of the other agents. It's good to get out there in the field and see how we do things. Do you have any questions?"

"No. Not yet. I'm excited though."

Rick grinned and stood. "Welcome aboard. I think you're going to love it!" He shook her hand and Sophie nodded. "I think I will, too. Thank you for the opportunity."

"I think you're going to make us both a lot of money, Sophie. See you in the meeting."

Sophie went back to her desk and felt like she was walking on a cloud—she was so excited and eager to start her new role. She logged on to her computer and checked email and kept an eye on the time. It was ten to eight. Tessa and Caroline walked in a moment later and Caroline came right over to the reception desk.

"Did you talk to him?" she asked.

"I did. It's official. As soon as they find a replacement for me, I'll start in sales. And I'm attending the morning meeting today."

"That's great. We'll see you in there then," Caroline said.

Tessa gave her a smile too. "Congrats!"

Sophie made herself a fluffy coffee from the Nespresso machine and a few minutes before eight, she went into the conference room and sat next to Caroline at the long oval table. At eight sharp, Rick breezed into the room, sat at the head of the table and looked around the room. "Okay, what updates do you all have for me?"

Sophie clicked on her phone to record the meeting and opened a notebook as well to jot notes as people talked.

"I signed a new listing end of day yesterday," Troy said. He was one of the more senior agents. Sophie guessed he was close to Rick's age. "It's a three-bedroom condo in Murray Hill. Monthly fees aren't too bad, just five. They want three point five million for the unit."

Rick nodded. "Good job. What kind of condition is it in?"

"Excellent. It was renovated a year or so ago, but the owner got transferred to the West Coast, so they need to move. It has a small room that could either be an office or a den and some nice distant views of the Hudson. And a balcony off one of the bedrooms, decent size too. You can fit king-size beds in the bedrooms and they're all similar size. Hardwood floors."

"That should go fast," Rick said. "Does anyone have a buyer for it?"

"I might," Caroline said. "I'll call her right after the meeting."

Troy nodded her way appreciatively. "They're on the West Coast this week. If anyone wants to look at it today, we can run over."

"Good job, Troy," Rick said. He glanced at Sophie. "I have some news to announce, too. In case you're wondering why Sophie is here today, she's going to move into a sales role as soon as we can find a replacement for the front desk. I know you'll all help to encourage her and show her the ropes. I told her we'll have her take turns shadowing different people."

There was a chorus of congratulations and more than a few surprised looks as the dozen or so realtors turned their attention Sophie's way. She smiled and somewhat nervously said, "Thanks everyone. I'm excited to join you." It was a little intimidating to join a group of mostly experienced realtors. She hoped that they wouldn't mind a newbie and her questions. She knew she had a lot to learn.

There were two more new listings from two different agents and Sophie paid close attention as they described the units and the neighborhoods and amenities. Rick then asked for progress updates.

"My client is seeing a condo this afternoon and is going to make a decision and hopefully an offer later today," Caroline said.

"Good, go get 'em Caroline. Who else?" Rick said.

"I had an accepted offer last night, on the Simon property," Tessa said proudly. Sophie was excited for her. Tessa had told Sophie and Caroline about the offer which had been a tough negotiation. They'd gone back and forth, and Tessa hadn't been sure they'd actually come to an agreement, but they had.

Rick looked impressed. "That's fantastic, Tessa. Is that your biggest sale so far?"

She smiled. "It is. The final offer was twenty-one million."

"Someone needs to ring the bell! Well done!" Rick said.

Tessa got up and walked to a large bell that hung on the wall and she pulled the leather strap hard, and the clang of the bell rang out. Everyone in the room clapped and cheered.

"Okay, anyone else have an update?" Rick looked around the room.

They were all quiet. "All right, let's have a great day everyone!"

Sophie went to the front desk and turned the phones on to start the day. She had taken good notes, so she didn't need the recording after all. She typed her notes up quickly and mailed them off to Rick. It had been exciting to sit in that morning meeting. The energy was high, and it was so interesting to hear about the new listings and activity. And Tessa's sale. Sophie mentally did the math and worked out that the commission on that sale was just over two hundred and fifty thousand for Tessa. The full commission was just over a million at five percent and that was split between Tessa and the listing broker and then Tessa's share was split again with the office.

It was hard for Sophie to fathom making that much commission on a single sale. She knew though that most of Caroline's and Tessa's other sales were much lower, more in the two to five million range. But still, on a two million sale, that meant her share would be about twenty-five thousand. Unless of course she was also the listing agent and found the buyer too, which was unusual, but if so, then she would make double her normal commission as she would get both sides.

It sounded like Monopoly money to Sophie. She liked Caroline's suggestion to start out focusing on rentals. The total commission was much lower, but the transactions went faster and the money came in sooner. There was a lot to it, and she was excited to learn as much as possible and do both rentals and sales. First though, she had to pass the real estate exam to get her license.

Andrea came out to the front desk a few minutes before noon to cover for Sophie's lunch.

"Congrats on your new role! Rick filled me in. I called the agency and they just got back to me to let me know they've found someone that can start tomorrow. So, you can head right into the back tomorrow and I'll have a desk set up for you. Good luck!"

"Thank you." Sophie was a little dazed by how fast things were moving.

Caroline, Tessa, Troy, and a few others walked toward the front desk.

"We're going to look at Troy's new listing. Do you want to come?" Caroline asked.

Sophie did. But she wasn't sure she'd make it back in an hour. She glanced at Andrea, who nodded. "Go ahead. If you're a few minutes late, I can handle it."

"Thank you!"

Sophie followed the others out the door and they took the subway to Troy's listing. "It's almost always faster than driving," Caroline explained.

When they reached the listing, Troy let them in and showed them around. It was a beautiful unit, and in the distance, the sun glimmered on the water of the Hudson River.

"That is a great view," Caroline said.

"Check out the balcony," Troy opened the door, and they stepped outside. It was a really nice outside space. Bigger than most balconies that Sophie had seen.

The kitchen was on the small side, but the bedrooms were big, with high ceilings and lots of closet space and the living room had exposed brick walls and a gas fireplace which made the room cozy.

"I think this will go fast," Sue, one of the more senior agents said.

"I'll mail it out to my buyers," Tessa said. "I have to get a newsletter out this week anyway and this is a great property to showcase."

Troy looked at Sophie and grinned. "What about you, Sophie, do you have a buyer for me?"

She laughed. "I wish I did. I can't wait to have some buyers."

"Buyers are great, but my advice is to focus on getting listings. That's where the real money is," Troy said.

"He's not wrong," Tessa agreed.

They headed back to the office and Sophie was relieved that they made it back five minutes early. Andrea disappeared into her office and Sophie fished around in her purse for an energy bar that she'd stuck in a pocket over a month ago. She was too late to eat her salad, but she could quickly eat the bar and that would hold her until dinner. She was almost too excited to eat her salad anyway. She couldn't wait to get going and start finding buyers and listings of her own. Even though she had no idea of where to start.

CHAPTER SIXTEEN

Andrea found Sophie after the morning meeting the next day and showed her to her new desk, which was in the middle of a huge room. There were no private offices for the agents, it was what Caroline called 'the bullpen'—just over a dozen desks, a few feet apart. Along one wall there was a giant whiteboard where people wrote pending activity and deals closed for the month.

"Here you go," Andrea said. She pointed to a stack of books and a binder. "That is your study material for the real estate exam. There is a course starting next week we can get you into if that works for you."

"That works," Sophie said. She had no plans and was eager to get started.

"Perfect. I'll email you the details of where to go. Until then, if you want to get a head start, you can read over these books and the info in the binder. Rick wants you to join him in his office at once. You'll spend the afternoon shadowing him."

Sophie nodded. She felt both intimidated and excited

to be following Rick so soon. He was a dynamo of energy, and she knew she could learn so much from him.

"All right, I'll leave you to it," Andrea said.

She walked off and Sophie looked around the office. Everyone was at their desks, either checking email or talking on the phone. Both Caroline and Tessa were on the phone talking to clients.

Sophie looked at the sales board and saw that for year-to-date sales, a woman named Melissa was by far the top seller. Troy was right behind her. Followed by Sue, and then a little further down, Tessa and Caroline were neck and neck. They were right in the middle of the pack with six other agents below them at various levels. Sophie's name was already on the board, at the very bottom, with no numbers next to it. She hoped that soon, she'd be able to put something on the board, even if it was just rental dollars.

She flipped her book open and started reading. There was a lot to learn about the industry itself and selling real estate in New York. Each state had slightly different rules that had to be followed. As she read, Sophie listened to all the activity around her—agents on the phone with clients, and their interaction with each other as they discussed new listings and brainstormed approaches for working with buyers and helping them to make offers that would be accepted. The market was still hot, and Sophie knew that many properties immediately generated multiple offers.

The office emptied out as the agents all left for appointments to show properties to their buyers and to meet with potential new clients. Sophie ate her salad at her desk and was only one of two agents in the office at that point. The other was Troy, who was the agent on duty who would work with any walk-ins or calls that came through.

As Sophie ate her salad, she listened to Troy on the phone with someone who had called in for information on a listing. He was patient and asked a series of questions to determine what the buyer was ultimately looking for. By the time he ended the call, he had an appointment set up to meet with the caller that afternoon and to show the listing soon after. He turned to Sophie and grinned.

"Did you overhear any of that?"

She nodded. "It sounded like a good call."

"It was. Normally I wouldn't agree to a showing until I meet the buyer in person, but I've been doing this for a while and based on how they answered all my questions, I could tell they are a serious buyer. So, we'll meet here and then head right out to the property."

"Is it your new listing? The one we saw yesterday?"

"Yeah. I made sure it went online yesterday and there have been a few calls already. I think this one might go fast. The price is good and it's an in-demand neighborhood that doesn't have a lot of inventory."

"Good luck. I wish I had a buyer for you," Sophie said wistfully.

Troy laughed. "You will soon enough. Got to get that license first." He glanced at her stack of books and made a face. "It's a necessary evil, but we all had to do it. Get it over with and take the test right away while it's still fresh. Don't panic if you don't pass it the first time. Some of us need two tries."

Sophie nodded. "I'm starting the course next week." She was determined to pass the test on her first try.

Troy's phone rang and he turned around and took the call. Sophie focused her attention back to her lunch. A few minutes before one, she closed the book she was reading, and headed to Rick's office.

When she reached his door, it was ajar, and she could see that he was on the phone. He looked up and saw her and waved for her to come in. She did and sat in the chair across from his desk while he finished his call.

"Ted, we've got this. We'll schedule a broker's open house this week and get as many eyes as possible on the property and then we'll do our thing. I'll keep you posted and thanks again. We appreciate your business."

He ended the call and pumped his fist in the air. "We just got an incredible new listing. A forty million dollar penthouse condo. Want to see what a forty million penthouse looks like? It's on Fifth Avenue right across from the Met. Fantastic location. I need to kill a little time before a showing."

Sophie smiled. She didn't mention that her apartment was nearby. "I'd love to see it."

They headed out and rode in Rick's private car which was always parked just outside the office. He had a driver, Evan, who was semi-retired and shared the job with another driver. Evan worked afternoons and Jose worked mornings.

"It works out great for everyone," Rick said as Evan pulled into the traffic. "By having a driver, I can still get work done while I'm sitting in traffic. And it's a write-off." He grinned and then his phone dinged, and he read and replied to a text message. For the rest of the drive, Rick took several calls and replied to emails and text messages.

Traffic was light and they arrived at the new listing a short time later. Rick led the way into the building which was beautifully maintained and had a doorman and marble floors in the lobby. They took the elevator to the top floor and when they stepped directly into the apartment from the elevator, Sophie gasped.

The entry way to the apartment had sleek black marble floors and opened into the living room which was expansive and overlooked Central Park and the Met and Fifth Avenue below. The ceilings were very high.

"Eleven or twelve feet, I need to double-check that, but isn't this awesome? I love high ceilings like this," Rick said. The rest of the apartment was stunning, too. The kitchen would make any chef happy as it had all high-end appliances and there was more marble on the counters and oversized island that had six chairs along one side.

"Too bad the owner never used the kitchen. His wife doesn't cook, and they mostly ate out or got takeout. But for someone who likes to cook, this is chef's kiss." Rick made a kissing motion with his hands to his lips and Sophie laughed. He was a big personality and he reminded her of a kid with his childlike wonder and high energy. Everything about the apartment was 'amazing' to Rick, though Sophie had to agree it was impressive.

There were five bedrooms and eight thousand square feet over two floors. The library was so beautiful with custom-built bookshelves and a ladder that was attached. There was also a big bay window that looked out over the street and window seat cushioned in ivory velvet. There was a gas fireplace and two oversized mahogany-colored leather club chairs—perfect for curling up and reading by the glow of the fireplace.

"What do you think?" Rick asked as they finished the tour and waited by the elevator.

"It's incredible." This unit was slightly more than twice the size of Sophie's apartment, which felt huge. She wondered who would buy such an expensive apartment. "How do you find someone who can afford this?" she asked.

The elevator opened and they stepped inside. "There are many people who can easily buy something in this price range. There's a lot of money in Manhattan. Could be old family money, or someone that hit it big in the tech market or hedge funds or a celebrity—especially musicians. When they go on tour the money is insane. And they value their privacy—a building like this could be perfect." He grinned. "Do you know any celebrities, Sophie?"

"Just one. He's an author, Max Bennett, and he has a supermodel girlfriend. I don't think Max makes that kind of money though. He's my neighbor," she added.

Rick looked interested though. "No kidding? Where do you live?"

"A few blocks from here actually. I was staying with my aunt, and she left the apartment to me."

Rick whistled softly. "That's a hell of an inheritance. That could be your first listing if you are planning to sell."

But she shook her head. "I'm not. Not any time soon. I love it there. And I just signed one year lease agreements with Tessa and Caroline. They're my roommates now."

Rick nodded. "That's smart. Their rent might cover some of your monthly maintenance fees."

"It covers most of it. It's an older building and the fees aren't too high. Though it's all high, really."

"The monthly fees and taxes are crazy in Manhattan, but anyone that can afford to pay the asking prices for these apartments can handle the fees," Rick said matter-of-factly.

Evan was waiting out front and they climbed into the car and headed to their next stop.

"I have a showing in Brooklyn. It's a gorgeous brownstone and if these buyers take it, it will be the third house I've sold to them in ten years," Rick said proudly. "First it was a studio apartment, then a two bedroom and now they're expecting twins and need more room, both inside and out. This townhouse has a great back yard and small garden. It's a gem." Rick paused for a moment, and then added, "If you treat people right, they come back and they refer their friends and family. And that's how you get your income to the next level."

Sophie nodded and felt a moment of discouragement as she really had no friends or family to speak of in the city.

"How did you start out, before you knew a lot of people?" she asked.

"It was hard at first. I'm not going to lie. I almost gave up a bunch of times," Rick admitted. "But I'm stubborn and I was determined to make this work. I saw other people doing it and I figured why not me? I didn't know many people then, but I knew I had the work ethic. That's key. I made sure that everyone I met knew that I sold real estate. It's all timing. If you talk to enough people, eventually you'll bump into someone who is ready to buy or sell."

Rick's enthusiasm was contagious. Sophie's twinge of doubt disappeared. She could do this. She had all the time in the world, and she wasn't afraid of hard work.

When they reached the Brooklyn property, Sophie paid close attention—to everything. She noticed the difference in the feel and size of the Brooklyn townhouse. It did seem to be a nice option for a family as it had a real backyard and plenty of space and the prices were lower than in Manhattan proper.

She also paid attention to how Rick interacted with his buyers. They were a married couple, Bill and Emma Sousa. Rick introduced Sophie as a new associate, and she followed along as they toured the space and he pointed out the benefits of the property. She also noticed that Rick was a very good listener, too.

"Bill, has anything changed since we last talked? Have you seen any other properties in person or online that you've liked?" Rick asked.

"We've been to a few open houses, and we look online all the time, but it has only confirmed that we want something more like this. The open houses were condos in midtown, and they just aren't big enough, for what we want to spend."

Rick nodded. "You really can't beat Brooklyn. It's a great area for families."

When they finished touring the townhouse, Rick asked if they wanted to make an offer. Sophie wondered if that was too pushy, but Bill didn't seem to mind.

"We might. We just need to talk about it tonight and

then I'll call you first thing in the morning." He smiled at his wife. "I am pretty sure we're going to want to offer." She nodded happily.

"Fantastic. You know how to reach me." They said their goodbyes and Sophie and Rick found Evan parked a little ways down the street. They climbed into the car and headed back to the office.

"And that's the job," Rick said. "In the office in the morning and then out in the field most of the day, showing properties and getting listings. If you can get yourself a listing or two, you'll build momentum faster. Because everyone in the office can help you find a buyer for it. It's great to have buyers too of course, but right now it's still a seller's market and there are often multiple offers." Rick's phone dinged and he glanced at it and then typed someone back. He looked out the window and then back at Sophie.

"Your buyer won't always get the property they want, and they won't necessarily buy it from you. Unless you have a solid relationship established. Buyers sometimes work with lots of agents, and just call on whatever property they see or go to open houses."

Sophie nodded, taking it all in. "Do you do a lot of open houses?"

"It depends on the property. For the ones that are in the most demand price points, we don't always need to, because they will sell quickly. But for some properties, they can be good to get the word out. We sometimes will just do broker open houses to get more agents to see it and then bring their buyers. "

It was after four when they returned to the office.

"Great job today, Sophie, see you tomorrow," Rick said as they walked through the door.

Sophie returned to her desk and opened her textbook. The office was busy now with agents returning calls and working on their computers. She read for another hour and then headed home, taking the textbook with her to continue her reading that evening.

Tessa and Caroline had plans with their boyfriends that night, so Sophie heated up some leftover pizza and curled up on the living room sofa with her textbook and Charlie by her side. She read for a while, until her eyes grew heavy and then headed to bed.

CHAPTER SEVENTEEN

Sophie spent the next two weeks taking her real estate course and studying to pass the exam. The classes were in-person and were all day Monday through Friday. When she finished, she signed up to take the test the following week and spent most of that week studying, attending the weekly meeting and spending a few hours a day shadowing a different agent.

She studied as hard as she possibly could. She took good notes, reviewed everything multiple times and took a practice exam. She didn't know if she would pass but she felt confident that she'd prepared the best that she could. She made sure to get a good night's sleep and wore a watch so that she could check the timing as the test went along. Years ago, when she'd taken an important test, she had been in a room without a clock and had no sense of how much time she had left. This test was so important that she couldn't risk that.

And she passed! It took almost two weeks to get the results, and in the meantime, Sophie continued to shadow the other agents and learn as much as possible about all the office listings. She wasn't yet able to work with buyers or get clients until she actually had her license, so she watched what everyone else did and paid close attention.

She went with Caroline when she held an open house for one of her listings and it was interesting to see how that was done. Caroline advertised the open house online and on all her social media. She also emailed her list of buyers —even ones who had already bought some type of property.

"I send new listings to everyone," Caroline explained. "And I ask them to forward the email to anyone they know who might be looking. And they do. I generate a lot of referrals that way."

About a dozen people came to the open house. They were there for one hour on a Saturday afternoon. "Weekends draw the most people, definitely," Caroline said.

Sophie watched as Caroline encouraged each visitor to sign in her guestbook. "Please go ahead and explore. If you have any questions about the property, let me know."

"You don't walk around with them?" Sophie asked.

Caroline shook her head. "No. Most people don't like that. They want to see for themselves. If they have questions, they will find me and ask. And that's when I can get a better sense of how serious a buyer they are. Or if they're just bored and looking for something to do on a Saturday afternoon." She laughed. "There's a lot of that too. People who are just curious but not in the market to buy, at all."

"Do you usually sell the house from an open house?"

Caroline shook her head. "Sometimes, but not usually. The value of the open house is the marketing—it gives the property exposure, and the agent—most of the sales generated from an open house are for other properties. Someone might stop in, but that property isn't the one they end up buying. But, if they are seriously looking, I can pick them up as a buyer and show them other things. And there's also broker open houses which are for other realtors. The more agents that know about a property, the better."

As they packed up Caroline's marketing materials and prepared to leave, Caroline turned to Sophie. "When I started out, I did a ton of open houses—for other agents. The more senior agents don't love doing them as much and they are happy for junior agents to hold them at their properties. And the property owners love it—especially if it's a vacant property. It's the most visible marketing to them."

"Oh, I'd love to do that," Sophie said.

Caroline smiled. "I'm sure you'll have plenty of takers. That's one of the ways I built up a solid list of buyers when I was starting out. Also, keeping in touch with people that rent—they often turn into buyers a year or two later."

Sophie got the good news about passing her exam on a Friday and hit the ground running on Monday. Although by the end of the week she felt like she was running in circles. She was anxious to start working with buyers but by the end of the week she didn't have a single buyer. And she'd done everything suggested. She'd let everyone in her building and everyone that she came across, like Tony and Richard at the restaurant, know that she was starting a career in real estate. Everyone wished her luck, but no one seemed to be looking to buy or sell. It was a bit discouraging.

The following week though she got her first ad call forwarded to her and it was someone interested in one of their rentals. She was so nervous and excited at the same time and stumbled her way through the call. She referred to the list of questions Rick had given her to cover with people interested in renting and everything seemed to fit.

"It's for me and my boyfriend, I mean my fiancé, I'm not used to saying that yet," Liza the woman on the phone said. "Our lease is up in a few weeks, and we want a bigger place." They were currently in a small one bedroom.

"We both work from home now so depending on the property a two or three bedroom could work." The one she was calling on was a two bedroom with a small office.

"It sounds ideal. I like the location and we can turn one of the bedrooms into an office slash guest room."

Sophie invited her to come into the office and then they would head out to see the property.

Liza came in at three and Sophie took her into a small conference room and had her fill out a rental application so they would have the paperwork ready to go if she liked the listing. "If this one doesn't work for you, we may have others coming in," Sophie said. She liked Liza, she was friendly and professional. She and her boyfriend both had good jobs in the tech industry and they'd received bigger salary increases and bonuses than expected, and were anxious to move into a bigger place.

They headed out to the rental, located in the East

Village, which Sophie had learned was one of the more in-demand neighborhoods.

"Neither one of us cooks, so we go out to eat a lot or get takeout and the East Village has so many great restaurants," Liza said as they reached the building. Sophie unlocked the door of the apartment and held it open for Liza to step inside. Sophie had seen pictures online, but it wasn't the same as seeing a property in person.

Sunlight streamed through big windows, and while the kitchen was a typical small galley size, the living area was spacious, and the primary bedroom had its own roomy bathroom. The other bedroom was a bit smaller but still a decent size.

"This would make a great office," Liza said. "And if we put a pullout sofa here, we can use it as a guest room, too."

They walked into the smallest room, which was currently being used as an office. "This is perfect. It's on the opposite side of the apartment, so we won't be on top of each other. This just hit the market, didn't it? I just saw the listing last night."

Sophie nodded. "Yes, it's brand new."

"I don't want to risk losing it. Brandon told me I could write a check if I liked it." Sophie was stunned that it was moving so fast. She smiled and nodded.

"Of course. We have your paperwork and I'll submit the application immediately. It should just take a day or two to process the background check and I will let you know asap."

Liza wrote Sophie a deposit check and they went their separate ways once they reached the street. Sophie felt like skipping as she made her way back to the office and Caroline could tell the minute she saw her face that it had gone well.

"She liked it?"

Sophie grinned and held up the deposit check. "She loved it."

"Fantastic! Once she passes the background check and it's a done deal, we'll celebrate."

They celebrated that Thursday night with after-work drinks at Champers Social Club. Sophie was on a high from having her first deal close, even though it was just a rental.

She'd been thrilled that morning in the bullpen when she'd been able to announce that she'd closed her first rental. When she'd checked her emails first thing, she'd received notification that Liza had passed the background check and the apartment was hers.

"Well done, Sophie. It's your first deal, so go and ring the bell!" Rick told her.

She'd done so and it was a thrill to hear the bell clanging and the claps and congrats from the other agents. She knew it was a small step, but it was a big one to her. It was proof that she could actually do this.

Caroline was so encouraging. Sophie had leaned on her quite a bit with her newbie questions, and Caroline was patient and answered all of them. She never bothered Tessa with questions as she was always on the phone or deeply focused on her email. There was a strong 'don't bother' me vibe around Tessa. She was very intense and competitive with the other agents.

Sophie had noticed the dynamics in the office and found them interesting. Most of the agents were encouraging and collaborative, but a few of them, like Tessa, were a bit competitive. While Caroline always cheered when someone rang the bell or announced a new listing, Tessa often seemed to bristle.

Sophie knew that Tessa and Caroline had started at the office within a week of each other. Tessa had been brand new with no experience at all, while Caroline had worked for her family's real estate office. But she still had to learn the Manhattan market, which she'd said was very different than upstate New York.

At the moment Tessa was slightly ahead of Caroline on the sales board, thanks to her recent big sale. Caroline didn't seem to care much about that, but Sophie could see that it mattered that Tessa be in the lead. Sophie was just glad she was finally on the board, even if very solidly in the bottom slot. At least she had some numbers up.

The restaurant was packed and there were no seats open at the bar, so they just had one round and decided to head home and pick up a pizza along the way. Sophie opened a bottle of prosecco since they'd all been drinking champagne at Champers. They set the pizza box on the living room coffee table and all helped themselves to slices. Caroline and Tessa got comfortable on the sofa while Sophie settled into Aunt Penny's favorite club chair.

They continued chatting about work stuff, which Sophie found endlessly fascinating.

"Troy got another incredible listing. He sold that Murray Hill one so fast," Caroline said. A moment later she added, "You should ask him if you can do an open house. He might let you."

"Good idea. I'll ask him on Monday."

"Did you notice that Rick gave Sue another listing? I swear she's his favorite and it's so unfair," Tessa complained.

"I don't think he really favors her," Caroline said thoughtfully. "I think it was just her turn."

"Her turn seems to come up more often than anyone else. And Rick knows the owners of that property. He handed it to her on a silver platter. I've never been handed a listing like that," Tessa said.

Caroline changed the subject. "We should have a dinner party soon. You could have Cody over and I'll have Ed and Sophie you should ask Max and his girlfriend."

"That would be fun. I'd love to chat with Millie. Her life sounds so fascinating with all that travel," Tessa said. "I can't do this weekend though. Cody's taking me to Vermont to meet his parents."

"Oh, that's a big deal. Are you nervous?" Caroline asked.

Tessa smiled. "Not really. I'm good with parents. They usually love me. We're not staying with them, though. We're staying at a bed and breakfast nearby. It should be fun."

"A dinner party does sound fun. Does anyone know how to cook?" Sophie asked. So far, they'd eaten a lot of takeout and heated up very simple things, like store-bought rotisserie chicken.

Tessa laughed. "Kitchens and I don't get along very well."

"I can cook a little. Easy things like chicken parmesan or lasagna," Caroline said.

"I do know how to make a good garlic bread," Sophie said. "Either of those options sounds good to me."

They decided to aim for the following weekend, Saturday night, and to make lasagna. "I'll show you how my mother makes it. It's time consuming, but pretty simple," Caroline said.

"Perfect," Tessa said. "I'll pick up some red wine. Looks like we're running low."

CHAPTER EIGHTEEN

After closing her first rental, Sophie started the week expecting wonderful things. She kept busy, doing everything Rick and the others recommended. She'd chosen a farm area, the neighborhood of her aunt's apartment.

"You might as well take advantage of living there. It's a tough market to crack but people knew your aunt—you should make a list of everyone she knew. You said she volunteered on a few boards and was active at the Met. Send a nice postcard to all of them letting them know who to call if they're in the market to buy or sell," Rick had said.

Sophie did that and was optimistic that she'd hear back from someone who might be looking for real estate help, but she heard crickets—nothing at all.

"It's a numbers game and timing. Where most people mess up is they reach out once and never follow through. Put everyone on a regular rotation, where you are reaching out to them with information about the market," Caroline advised. "They will remember your name when they finally have a need, and you might get a call or email out of the blue."

"Always have lots of balls in the air, because you'll drop most of them," Rick advised. Sophie had heard that same advice from most of the agents about the danger of getting one deal moving along and focusing all your energy on that and then when it falls apart, you're left with nothing.

Troy agreed to have Sophie do an open house on one of his listings. It was a slightly overpriced property, but the seller didn't want to lower the price.

"This will calm them down for a while. Doing open houses will keep them happy. Sellers think they are the magic sauce—when in reality, if they just priced better, they'd sell quicker," Troy said.

"Do you ever refuse to take a listing if the seller's price isn't realistic?" Sophie asked.

He nodded. "Yes. I hate doing it, but I've learned the hard way that it can be a complete time waster. When the listing period is up and the property hasn't sold, they blame the agent and give it to someone new, at a lower price and then it sells. It can be frustrating."

Sophie wondered why he'd taken this one if he felt it was overpriced. She didn't ask, but a moment later he volunteered the information. "I told him it was too high, but he promised to give me another chance if we don't sell it at this price. And I've worked with him before. So, it was a risk, but a calculated one."

Sophie set up an open house for that Saturday. They'd had to postpone the dinner party again because Caroline's grandmother fell, and Caroline went home for the weekend to see her family and visit her grandmother in the hospital. Tessa had mentioned that she'd probably spend the weekend at her boyfriend's apartment, so the weekend stretched ahead of Sophie, long and empty. She was glad to have the open house, and when Caroline asked if she'd cover her open house on Sunday, too, she happily agreed.

Sophie baked cookies Friday night. She wasn't much of a cook, but she could bake a really great chocolate chip cookie. She made a big batch and divided them to take to both open houses. She also printed up a bunch of brochures and brought a notebook for people to sign in with their contact information.

The weather cooperated and was clear and sunny, though cooler than Sophie would have liked. She got to the first open house on Saturday a bit early and turned on the oven. She put the cookies on a tray she'd brought with her and popped them in the oven to warm up and hopefully make the kitchen smell homey.

She arranged the warm cookies on a platter, along with a pitcher of cold water and nice paper cups. She walked around the apartment and made sure the lights were on in all the rooms and the curtains were open to let in as much light as possible. She also put balloons and a sign outside of the building, letting people know there was an open house. Now she just had to wait.

The open house started at two and went for one hour. A few minutes past two, the first potential buyers walked through the door. They were a young married couple in their early thirties and Sophie was thrilled to see when they signed in that they weren't working with an agent yet.

"We're just starting to look," the husband said.

"We are preapproved though," his wife added.

"Please look around and let me know if you have any questions," Sophie said.

"This listing has been on the market for a few weeks now. Do you think the owners are flexible on price?" the husband asked after they'd walked all through the apartment.

"I think he'd welcome an offer," Sophie said truthfully. She wasn't sure how flexible the owner would be, and she worked for the seller, so it was her job to get the best offer possible.

"This is a little higher than we'd hoped to pay," the wife said. "Do you have any other listings we should know about?"

Sophie smiled. "Of course. What's most important to you and what areas are you interested in?"

They chatted for another fifteen minutes or so and Sophie jotted down notes on what the couple wanted and what their ideal price range was. She agreed to follow up after the open house to set up some more showings for them.

About ten others came through, but none of them seemed like serious buyers. Still, Sophie was friendly and made sure to get contact information to follow up with those who weren't already working with realtors.

The open house the next day for Caroline was more of the same. Though there was one woman who seemed like she was ready to buy soon, and they agreed to touch base on Monday about seeing more properties. By Sunday evening, Sophie was tired but encouraged. She had two buyers to work with now and she figured that the odds were good she might have her first sale soon.

CHAPTER NINETEEN

S ophie was on a high all week, showing listings to her
two buyers and trying to drum up more buyers and
possible listings. She felt good about both buyers and set
up showings on both Thursday and Friday. Both said they
would call her over the weekend or on Monday with their
decisions.

So, she was on pins and needles when she checked her
email first thing Saturday morning before heading to the
store to pick up groceries for their dinner party that night.

First came the email from the young couple, who she'd
really liked.

"Sophie, we're so sorry, but we saw another listing last
night and we both fell in love and made an offer that was
accepted. You were great to work with and we'll be sure to
call if we're ever looking again."

And before that could sink in, another email came
through fifteen minutes later from the single woman that
had seemed like such a solid buyer. Well, she was, but like

the couple, she wasn't working exclusively with Sophie either.

"Sophie, I really liked the last listing you showed me, but I had dinner with a friend last night and she's decided to move, and her place is perfect for me. There's no realtor involved. I'm sorry this didn't work out, but I'll definitely tell my friends to call you. I did enjoy working with you."

Tessa walked into the kitchen as Sophie finished reading the email. She stopped and took in Sophie's face.

"Everything ok? You look like someone just died."

Sophie sighed and told her about the two emails. Tessa's expression softened and she made herself a cup of coffee and one for Sophie too. She set it down in front of her.

"I'm sorry. That's the worst. Especially when you're so sure you have a good one. It happens more often than we'd like—and always when you'd least expect it. I mean, the friend moving, that's just fate. The other couple though, unfortunately some buyers do that. They just call on different listings instead of working with one agent."

"Is there anything I can do to prevent that?"

Tessa shrugged. "Some people try to force buyers to sign exclusivity agreements. I don't believe in that. I prefer to just provide excellent service, so I deserve their loyalty. Most buyers won't do that to you. Some will, but in the long run, I think it works out better this way."

Sophie nodded. "I thought I was so close."

"Did you ask them if they were working with any other realtors?"

"I did. I got them both through open houses."

"Be more specific when you ask them. I ask if they have seen any other houses through a realtor. Because some buyers don't understand what working with a realtor means. At least if you know they are using other people, then you can decide how much time to spend on them."

"That makes sense." Sophie shook her head, still feeling horribly discouraged that her potential sales had disappeared. "Is it always this up and down?"

Tessa grinned. "It gets better as you gain more experience. You'll have a better sense about people, and really you just have to focus on generating as much activity with as many people as possible. So, if one thing blows up, or two, you just move on to the next deal."

Sophie appreciated that Tessa was being so kind and encouraging. She hadn't seen much of this side of her, and it helped lift her mood a little.

"How was your week?" Sophie asked her.

"It was good, really good actually. I had a couple of referrals, one for a buyer and a new listing and the buyer might be into the new listing. That almost never happens. But I'm still doing an open house and emailed my list. I'm not counting on that happening. But it would be great if it did—it's like a double deal."

"That's awesome. How much is the listing?"

"Just under four million," Tessa said.

Sophie did the math quickly in her head and the size of the commission was staggering.

"That's so much money. Are you saving a lot?"

"I'm starting to. Last year I paid off my college loans and my car. Now I'm saving to buy something." She grinned. "But I want something really nice, like this place. So, it may be a while."

A few minutes later, Caroline padded into the kitchen and murmured hello on her way to the coffee machine. She made herself a cup, took a sip and leaned against the kitchen counter. And then she noticed Sophie and Tessa sitting side by side at the island.

"What are you two up to?"

"Sophie just got some bad news," Tessa said.

"Both of my buyers just made offers—not through me." Sophie filled her in, and Caroline looked so sympathetic that Sophie almost felt like crying. She appreciated the support though.

"That stinks. Don't let it get you too down though. Just keep moving forward," Caroline advised.

"That's what Tessa said, too. It's good advice."

Tessa grinned. "You could always go back to the reception desk."

Sophie smiled. She knew Tessa was teasing, but she did keep it in the back of her mind, that if this didn't work out, she could always go back to reception or temp elsewhere. But she wasn't anywhere near ready to give up yet. If anything, she was even more determined to make this work. She really believed it was possible.

Sophie put all thoughts of real estate out of her mind for the rest of the day and went with Caroline to the grocery store to get everything they needed to make lasagna. Caroline had her mother's recipe in an old cookbook on a sheet of paper that was oil-stained from frequent use.

"I almost know this recipe by heart I've made it so many times," Caroline said. "But I still like to double-check and make sure I don't forget anything. She showed Sophie how to make it and the kitchen smelled so good when Caroline pulled the lasagna out of the oven. It was late afternoon and they planned to reheat it before everyone arrived.

Sophie got her garlic bread ready to go into the oven at the same time. She split a loaf of crusty Italian bread and slathered softened butter, crushed garlic, parsley and a little parmesan over it, then she put the two loaves together again and wrapped it all in foil. When she baked it later the outsides would be nice and crusty and the tops all soft and buttery.

Tessa had a showing that afternoon and then hit the gym before stopping at the wine store and coming home with an assortment of red wines.

"They were having a tasting in the store, so I tried a few and got the ones I liked. I need to go jump in the shower now." She was still in her gym clothes.

An hour later, they put the lasagna and garlic bread in the oven to warm up. Tessa opened two of the bottles of wine. "We can let them breathe a little and open up before everyone gets here," she said.

Sophie found a big bowl and pulled a tossed salad together and set it on the counter. Everything was ready and a few minutes later, Caroline's boyfriend arrived, followed five minutes later by Cody and last of all, ten minutes later, Max knocked on the door.

Sophie let him in and noticed immediately that something seemed off about him. He wasn't his usual cheery self. He seemed quieter than usual and looked a little down. She registered that all in a few seconds and realized she might be making the wrong assumptions. It's just that Max always greeted her with a big grin, he was generally sunny and upbeat. But not today.

"Hey there. Come on in. Millie couldn't make it?"

He shook his head. "No." He didn't elaborate and handed her a bottle of red wine. It was Austin Hope. He'd remembered that it was one of her favorite 'splurge' wines. It usually ran about $50 a bottle, so as much as she loved it, she didn't have it often.

"Thank you, Max. That's so nice of you." Sophie brought it in the kitchen and set it with the others on the counter. "We have some red already open, would you like a glass?"

He nodded, "Sure."

Sophie poured him a glass and introduced him to Cody and Ed. Caroline had set out a bowl of salted mixed nuts and they nibbled on those while they sipped their wine, and everyone chatted while the food heated up.

When it suddenly smelled amazing, Sophie guessed that it was time to take it out of the oven. Caroline was already on it and checked to see if the lasagna was ready. It was, so she put it on the stove top and set the garlic bread next to it. She cut the lasagna, while Sophie sliced the garlic bread. Everyone helped themselves and settled at the dining room table.

The lasagna tasted as good as it smelled and everyone raved about it and the garlic bread, too. The conversation over dinner was lively as they talked about everything from football to real estate and concerts that they'd seen recently.

The guys all went back for second helpings of lasagna. Sophie reached for another slice of garlic bread. When Max sat back down, Tessa looked at him curiously. "I thought Millie was going to come tonight. Is she traveling somewhere exotic again?"

Max sighed. "I don't really know where she is. We actually broke up yesterday." He reached for the garlic bread and ripped a piece off. There was a sudden, awkward silence at the table.

Sophie looked at him sympathetically. Now she understood why he seemed off. "I'm sorry, Max."

He looked at her gratefully. "It's fine. It was a long time coming." He glanced Tessa's way. "Last I knew she was in London hanging out with Rodney Blake."

"The Rodney Blake?" Tessa was clearly impressed. Rodney was one of the biggest pop stars in the world and was insanely handsome in a sexy, charismatic way.

"Yep. She swears they're just friends. But it doesn't matter. It hasn't been right with us in a while. I never see her. The traveling gets old after a while."

"I'm sorry, Max. Breakups are tough," Caroline said.

He nodded. "Thanks. I'll probably be in my hermit stage for a while, where I lick my wounds and lose myself in stories that are darker than usual."

"Well, that sounds depressing," Tessa said.

Max laughed. "I'm being dramatic. But seriously, every time I've had a breakup it is usually good for my writing. So, it's not all bad."

It didn't sound overly healthy to Sophie, but if it helped him to deal with the breakup maybe it was a good thing.

"Did anyone save room for dessert?" she asked. "We have tiramisu from the Italian bakery."

"I think there's always room for tiramisu," Max said.

Sophie and Caroline cleared the table while Tessa set out the tiramisu and dessert plates. Everyone had a little and it was so creamy and delicious. It was one of Sophie's favorite desserts. She loved the coffee and liqueur-soaked ladyfingers and the smooth mascapone and whipped cream filling. She was too full to have more than a bite or two, but she was already planning to have a bigger slice with her coffee in the morning.

They sat around the table chatting for another hour or so before Max yawned and said he needed to get going. Sophie immediately yawned too and then laughed. "Why is it that yawns are always contagious?"

Max thanked them and said goodbye to everyone. Sophie walked him to the door. "If you need anything, let me know. Maybe we can watch *Murders* tomorrow night, if you feel up to it?" she suggested.

Max smiled and pulled her in for a goodbye hug and squeezed her tight for a quick moment. "You're the best, Sophie. It was good for me to get out tonight and get my mind off things. I'll text you tomorrow about *Murders*."

"Night, Max, sleep well."

Sophie joined the others at the table and Tessa raised her eyebrows. "So, Max is single....you should go for it."

Sophie didn't think of Max that way and said so. "We're just friends, and I think that's what he needs right now. He seems pretty upset about this breakup. I'm sure dating is the last thing on his mind."

Tessa looked skeptical. "He's a guy. He'll be ready to date someone soon, might as well be you, unless you're not interested? He's a catch though."

"I can't think of him that way. You're right though. He is a great guy." She yawned again and stood up. "I think I'm going to call it a night."

CHAPTER TWENTY

Sophie's mother called a little after ten Sunday morning. Sophie hesitated when she saw the familiar number on the caller ID. She loved her mother, but they really weren't close, and she hadn't talked to her in well over a month when she'd still been trying to convince Sophie to sell the apartment. But she felt more guilty not answering. She took a deep break and said hello to her mother.

"Hi Mom, how are things in Hudson?"

"Everything is fine here. How are you doing, Sophie? Did your roommates move in?" Sophie had told her when they last spoke that she was going to rent rooms to Tessa and Caroline.

"Yes, they moved in not long after we last spoke. It's going well. We had a dinner party last night."

"A dinner party? Who did the cooking?" Her mother's tone made it clear that she didn't think it would be Sophie.

"Caroline made lasagna. But she showed me how to do it and I helped. It came out great."

"Well, it's good that you're finally learning to cook. What about your job? Have you sold anything yet?"

Her mother's timing couldn't possibly be worse. "I almost had two sales this week, but they both fell through," Sophie admitted.

Her mother was quiet for a moment. "I don't know how people can work on all commission. That seems ridiculous. Maybe they will give your old job back to you if you ask them? Or you could always temp again?"

Sophie felt the beginning of a stress headache. "Mom, it takes most agents a while to get going. I did close an apartment rental, so I'll get some commission on that. And even if I were to make a sale today it would still be three months on average before I'd see a commission check. I'm looking at the big picture here and just working hard."

"Three months! I really think you should reconsider this job. I never pictured you in a sales role."

Sophie hadn't either. But she didn't want to admit that to her mother.

"Mom, I'm fine. I don't spend a lot and with the rent money from Caroline and Tessa and Aunt Penny's bank account, I can manage for at least a year even if I don't make any sales. It's the perfect time for me to try this."

Her mother sighed. "Well, you know what I think. I only want the best for you."

"I know. Please tell Dad I said hi."

"I will."

"I should run, Mom. I'll talk to you soon."

Sophie ended the call feeling exhausted. She'd already been full of doubts. But in a strange way, having the conversation with her mother strengthened her resolve to keep going. She really wanted this to work out and for her mother to see that she could be successful in real estate sales.

Max texted her later that afternoon around three.

Are you still up for Murders at 7? If so, do you want to come here? I don't think I'm in the mood for a lot of people.

Sophie smiled. She didn't blame him for not wanting to be grilled by Tessa again. And she was curious to see his apartment. So far, he'd always come to her aunt's place.

Sure, what can I bring? she texted back.

Nothing. Or maybe wine. I'll get pizza if that works?

Perfect. See you at 7

"I'm heating up the leftover lasagna, do you want some?" Caroline asked a little before seven. They'd had a lazy afternoon, doing laundry and watching TV after Caroline's and Tessa's boyfriends went home.

"I'll have some," Tessa said. She was sprawled out on the sofa, reading a magazine.

"I'm actually heading over to Max's. We're getting pizza and watching *Murders*," Sophie said.

Tessa sat up and she and Caroline exchanged looks. "He usually comes here for that," Tessa said. "Did you change your mind about going after him?"

Sophie laughed. "Not at all. I just think he's still kind of down. He wasn't up for being around everyone."

Caroline nodded. "I'd probably feel the same. I'll save you a piece of lasagna. You can have it tomorrow."

"Thank you."

Sophie grabbed the bottle of Austin Hope that Max had brought over the night before. She walked down the hall to Max's apartment and knocked twice.

He came to the door a moment later and smiled when he saw her and the wine. He was wearing sweats and his hair was still a little damp from a recent shower. When he smiled a dimple popped in his left cheek and Sophie wondered why she'd never noticed that before.

"Come on in. Thanks for bringing the wine."

She smiled. "I thought it seemed appropriate as we never got to it last night. And I know it goes really well with pizza."

He laughed. "I think it goes pretty well with just about everything."

Sophie followed him into his kitchen and looked around the apartment as she walked. The layout was similar to her aunt's apartment but the decor and overall feel was totally different. Max's place had a much more masculine feel with leather sofas and walls painted deep hunter green and blue gray.

The kitchen had burgundy walls almost the same shade as the wine and smoky black granite counter tops. His appliances were stainless steel and the stove was chef quality—an Aga—with six gas burners. Even though Sophie wasn't much of a cook, she still recognized high-end names.

"Your kitchen is gorgeous. I didn't realize you were into cooking. Or was it your mother that got the Aga?"

He looked amused. "I'm not sure my mother would know what an Aga is. I totally renovated the apartment when I bought it. And in the past few years, I've gotten more into cooking. Though I still mostly eat pizza and takeout."

"What are your specialties? Maybe you can give me a few tips. My cooking abilities leave a lot to be desired."

He thought for a moment. "I make a pretty delicious steak au poivre and short ribs and meatballs." He laughed. "Mostly red meat, I guess. Oh, and salmon. I've been experimenting with that some lately."

Sophie's stomach rumbled at the mention of the different dishes. "I don't know how to cook any of that. It all sounds delicious, though."

"Are you hungry? The pizza just arrived a minute before you got here, and it looks pretty good. We could eat while it's hot. Once you open the wine, of course." He handed her a wine opener.

"Of course. I'm starving, actually."

They took the wine and pizza into Max's living room and sat side by side on his chocolate brown leather sofa. Max clicked on the TV and found their show. Sophie sipped her wine and felt an awareness of Max that she hadn't felt before. He was just inches away from her on the sofa and she caught a whiff of the soap he'd used in his shower. She noticed how his hair fell in natural dark waves and how there was a hint of stubble on his jaw. He clearly hadn't shaved, but the look worked on him.

She'd always noticed that Max was good-looking of course—she wasn't blind. She'd just never thought of herself as attracted to him before. He'd had a girlfriend, so she'd automatically put him firmly in the friend bucket. She'd assumed that was where he'd stay. This new attraction complicated things. As Max had made it clear that he wasn't even thinking about dating yet. And if he was—he'd never given her any indication that he saw her as anything other than a friend.

Sophie pushed the silly thought away and reached for another slice of pizza. She could be secretly attracted to her next-door neighbor. No one had to know. She knew Caroline and Tessa would be pushing her to do something about it if they had any idea how she felt. And she didn't even know if this was a real attraction or just a sudden awareness now that she knew he was single. No, what Max needed from her now was friendship, nothing more.

CHAPTER TWENTY-ONE

W hen everyone went around the room giving updates on pending deals Monday morning, Sophie cringed when it was her turn.

"Both of my possible deals fell through. They both bought houses, but not through me."

There was an awkward moment of silence and then Rick looked around the table and grinned. "Sophie, I'm sorry to hear that. But as everyone around this table can confirm, it has happened to all of us. Just keep going. Remember, focus on generating as much activity as possible and the deals will happen."

Sophie tried her best all week. She did everything imaginable to drum up some business, and by Friday morning, she was deeply discouraged again because nothing seemed to be happening. No one returned her calls or her emails and even the one ad call she took the day before sounded like a good buyer, but he was a no-show for a meeting she set up.

She sipped her coffee in the meeting and tried to will

herself into a better mood. It was hard though when everyone around her had exciting things happening and she had no updates at all to share. She hoped that Rick wouldn't think she wasn't trying because she was. She was starting to wonder though if maybe she just wasn't cut out for this business. Maybe she wasn't meant to do sales.

She was starting to worry about the money a little bit, too. Her aunt had left her a bank account that, with what Caroline and Tessa paid her each month, would cover the management fees, but she'd just had a letter this week informing her that all units were going to be assessed fifty thousand dollars for unexpected building repairs. That was above and beyond what the monthly fees covered. There was enough in her account to cover it, but it would be a significant decrease to her balance.

If she didn't start generating some income soon, when Tessa's and Caroline's year was up, Sophie might have to sell the apartment. She hated even thinking of it, but realistically it might come to that, unless she was able to make a go of this. If she went back to temping, that wouldn't be enough to stay in the apartment long-term—eventually, she would have to sell. The thought was depressing.

They were going around the table doing updates on new activity and it was almost Sophie's turn. Once again, she would have to say she had nothing new to report. Her phone dinged with a new text message, and she glanced at it, then reread it, and smiled.

"Sophie, anything new to report?" Rick asked.

She looked up. "I might have my first listing. I just got a text message, a referral from the couple that bought from someone else. She has a condo she wants to sell."

"Fantastic news! You didn't make that sale, but they liked you enough to refer their friend. Well done," Rick looked pleased to hear it.

And just like that, Sophie's mood shifted and she felt excited and hopeful again.

Sophie met with Renee Hall that afternoon at her condo in the East Village. Sophie had done as much research as possible before heading out to the meeting. She looked the property up online and saw what others nearby had recently sold for. And she consulted with Rick to make sure her suggestion for pricing was right. She gave him all the information and waited for him to weigh in.

He looked everything over and then nodded. "This is a great listing, Sophie. I agree with your thoughts on pricing. Two million sounds exactly right for the market. And that's a price point that will move quickly, especially in that neighborhood. Do you know what she's thinking for price?"

"She said she wasn't sure and wanted me to advise her."

"Good. She'll probably still have some idea, hopefully she'll agree. Don't be surprised if she wants you to go higher. You could try a little higher if she really pushes back, but I wouldn't go more than two hundred over. And that's only if she agrees to lower it if we don't have offers right away."

"Great, thank you."

Sophie gathered her materials together—she'd printed out a presentation for Renee with detailed comps from other recent sales to support her suggested price. She headed out and hoped that the meeting would go well. Renee had sounded super nice when they spoke briefly after the meeting.

She arrived a few minutes early and took a good look at the outside of the building before going in. It was on a quiet street and the building was well maintained and there was a doorman. That was a plus.

Sophie went in and told the doorman she was there to see Renee. He buzzed her and Renee confirmed the meeting. Sophie went in the elevator to the sixth floor. There were seven floors in total.

She knocked on Renee's door and she opened it immediately.

"Hi Sophie, come on in."

She stepped inside and noticed the scent of something delicious coming from the kitchen.

"Are you cooking? It smells amazing," she said.

Renee laughed. "Thanks, it's a chicken stew. I work from home and when I went to the store earlier today, it was so cold and raw out that I wanted to make something cozy and warm. Let's look at the kitchen first."

Renee led her into the kitchen, which was a decent size, not just the usual galley kitchen. It had nice features too including a backsplash of smoky gray glass subway tiles, a Viking gas stove and wood paneled appliances that gave the kitchen a pretty, high-end look.

The kitchen opened into the living area, which had exposed brick along one wall and ten-foot ceilings which made it feel more spacious. There were two bedrooms and two bathrooms, one of them was in the primary. Both bedrooms were big enough for a king-size bed, which was a plus and the primary also had a walk-in closet. The final room was an office, and while it was small, it had a calming view of the building's courtyard with its leafy trees.

They made their way back to the kitchen and Renee suggested they sit at the island, which had three chairs and a creamy white quartz countertop that at first glance looked like marble.

"I really wanted marble, but my mother talked me out of it. She said marble is best for people that don't actually cook. It stains so easily."

"It's beautiful. It looks so much like marble," Sophie said.

"Would you like a cup of tea? I'm going to have one," Renee offered.

"Sure, I'd love one."

Renee had an electric kettle, and the water was already hot. She poured two cups of water and added teabags to each.

"It's Autumn Harvest, an herbal tea," Renee said as she set the cup in front of Sophie.

Sophie thanked her and took a small sip. It smelled amazing and tasted of apples and cinnamon. Once Renee was settled, Sophie walked her through the listing agreement. The final step was deciding on the price.

"Did you have a price in mind?" Sophie asked her.

"I really wasn't sure, but I did some research too and saw a lot of the listings you mentioned here. Given the high-end appliances and condition of my unit I thought maybe a little over two million, maybe a hundred thousand over?"

Sophie nodded. "My initial research before seeing your unit would have suggested right around two million. Now that I have seen it, I agree with you and think that sounds like where we should be. We can reevaluate in a few weeks once we've had some showings and collect feedback—and hopefully some offers. If we don't have offers and have feedback that the price seems high, we might want to consider lowering it at that time. Does that work for you?"

Renee nodded. "That seems fair. Will you want to do an open house?"

"I'd like to. If that is okay with you? We usually do them on the weekends and I can give you plenty of notice, of course."

"That's fine. I'll make sure I'm elsewhere."

Renee signed the listing agreement which was for ninety days, and Sophie drank a little more of her tea and then headed back to the office to get started on her new listing.

CHAPTER TWENTY-TWO

Sophie went back to the office and turned in her paperwork for the listing and input all the information into the computer. She set up an open house for that Sunday and posted all over social media and emailed everyone in the office and her tiny list of personal contacts.

Both Caroline and Tessa were at their desks. Caroline was in a fantastic mood and was writing up an offer for a condo she'd shown a few days ago. When she saw Sophie, she asked her how it went, and Sophie told her all about the new listing. Tessa sat two desks over and didn't even glance their way, which wasn't like her.

"Oh, that's a good one. Great price. There should be lots of interest, especially in that location. I may have someone, actually. I'll call and run it by them."

"Thank you!" Sophie glanced at Tessa who had her back to them. She raised her eyebrows at Caroline, and she sighed and spoke softly. "She's having a bad day. Her big double sale—the buyer didn't get co-op approval. She's back to square one on the listing and they are furious with her."

"Oh, that's awful. Does that happen often?" Sophie asked.

"Not usually. We know what the co-ops need to see, which is typically more money down, lower debt ratio and three years of funds in the bank to cover the monthly fees." Caroline paused. "It wasn't a money issue. Two of the people on the board know the buyer and don't like him. So, they vetoed him moving in. That doesn't happen often."

"That doesn't seem fair," Sophie said.

Tessa spun around in her chair. She'd obviously been listening. "It's beyond not fair. I've never had someone get declined just because they don't like the person. It's total BS. And now the seller is furious. He knows it's not my fault, but he's not happy and says if I don't find a buyer in the next few weeks, he's going to give the listing to someone else."

"I'm so sorry, Tessa," Sophie said.

"And I lost the buyer completely. I think he's embarrassed and just doesn't want to deal. He said he's going to stay in LA and will let me know if anything changes. I don't expect that I'll hear from him again."

"You might," Caroline said. "He might just need to calm down."

"Maybe, but I'm not holding my breath for that," Tessa said.

"We should go for after-work drinks. I think we all deserve a cocktail," Caroline said.

"I could definitely use a drink," Tessa said grumpily.

"We can celebrate Sophie's first listing," Caroline said.

Sophie felt bad celebrating, given what had just happened to Tessa.

Tessa laughed. "Hopefully she'll have better luck than I did."

They decided to go to a dive bar on the way home from the office. It was dark and smelled a bit of beer and it suited their moods. It was crowded but not packed and they easily found seats at the bar. It didn't seem like a fancy cocktail kind of place, so they stuck with basic things—Tessa had a vodka and soda water with cranberry, Caroline had a gin and tonic and Sophie went with a cosmopolitan.

Tessa's first drink went down quickly, and she ordered another. Caroline and Sophie had barely taken more than a few sips of theirs.

"That helped take the edge off," she said. "I still can't believe this deal fell through. I thought it was so solid. It never crossed my mind that they'd reject him just because they don't like him."

"These co-op boards can be tough," Caroline said. "It's a gorgeous property, hopefully we can find someone else for it."

Tessa nodded and launched into office gossip. "So, did you happen to notice that Rick gave Sue another referral? This time it's an actual listing. I hate the way he plays favorites." She took a big swig of her drink and looked mad at the world.

Sophie glanced at Caroline. "Does he favor people?"

Caroline hesitated. "I didn't think so. Sue is one of the top billers and he rewards people sometimes with referrals that come in."

"He handed her a three million dollar listing. Must be nice," Tessa said bitterly.

Sophie could tell that Tessa was just miserable in general and that it was probably best to change the subject if possible.

"What are you guys up to this weekend?" she asked.

"I'll be holding an open house on Sunday. Three of them actually, back to back. I need to get more activity going," Tessa said.

"Are you doing anything fun, though?" Sophie asked.

"I don't know. Cody mentioned something about dinner somewhere. I have no interest in food at the moment, though. When I get stressed, I lose my appetite totally."

"I wish I did," Sophie said. "I'm the opposite—a stress eater. I go looking for comfort food, mac and cheese, potato chips."

"We have tickets to the Jets game on Sunday. I still have one open house though, at eleven and the game is at four," Caroline said.

"That sounds fun," Sophie said.

"I'll probably spend the weekend at Cody's. I'll let him spoil me and try to get my mind off this horrible day," Tessa said.

Sophie felt badly for Tessa but was somewhat relieved that she was going to be away for the weekend. With just her and Caroline, the energy in the apartment would be calmer and quieter. Sophie thought she would probably have a quiet weekend, too. Which was fine with her. After working all week, she didn't mind hunkering down on the weekend. And she had her open house to look forward to on Sunday. She liked that the open houses in Manhattan were typically just an hour, unlike the ones in her hometown that were always two or sometimes three hours long.

"Why are open houses only an hour in Manhattan?" she asked.

"It creates more of a sense of urgency, and it seems like more people are interested, which can mean they will move faster to an offer," Caroline said. "We also don't want to waste our time, and this way we can do multiple open houses the same day."

"That makes sense," Sophie said.

"Sometimes we can create even more urgency by holding all showings until the first open house. I've done that a few times," Tessa said.

"Should I do that?" Sophie asked.

Caroline shook her head. "I wouldn't. Just get the listing up and show it to anyone that will look. What you may want to do is to email some of the brokers we work with often from other offices and invite them to stop by as well and to bring any buyers they might have."

"I'll do that first thing tomorrow morning," Sophie said.

Caroline and Sophie had another round, and Tessa ordered her third drink. She was in a better mood now and had shifted from being upset to laughing at the absurdity of it.

By the time they left to walk home, they were all in a relatively good mood and Tessa's appetite had returned. They decided to pick up some Thai takeout on the way home and to relax and watch a gossipy real estate reality show. It was so ridiculous that they laughed constantly.

"Thank goodness it's not really like that," Caroline said.

"Well, it can be cutthroat at times," Tessa said. "But nothing like these shows make it out to be."

Even though it was over-the-top, these reality shows were guilty pleasures, and they were addicted to them.

"Tomorrow will be a better day, Tessa. We'll all try to find you a buyer," Caroline said.

"Yes, I don't have many buyers yet, but I'm trying to get more, and I'd love to find someone for you, too," Sophie said.

"Thanks guys. It's all good. I have almost a month to find someone. I am determined to get this under contract ASAP."

CHAPTER TWENTY-THREE

Sophie was excited to start the volunteers training program Saturday at the Met. It was a combination of online and onsite training, and the program was six months long. By the time they finished, they'd know enough to answer questions from people visiting the museum. And Sophie had been accepted into the weekend program which would be a shift every other weekend once she finished the training.

During the break between their first and second lecture, the attendees chatted amongst themselves and introduced each other.

There were six people in her class, and they were a mix of ages and backgrounds. Two were younger and were art history students at nearby colleges. Two were retired and were excited to learn more about the museum they'd loved for years. And the other was a woman about Sophie's age. Her name was Emily. Her hair was a sleek, shiny brown bob that fell to her collarbone and Sophie loved her outfit. She was so elegantly dressed in a cream cashmere turtleneck and wool caramel-colored pants and boots. She had stunning diamond solitaire earrings and a thick gold bangle bracelet.

"I just had my second baby recently and am a stay-at-home mother now. But I really miss working. I've always loved art, so this will let me get out of the house and feel useful."

"How old are your children?" Sophie asked her.

"The baby, Leo, is just six months and my girl, Mariah, is four. What about you?"

"No kids yet. I'm new to the city. I just started working in real estate recently. My aunt was a volunteer here for years and loved it so much. I live close by and thought I'd follow in her footsteps. And it's something to do on the weekends. I still don't know many people here yet," she admitted.

Emily smiled. "The weekends are perfect for me too, because Jim is home and can watch the kids for the afternoon. Where do you live?"

"Just a few blocks down from here. My aunt had an apartment and recently passed, and she knew how much I loved the city."

"Oh, I'm so sorry. How wonderful though that you get to stay here now. We live nearby, too. I love our apartment, but now that the baby has come, it's feeling a little small. Eventually we may want to get a bigger place. But we're in no rush," Emily said.

"Moving is stressful," Sophie agreed. She'd already mentioned that she was in real estate so she didn't want to be pushy and offer to help. She knew she probably should, but it didn't feel right. Not yet.

Emily laughed. "It really is. I'm just not ready to deal with it yet. Maybe in a few more months. We'll see. How is the market right now?"

"It's busy. We have a lot of beautiful properties. I'm sure there will be plenty when you're ready to look," she said.

Emily nodded. "That's what Jim says, too. He's not in any hurry, but he said it's my call. Whenever I'm ready, we can start looking. Maybe I'll pick your brain then."

Sophie smiled. "Of course. I'd be happy to help."

Their instructor started speaking again and they brought their attention back to the next lecture.

When the training was over everyone went their separate ways, and Sophie stopped off at the grocery store. She had the apartment to herself as both Caroline and Tessa were off with their boyfriends. She decided to try and cook something and was craving risotto. She'd looked up a recipe online and it didn't look that hard. There was half of a rotisserie chicken in the fridge and a wedge of parmesan cheese. She bought arborio rice, chicken stock, mushrooms and spinach. The recipe also called for a little white wine, so she decided to have a glass of that as well and picked up a bottle of chardonnay.

When she passed by the bakery section of the store, a box of bite-sized brownies called to her, and she added those to her cart. She carried her bag of groceries home and was glad it was a short walk.

When she walked out of the elevator, Max was coming down the hall towards her. She hadn't seen him since they'd had pizza at his place the previous Sunday night. He smiled when he saw her and glanced at her bag of food. "What are you up to?"

"I'm going to try and make risotto tonight. My first time."

"Oh, that sounds good. What kind?"

"Nothing fancy, leftover rotisserie chicken and mushrooms and spinach." She grinned. "And lots of cheese."

"Perfect. I'm sure it will be great. Risotto is easy. A little time-consuming, but not too bad."

"Where are you off to?" she asked. She assumed he was heading out to do something interesting.

"I'm heading to Duane Reade actually. Very late night with the guys yesterday and I've run out of Advil. Coming straight home and in for the night after that."

He did look tired. Sophie felt for him. Being hungover was no fun.

"If you're up for it, I could use some help eating the risotto. The recipe makes a ton," she said.

He nodded. "Sure. I could come while you're making it if you like and give you a few tips."

"I'd love that. Why don't you come around five thirty? I'm guessing no wine for you tonight?" she teased.

Max made a face at the mention of wine. "Not a drop. I'll bring my bottle of Gatorade."

Sophie sympathized. "I'm sorry you're feeling so lousy. I also picked up brownies and we have vanilla ice cream. That might help you feel better."

He grinned. "It just might. See you in a bit."

CHAPTER TWENTY-FOUR

Sophie had all the ingredients lined up on the counter for the risotto. She found a big cast iron soup pot that her aunt had that looked about the right size for the risotto. The recipe called for a half cup of white wine, so she'd chosen one of her favorite chardonnays. She'd read somewhere that if a recipe called for wine that you should pick one that you enjoyed drinking. She measured out a half cup and then poured herself a small glass as well, to sip on while she cooked.

At a few minutes past five thirty when she was about to start chopping the onion, there was a knock on the door. Max stood there, holding a giant blue bottle of Gatorade. He'd showered and looked more alive.

"Are you feeling better?" she asked as he followed her into the kitchen.

"Yes, much. It's amazing what a shower, lots of water and Gatorade can do. I'm actually getting a little hungry, too."

"I was just about to get started, so it shouldn't take too long, I don't think."

"Maybe a half hour or so once you have the rice in the pan," Max said.

He watched as Sophie measured out two tablespoons of butter and one of olive oil and added both to the big pot on the stove. A few minutes later, she added the chopped onion.

"Does your recipe suggest warming your broth? That makes it all go faster. I put a separate pot on the stove and dump the broth into it," Max said.

Sophie glanced at the recipe. "No, it doesn't mention that. I'll do it, though." She found a small pot and poured the chicken broth into it and set it on the burner over low to medium heat.

"Those onions look ready. You can add the rice now," Max advised.

The onions were soft and translucent. Sophie dumped a cup and a half of the arborio rice in the pan and stirred to coat. The directions said to add the wine a minute later. She did that and gave it a good stir.

"As the liquid is absorbed, you just add another half cup or so and give it a stir. Keep an eye on it though and turn the heat down or up if it's getting absorbed too fast and sticking on the bottom of the pan," Max said.

Sophie smiled. "You sound much better. Are you sure you don't want a glass of wine? This chardonnay is really good."

Max looked horrified at the thought. "I couldn't be more sure. No wine for me tonight."

She laughed, not surprised by his answer. "So, tell me

about last night. Where did you guys go and why did you drink so much?" Max didn't usually overdo it from what Sophie knew of him.

He sighed. "It started out as a fun night. A bunch of us met up at a bar in Brooklyn, had a few drinks and then got some food. As we were finishing up, a few of the guys were going to head home, two others wanted to head to another bar. I didn't have any reason to rush home, so I went with them." He paused for a moment and took a swig of his Gatorade.

"As we walked to the bar I got a text message from Millie saying she missed me and wanted to know if she could come over and if we could talk. It killed me to say no, but I did. And then spent the rest of the night obsessing over it with the guys and wondering if I'd made a huge mistake. That led to doing shots and staying out much too late."

Sophie watched him closely. "Do you regret it? Not agreeing to see her and talk about it?" He still seemed pretty torn up about it.

But Max shook his head. "No. I woke up and felt calm about the whole thing, but last night I had doubts. The only reason to have her over and talk would be if I was open to getting back together. And I'm not. So, it didn't feel like the right thing to do—for either of us. I didn't want to lead her on or agree to something that I really don't want."

"Did you tell her that?"

"Yeah. She understands it even though she doesn't like it. When we talked initially about this, I asked her if she planned to cut back on her travel. That was one of my main issues. I just didn't see her enough and didn't see that changing. And she said no. It won't change. Not anytime soon. So, that settled it."

"I'm sorry, Max. Breakups are hard."

"Yeah, they are. But it's all good." He smiled. "Or it will be soon. You might want to add some broth to that."

Sophie glanced at the risotto. It was looking a little dry on top with lots of holes that used to be bubbles. She scooped up some of the warm broth and added it. When she stirred the rice, her spoon stuck on the bottom, and she scraped it up and lowered the heat a little.

"So how was your day today, before you went grocery shopping?" Max asked.

"Oh, it was really good. I started training for a volunteer role at the Met and it was fun."

"Your aunt used to love volunteering there. She would definitely approve."

"Yeah, I think she would. I used to love going to the Met with her. I could stare at the paintings for hours."

"Well, that sounds like the perfect volunteer job, then. The Met is a cool place. It's been a few years since I've been. I should go again. I know they change up the exhibits all the time."

"You really should. I'll go with you anytime," Sophie said. "Oh, and I got my first listing this week. I'm doing an open house for it tomorrow."

"Cool, tell me all about it."

She did and when she finished describing the co-op, he agreed that it sounded like a great listing.

"Tessa had a rough week." She told him about her sale falling apart and the co-op board rejecting her buyer.

"That stinks. Co-op boards can be brutal like that.

Really petty if they just don't like someone. Those deals always take longer to close too as the co-op approval process can drag on. My mother was on the board here and she told me some stories over the years," Max said.

"I'll keep my fingers crossed that the co-op board on my listing is nicer!" Sophie laughed as she added more broth to the risotto and gave it a stir.

"I hope you have beginner's luck and sell it super fast. Maybe the perfect buyer will come to your open house tomorrow," Max said.

"Thanks. That would be awesome. I'm not counting on it. Did you know something like only three percent of sales come from open houses? But it is a great way to find buyers for other houses. If I get a buyer at all tomorrow, I'll be thrilled."

"Maybe I'll stop by and check it out. I have nothing going on tomorrow."

"If you could, that would be great. The more people that come, the better and I'd love your opinion once you see it."

"Will do. You might want to add your mushrooms now, give them a little time to cook down," Max suggested.

Sophie dumped the mushrooms and some more broth into the pan and took a sip of her wine. After another ladle of broth was absorbed, she added the spinach and chopped cooked chicken. The final step was to add the last bit of broth, more butter and about a third of a cup of freshly grated parmesan cheese. She stirred it all together and then handled Max a forkful to taste. "Can you let me know if this needs anything?"

He took the bite and swallowed. "That's good. Did you use low sodium broth?"

She nodded. "I did. Does it need salt?"

"Yeah, a little salt and pepper and maybe another pinch of parmesan. It's good though!"

Sophie added the seasoning and grated more cheese over the risotto and gave it a final stir. She took two plates from the cupboard and scooped a big mound of risotto on each. They ate at the island, and both went back for seconds. Sophie was happy with how it turned out.

"It's really not hard at all. A great way to use up leftovers," she said.

"It will taste great tomorrow, too," Max said.

"You might have to take some home with you. I can't eat all of this." The recipe made a huge amount.

"I'm happy to help you out with that," Max said.

After they finished eating and Sophie put everything away. She turned to Max.

"How are you feeling now that you've eaten? Any better?"

He grinned. "All better. Did you mention something about brownies?"

She laughed. "Yes, I'll get them. Ice cream, too?"

"What do you think?"

"Right. Silly question." She got the carton of vanilla ice cream out and the box of brownies and two bowls. "Here you go, help yourself."

They filled their bowls with ice cream and mini-brownies and took them into the living room and settled on the sofa. Sophie clicked on the TV and surfed until she found a movie on Netflix that they both wanted to watch—a humorous action film.

The movie was good and by the time it ended, Max was yawning even though it wasn't even nine yet. Sophie guessed that the day had caught up to him and that he probably hadn't slept well the night before and then woke up feeling awful from being hungover.

"I'm sorry. How lame that I'm ready for bed already," Max apologized.

Sophie picked up their ice cream bowls and brought them to the kitchen sink.

"Don't be silly," she said. "You had a rough night or rather day. I bet you'll sleep well tonight."

"Thanks, Soph. For dinner and for understanding. You're a good friend." He pulled her in for a goodbye hug and squeezed her tight.

"Goodnight, Max. See you tomorrow."

She closed the door behind him, rinsed the bowls and put them in the dishwasher and tidied up the rest of the kitchen. It was still early, and she was wide awake, so she headed back to the sofa and clicked over to the Hallmark Channel. After the action movie she was in the mood for cozy Christmas. She thought about what Max had said, how he considered her a good friend. That made it clear how he felt about her. She did value his friendship. He was one of the few friends she'd made so far in the city. She didn't want to ruin that by crushing on him too obviously.

CHAPTER TWENTY-FIVE

Sophie's open house was at one the next day and she headed out early to make sure she had time to heat up her cookies in the oven. She'd made the cookie batter that morning, shaped it into balls and froze them. Then she brought the frozen dough balls and a cookie sheet to the open house and popped them into the oven. She got there a half hour early and baked two batches. The first batch was cool enough to eat, but still warm and the smell of baking cookies was tantalizing and gave the apartment a cozy feel.

She'd just finished piling the cookies on a platter when the first person arrived. It was a sunny, clear day and she was surprised by how many people came to see the apartment. Some of them were with brokers, who were also curious to see it. One of them stopped and chatted with her while his clients were walking around.

"This is a great listing. If the people I brought don't offer, I may have several others that could be interested. Will let you know ASAP," he said.

A few of the people looking were curious neighbors. Caroline had told her that often happened with open houses. But there were also two interesting buyers that were not currently working with realtors, and both agreed to speak further with Sophie on Monday. They both loved the property but wanted to look at other things.

Max came by a little after one thirty. He walked around and then joined her in the kitchen and took a cookie. "Are these homemade? It smells like you baked them here."

She nodded. "They are and I did."

He took a bite. "Impressive." He glanced around the room. "It's a great listing, too. Seems decently priced, considering the appliances and some of the built-ins in the living room and office." Both rooms had polished, custom-built wooden bookcases, that were staying with the unit.

"Thanks. The feedback has been pretty positive so far."

Sophie looked up as a familiar face walked through the door. It was Rick Fulton. She was surprised to see him.

"Afternoon, Sophie. I was in the area and thought I'd drop in and have a look and see how things are going," he said.

There was still a broker and two other potential buyers walking through the unit. Rick glanced at her sign-in sheet and saw that twenty-four people had signed in. Sophie wasn't totally sure, but she thought that seemed like a decent amount. The hour had flown by, and it felt very busy. She'd been fielding questions the entire time.

"It has been pretty steady," she said.

He nodded. "Nice turnout. I see a few broker names that I recognize too." He sniffed the air. "Smells fantastic. Did you bake something?"

She smiled. "I made chocolate chip cookies. Have one." She held the plate up.

He reached over and took one. "Well done. I'm going to have a quick look around."

He wandered off and Max raised his eyebrows. "Your boss, I take it?"

"Yes. I'm sorry, I should have introduced you. I will when he comes back. I was just a little flustered. I didn't expect to see him."

"No worries. He seemed pretty happy." Max grabbed another cookie and Sophie reached for one, too. The open house was over in ten minutes.

The broker and his client left, and the remaining potential buyer walked up to Sophie. He'd already signed in and seemed excited. "I didn't expect to like this place so much. I'd like to come back tomorrow with my wife if that's possible?"

"Of course! What time were you thinking?"

"We could come over at lunchtime if that works. I know you have a lot of people looking, so I want to move as fast as possible. We've lost out on two other properties," he admitted.

"Are you already working with another realtor?" Sophie asked.

"No. This was months ago. We were so disappointed that we put our search on hold. And we weren't crazy about the agent we were working with. The communication was frustrating. This is your listing, right?"

Sophie nodded. "Yes. But if your wife doesn't like it, we can look at other things. We can talk about that more tomorrow. I'll call the seller when I leave here and confirm that we can do that time tomorrow and I'll text you after."

"Excellent. I look forward to it. You don't have any offers yet, I hope?" He looked concerned.

Sophie shook her head. "Not yet. This is a new listing and first open house."

"Good. We'll see you tomorrow then. I'll watch for your text."

He left and Rick sauntered over wearing a Cheshire cat grin. "Well, that sounded promising. Were there any others that seemed interested?"

"A few actually. One of the brokers said if his clients weren't interested, that he might have one or two others to show it to. And I picked up two new buyers, well three counting this last guy."

"Excellent. You're doing a great job, Sophie. You'll be ringing the bell soon, I can feel it."

Sophie laughed. "Rick, this is Max Bennett. He's my neighbor."

Rick held out his hand. "Great to meet you. My sister loves your books."

Max smiled and shook his hand. "Please thank her for me."

"Will do." Rick turned his attention back to Sophie. "I'll get out of here so you can pack up. See you in the office tomorrow."

Rick left and once he was gone the apartment felt quiet.

"He's an energetic guy," Max commented.

"He is. It's nice that he took the time to stop by," Sophie said.

"Does he go to everyone's open houses?" Max asked. There was an edge to his voice that Sophie found curious.

"I don't know. I wouldn't think so. He said he happened to be in the area. I think he probably wanted to check and see how I was doing as this is my first listing."

"He seems very hands on," Max said.

"He is. He knows pretty much everything that is going on."

Max glanced at the platter of cookies. "Do you need a hand packing up?"

"Sure. Do you want to carry the cookie sheet, and I'll pack the cookies up?"

Sophie boxed them up, set them on the platter and handed Max the cookie sheet. She took a final walk through the apartment to make sure nothing was out of order, then they headed home. As they walked, she called the seller to let her know how the open house went.

"We had a good turnout. One guy seemed very interested and wants to come back tomorrow at one with his wife. Does that work for you?"

"I'll make it work. I'll head to the coffee shop around the corner for an hour or so. Come any time after twelve thirty."

"Great. I'll keep you posted with their feedback."

When they reached the apartment, Max waited to hand her the cookie sheet until she opened her door and set the cookies down.

"What are you up to for the rest of the afternoon?" he asked.

"Wildly exciting things—laundry, paying bills," Sophie said. "What about you?"

"I think I'm going to try to get some writing done. Do you want to watch the latest episode of *Murders* later tonight?" He grinned. "If you're not sick of me yet?"

Sophie laughed. "Not yet. I'll be over around seven."

CHAPTER TWENTY-SIX

S ophie brought half of the leftover cookies with her to Max's apartment, along with a bottled water she'd just opened. She smelled the pizza when Max opened the door and smiled. They seemed to have a routine now of pizza and an episode of *Only Murders in the Building* on Sunday nights. She looked forward to these nights, and she never got tired of pizza.

"What kind did you get this time?" She set the box of cookies on the kitchen counter.

"Half pepperoni and half sausage, onion and pepper. I hope that's okay?"

"That's great. I love both."

Max got paper plates for both of them and they each grabbed a few slices and settled on his living room sofa.

The pizza was delicious, as usual, and they both enjoyed the latest episode. When it ended, Max got up and returned a moment later with the box of cookies. They both took one.

"How'd the writing go today?" Sophie asked him.

Max made a face. "I said I was going to go home and write, didn't I? I thought about it. But then I did laundry, ran some errands, and read a book for inspiration. I finally opened the story I'm working on, reread the last scene I wrote and then stared at the blank screen for too long. I don't usually write on Sundays, and I guess my muse wanted a day off."

Sophie was fascinated by how Max's writing process worked. "So, you can't force it. You have to wait for inspiration to come?"

"Sort of. But not always. When I get closer to deadline, I can't be that precious about it. I have to sit my butt in the chair and make the words happen. And they do. I don't understand it."

"Did you always know you wanted to be a writer?" Sophie asked.

Max thought for a moment. "I think on some level, I did always know. I was always a big reader and I used to dream about writing books someday. I knew it wasn't a practical job, though. I mean most people don't make a living at it. I am grateful and feel very lucky that I am able to do that."

"It's more than luck though. You're incredibly talented," Sophie said. "How did you get started?"

Max took another cookie then leaned back and put his feet up.

"Thank you. I always wrote. I scribbled horribly bad stories in beat-up notebooks when I was younger. I had some great teachers in high school and college that encouraged me. But I still knew I needed a degree in something that could pay the bills. That led to the mutual fund job, which was a disaster."

Sophie laughed. "I would have died if I'd made a mistake like that."

"Yeah, it wasn't fun. I deserved to be fired. My mother was not thrilled when I went to bartending, though. She thought I was wasting my degree. But I liked it and the hours were great and freed up my days to write. Still, it was a few years before I got serious about it and really buckled down and tried to learn how to structure a decent story. I think I wrote three books before I felt like I had something worthy of being shown to an agent or publisher."

"And that was published right away?"

Max laughed. "Not even close. I landed an agent, a well-regarded one. She recognized the good stuff in the book, but also wanted a lot of changes made. I resisted at first, but then realized the goal was to make the book better, and more marketable. And they were good suggestions. Once I made them, she sent it out and two publishers wanted it, which was pretty crazy."

"And you were off and running," Sophie said.

"Sort of. My books didn't take off right away. I didn't hit *The New York Times* list until book four and that was the book that changed everything."

"That was *Not My Family*?" It was the first book of Max's that she'd read.

He nodded. "Yeah, it was a bigger book, and everything seemed to come together for it. Film rights were sold, and the movie actually got made. That alone made things go crazy. It's been a wild ride ever since. But enough about me. What about you? Did you always know you wanted to do real estate sales one day?"

Sophie laughed hard at that. "It had never crossed my mind. I guess I'm a late bloomer. I never had a career that I was passionate about. I worked in the legal field after graduating, but I never loved it. That's why I temped when I came here. I knew I wanted to be in the city. The first day on the job at Fulton, when I typed up the morning meeting notes and browsed the office listings, I felt a thrill. Like that was where I was supposed to be, and the industry I was waiting on."

"It's your passion," Max said.

Sophie hadn't looked at it that way before. "I think it is, actually. When we get a new listing, I get excited and start trying to picture who would want to live there. Who would it be a match for? I feel like what I do is matchmaking in a sense. It's finding out what someone wants and giving them the perfect new home that satisfies those wants. I don't want to jinx myself, but at the open house, that guy who said he wanted to bring his wife back on Monday—I can see him living in that unit. It fits. Hopefully it will be a match for his wife, too. It might not be."

"Well, if it's not, you can find them something else. He does seem ready to buy," Max said.

"He does. I don't want to get my hopes up though. I've already seen how things can fall apart unexpectedly." Sophie realized that sounded kind of wishy-washy and it didn't reflect how she truly felt. She tried again. "I really want this to work out, really badly. Not just this deal but real estate as a career. I am determined to figure it out and be successful."

Max held her gaze for a moment, then smiled slowly. "I think you're going to do just fine. You seem driven and I think that's the key to success with anything....putting in the effort needed to get to where you want to go. Because nothing is easy, and most people give up."

Sophie realized he was right. Most people did give up when things got hard. She'd thought of giving up herself more than once, but each time she pushed through and didn't give into her doubts.

"Is it harder for you to write now? Or are you able to channel the heartache and laser focus on your writing?" Sophie asked.

Max grinned. "I think my lack of writing today would say there is no laser focus going on here. It's a day-by-day thing. I'm trying to get better about not letting the breakup slow me down too much. And sometimes I can use it if I'm writing an emotional scene. While my books are never based on real people, there are bits and pieces of me and my life in all the books."

"Do you think you'll want to start dating soon? Is it better to get right back out there?" Sophie asked.

Max looked surprised by the question and Sophie immediately regretting asking it.

"I'm sorry. If that's too personal, never mind. I was just curious how it affects your writing," she tried to explain.

"No, it's fine. Honestly, I can't imagine dating anyone right now. I seem to need to wallow a bit and feel sorry for myself when I have a breakup. And I tend to lose myself in work for a while, weeks even a month or two, until suddenly I'm just ready. I'm nowhere near that point now."

"That's understandable. I'd probably take a long break too."

"Do you want to watch something else?" Max asked. It was still early, just a little past eight."

"Sure, I can stay for one more."

They found a new detective series that looked promising on Netflix and watched the first episode. When it finished, Sophie had to fight back a yawn. She stood. "I should head home. I have a big day tomorrow."

Max walked her to the door. "Good luck, hope the wife loves it."

"Thanks, Max. Hope tomorrow is a good writing day for you, too."

He hugged her goodbye. She loved the way his arms felt wrapped around her. The contact was brief though. Max pulled back and smiled down at her. "Sleep well, Sophie."

CHAPTER TWENTY-SEVEN

Sophie woke early Monday morning, showered and changed and made herself a cup of coffee. She'd only seen Caroline and Tessa for a few minutes the prior evening when she came home from Max's apartment. Tessa had raised her eyebrows when Sophie told them where she'd been. But Sophie ignored it. She'd already told them she and Max were just friends. And Sophie knew that wasn't likely to change anytime soon.

Caroline and Tessa both had good weekends and Sophie was glad to see that Tessa was in a better mood. She wondered if Tessa would be able to sell her twenty million dollar listing again in less than a month. Sophie knew that the high-priced properties often took longer to sell.

Sophie ate breakfast quickly—a bowl of cereal and almond milk, and then headed into the office. It was very early, and Tessa and Caroline were still sleeping, but Sophie wanted to get in and get started on researching potential properties for her new buyers. She had a very busy day ahead of her. She had calls scheduled with her two new buyers to go over what they wanted and to possibly set up some showings for that afternoon or the next day.

And she was excited and a bit nervous to show her listing to the wife of the buyer she met at the open house. When she arrived at the office, it was a quarter past seven and no one else was there yet except for Rick, who was in his office with his door shut. She could see through his all-glass walls that he was on the phone. His feet were up on his desk and his tie was loose around his neck. His hair was still damp. She guessed that he'd come straight from the gym, which she gathered was his usual routine. He saw her walk by, waved and flashed her a grin.

Sophie dropped everything at her desk and went to make a cup of coffee. She sat at her desk and sipped her coffee, savoring the rich flavor and fluffy foam on top. When she opened her laptop and pulled up her email, a new message came through. It was from one of the brokers that she'd met at the open house.

"Sophie, just a heads-up that my buyer wants to offer on your listing. We're pulling it together now. I'll be calling shortly with the details. Just wanted to check quickly by email to make sure it's still available to see if there are any other offers pending."

Sophie typed back, "No offers yet, but I do have a second showing today."

A few minutes later, the reply came, "Great, stay tuned."

Sophie felt a strange sense of excitement course through her. She had activity now, and there was serious interest in her listing. She hadn't expected that she'd get offers or a sale so quickly. She knew it still might not happen though. So, she turned her attention to her two other buyers. They were going to talk in depth that morning, but they'd both given her a sense of what they were looking for and their ideal location and price range. She spent the next half hour searching all their available listings and going into REBNY, the database of listings across New York offices.

Tessa and Caroline walked in together at a quarter of eight. They grabbed coffees and headed into the conference room for the sales meeting which started sharply at eight. Sophie joined them a moment later and slid into a chair next to Caroline who smiled at her.

"I never even heard you get up this morning. You must have come in here extra early," she said.

Sophie nodded. "I did. I finally have some activity going on and it's going to be a busy day."

Caroline looked happy for her. "That's really great, Soph."

Tessa just looked her way, nodded hello and picked up her coffee mug.

Rick strode into the room a few minutes later. His hair was dry, his tie was perfectly in place and as usual, he was smiling and full of energy.

"Okay, talk to me, team. What does everyone have cooking?"

They went around the room, talking about new listings and giving updates on pending deals. When it was Sophie's turn, she told them about the pending offer. "I have another showing today, too, so there's a possibility I might have two offers." She was excited but also a little nervous about managing that properly.

Rick looked pleased to hear it. "Fantastic job, Sophie. Stop by my office after the meeting and we'll strategize on how to handle multiple offers."

Sophie nodded. She was grateful that he was going to help her with how best to handle that.

When the meeting ended, Caroline looked thrilled for her as she said, "I didn't realize you were close to one offer, let alone two. That's amazing. And Rick will help you. Multiple offers can be a little tricky to navigate."

Tessa looked her way and said nothing. She went straight to her desk and pulled up her email. Sophie wondered if she was in a bad mood. She'd come to learn that Tessa could be very up and down with her moods, and it often mirrored how things were going with work.

Sophie went to Rick's office, and he waved her in. He was pacing behind his desk and talking on his Bluetooth. Sophie took a seat and waited for him to finish the call. He wrapped it up and sat.

"So, you're about to get not just one but possibly two offers?"

Sophie nodded. "Might just be the one. It depends on how my buyer's wife likes the property."

Rick was quiet for a moment. "It was the guy at the end at the open house, the one I overheard?"

She nodded.

"I'll be shocked if they don't make an offer. That guy wants it. Though sometimes a spouse does torpedo what looks like a sure thing. You never do know."

He leaned his elbows on his desk and told Sophie all

about multiple offers. She took it all in and hoped that she might actually get two offers. When he finished, he wished her luck. "If you have any questions, don't hesitate to call me."

Sophie headed back to her desk and the rest of the day was a blur of non-stop activity and meetings. She spoke with both of her two new buyers and went more in detail with both on what they were ideally looking for and budget. She set up several showings for both over the next few days.

The broker called her back and walked her through his client's offer. It was slightly below the asking price, but they were cash buyers and eager to move quickly. Sophie called her client and delivered the offer.

"The offer is good for twenty-four hours. Since it's a little below your asking price, I would suggest waiting to see if the buyers coming back today want to move forward as well. If not, then you can either accept this offer or counter it."

"Let's definitely hold off and see how your other buyers like it. And if they don't move forward, I think I'd be inclined to counteroffer. I know buyers often expect a cash discount, but I am not under any pressure to sell quickly."

Sophie agreed. "Perfect. I'll call you this afternoon as soon as I meet with the buyers."

Now she had a firm offer in hand, Sophie wasn't as nervous about this second showing. There was still a lot at stake as of course she wanted them to offer, but she felt a bit more confident since she had a solid offer. It was a little below asking, but not much, so she felt good that they could come to an agreement if her buyers decided to pass.

Sophie arrived fifteen minutes early and waited just outside the building for her buyers. They arrived at one o'clock sharp and they all went up to the unit. They were a married couple, Peter and Kate Ingram. As they rode up in the elevator Peter told her that he was a software architect, and his wife had a high-level role with an investment firm.

"We have invested in real estate over the years and just sold one of our properties, so we will be cash buyers," Peter said.

Sophie was glad to hear it. With the market being so hot these days paying in cash gave a buyer an edge over someone who needed to wait on financing or, even worse, who had to add the contingency of selling their own property first.

"We won't overpay, though," Kate said. "And we are very picky." Where Peter was warm and friendly, Kate was more reserved and was even a bit cold. Sophie got the sense that she would likely be the negotiator—if she liked the property enough to offer.

Kate smiled though as Sophie unlocked the door and they stepped inside. The unit did present beautifully as it was a sunny day and light streamed through the windows and onto the gleaming hardwood floors of the living area. "Peter is excited about this unit though, so I am optimistic," she said.

"Please, walk around and explore. I'll be here in the kitchen if you have any questions," Sophie said.

They walked off and Sophie pulled her phone out of her purse and checked her email and text messages. She was surprised to see an email from Emily, the woman she'd met at the Met volunteer training.

Sophie, since we chatted, I've been thinking a lot about starting to look. With the two kids, our place is feeling small. And life has calmed down enough, that I am ready to put some energy into this. Can we set a time to chat?

Sophie immediately texted back. *Of course. Would you like to come into the office this week? Let me know what day and time works best. And also if you could please give me an idea of what range you are considering and ideal location, I can start to pull together some preliminary properties for us to look at when you visit.*

Sophie didn't expect to hear back right away, but two minutes later another email pinged through. *How about tomorrow at ten? If that doesn't work, then Wednesday at ten? We like our current area, near the Met. Fifth Avenue would be first choice if there's anything available. Our target range is mid to high teens, but we could go as high as twenty for something really spectacular.*

Sophie almost dropped her phone. Emily could go as high as twenty million! Though she was initially shocked, when she really thought about it, it made sense. She'd mentioned that her husband was a partner in a hedge fund company, and they already lived in the area.

She immediately thought of Tessa's listing. She didn't know if it would suit Emily, but it was spectacular and it was right on Fifth Avenue. She would do a full search and see what she could find in the mid to high teens as well. She wanted to have as many options as possible, so that when they met and spoke about what was important, Sophie could easily hone in on the properties that best matched what Emily and her husband wanted.

She looked up as Peter and Kate walked into the kitchen, and they were both smiling.

"So, what did you think?" Sophie asked.

"She liked it!" Peter said.

Kate laughed. "More than I expected to, actually. It is a great location, and it has everything that we are looking for. Do you think the owner is flexible on the price?"

"No, I don't think she is" Sophie said. "She's pretty firm on the price. And there is another offer on it that just came in this morning."

"Can you share anything with us about the offer?" Kate asked.

Sophie hesitated. After she'd talked to Rick, she'd called the seller and asked what she would give permission for Sophie to share, if anything.

"I can't share the amount, but I can tell you that it is also a cash offer."

Kate frowned. "So, we can't expect a discount for cash then?"

"Sometimes you can, but this seller is firm on her price and there is a competing offer," Sophie reminded her.

"I don't want to offer above the asking," Kate said. She looked at her husband and smiled, "But I'm comfortable making a full-priced offer if you are?"

He nodded. "Absolutely."

Kate pulled her checkbook out and wrote a check for the deposit and handed it to Sophie.

"I'm heading back to the office now. I'll email the offer paperwork to you immediately so you can DocuSign it and then I'll present the offer to the buyer."

. . .

When Sophie got back to the office, she pulled the offer together, emailed it off to her buyers and as soon as she received the signed copy back, she called her seller.

"I have good news," Sophie said excitedly. "We have a second offer, and they are also paying cash and have offered the full asking price. What would you like to do?"

"That is great news. I actually didn't think it would happen this fast," Renee said. "What are my options?"

"You could accept one of these offers, or we could tell them both to put their best offer forward and give them a chance to improve their offers."

Renee thought about that for a moment. "I don't think I want to do that. The first offer was quite a bit below the asking price. And the second offer is exactly what I asked for. It doesn't feel right to ask them to improve their offer. They might decide not to offer at all, right?"

"That is possible, yes. They did tell me they didn't want to go above the asking price."

"I don't blame them. Please tell them that I happily accept their offer." They discussed the building's co-op approval process and set a closing date about ninety days out.

When they hung up, Sophie took a deep breath. She was thrilled at the first sale, and a double sale at that since she had both the buyer and the seller. She still had to get over the co-op approval hurdle first, though.

CHAPTER TWENTY-EIGHT

Sophie was dying to share her big news, but the office was pretty much empty—other than the on-call agent, who she didn't know well enough. Everyone, including Rick was out with clients.

So, she had to wait until she got home a little after six. The rest of her afternoon had been hectic, too, as she'd had two more showings with her new clients. Those had gone well, but they both had a few more set up over the next few days. Sophie didn't get the sense that things would move as quickly with either of them, but she was still happy to show them as many listings as they wanted to see.

When she walked into her apartment, she was tired. It had been a long day, but a good one. She was on a bit of a high and was tempted to call her mother but decided to wait until the deal actually closed.

"Did you get another offer?" Caroline asked as soon as Sophie walked in. Tessa was sprawled across the living room sofa, filing her nails. She looked curious to hear Sophie's news, too.

Sophie joined Caroline at the kitchen island and sat on a stool next to her. "I did. My buyers made a full-priced offer, and the seller took it. I'm still kind of in shock."

"Congratulations!!! That is so awesome. Your first sale is a double, that is incredible. I'm so happy for you." Caroline gave her a big hug.

Tessa congratulated her too. "Nice job. Hopefully yours will clear the co-op board," she said. She grinned though and added, "I'm sure they will. Mine was a weird situation."

"I think we need to celebrate. Do we have any champagne?" Caroline asked. She looked in the refrigerator. "We are out of everything." She closed the door and turned around. "We could go out. Let's go to that little Italian place that your Aunt Penny used to go to all the time. That feels appropriate. I think she'd want us to. And I'm sure they have champagne."

Tessa stood and walked over to them. "That works for me. We don't really have anything here to eat."

So, they walked a few blocks to the Italian restaurant and Caroline proudly bragged to Tony and Richard that Sophie just made her first sale.

"Congratulations!" Tony gave Sophie a big hug. "Your aunt would be so proud. You must celebrate," he said.

Once they were seated, he sent three glasses of champagne over on the house. They toasted to Sophie's sale and had a delicious dinner. And over dinner they talked about work, as usual.

"Do you have anything else going on?" Caroline asked.

"I'm working with two new buyers and am showing them properties this week. We're not close on anything though." Sophie thought about mentioning her meeting with Emily, but it hadn't happened yet, they were meeting tomorrow at ten, and she didn't want to jinx anything. She still couldn't believe it was real that she might have a buyer that could spend up to twenty million.

"What about you, Tessa? Any luck on finding another buyer for your big listing?" Caroline asked.

Tessa took a sip of wine and set her wine glass down. "Not yet. I'm working my butt off on it. Calling everyone I can think of, former clients, other brokers, and asking who they might know. And we have some new ads for it. Those can be hit or miss. The clock is ticking...I'm down to three weeks now."

Caroline smiled encouragingly. "If anyone can pull this off, you can."

"Thanks. I do have some other stuff pending, but nothing close, yet. What about you?"

"I might be getting a new listing in later this week. I'm not sure yet on the price, but it might be my biggest one yet. It's on Fifth Avenue."

Tessa looked intrigued. "No kidding? If you do an open house maybe you'll find some new buyers that might be good for my listing, too."

Caroline nodded. "That's what I'm thinking."

Sophie was tempted to mention her new buyer again but kept quiet. She was excited though, about Caroline's new listing, given the location.

They all decided to splurge and ordered cannoli for dessert. Sophie loved the classic Italian dessert with the crispy pastry shell and creamy ricotta filling. They all had leftovers and walked home carrying their to-go bags. It had been a fun night and overall, one of the best days Sophie could remember. She felt full and happy and grateful for her new friends. When they reached the apartment, they watched TV for a bit. The delicious food and wine made them sleepy, and they all went to bed early. As Sophie drifted off, she sighed happily and looked forward to what tomorrow would bring.

CHAPTER TWENTY-NINE

Sophie went in early the next day. She wanted to pull together as many potential properties for Emily as possible. Based on their brief conversation, she found about eight potential units, plus the upcoming listing later that week from Caroline. She put them all into a folder and planned to have the laptop with her in their meeting and, based on Emily's must haves, she would show her whichever listings most closely fit her wish list.

But at nine thirty, her phone rang, and it was Emily.

"Sophie I am so, so sorry to do this, but I need to push our meeting out a week or two. Things have suddenly gotten crazy here and I need to wait a bit. I hope that's ok?"

"Of course," Sophie answered automatically. It was the only thing she could say. She hoped that they would reschedule. "Just let me know when you have time and we'll set a new meeting."

"Will do. Thanks so much. I won't be at the in-person training on Saturday either. We're heading out of town to Jim's family in Connecticut." She sounded anxious and worried, and Sophie guessed that maybe a family member was ill.

"It's no problem at all. We'll talk soon," Sophie said.

"What happened? Did your big deal fall through already?" Tessa teased her as she settled at her desk.

Sophie laughed. "No, not yet. That was a new client that just pushed out our meeting. She said she'll call when she's ready to come in. Hopefully in a week or two."

"That happens. As much as we like to think we are everyone's top priority, we're not," Tessa said.

Sophie realized it was very true. Especially when there were other more important things happening in someone's life. Buying a new house could go on the back burner.

That Sunday, after spending the weekend at her boyfriend Cody's house, Tessa came home in a mood. She stormed into the apartment, glared at Caroline and Sophie and went straight into her room and didn't emerge for a half hour. Sophie and Caroline had looked at each other in confusion. Neither of them had any idea what she was upset about.

When Tessa came out of her room, she had calmed down a little and walked into the kitchen and opened the refrigerator. She found an unopened bottle of chardonnay that Sophie had bought the day before and glanced at her. "Do you mind if I open this?"

"No, go ahead." It was clear that Tessa could use a drink to calm her nerves.

"Does anyone else want some?"

"Sure," Sophie and Caroline said at the same time.

Tessa poured glasses for all of them and as soon as they'd taken their first sip, she blurted out, "I ended things with Cody."

Sophie was shocked and Caroline looked like she was too. They'd both been under the impression that things were strong between the two of them.

"Why? What happened?" Caroline asked.

"I'm tired of wasting my time. We've been together just over two years and Cody hasn't mentioned marriage once. So, I brought it up and he seemed taken aback. Said he was happy with how things were going. I let him know that I can't wait around forever and if he wasn't even thinking about it, then there was no point to us being together."

"What did he say to that?" Caroline asked.

"He didn't have much to say. He seemed confused and said he loves being with me, but if I need to get engaged now, he's not on board with that. Not yet. So, I left." Tears of frustration welled up in her eyes and Caroline handed her a tissue. Then hugged her.

"I wouldn't consider it truly over. He probably just needs to digest this, and you two can talk again," she said.

"I'm not sure there's anything to talk about. I think we may be too far apart on this," Tessa said.

"I'm so sorry, Tessa," Sophie said. She didn't know what else to say. She certainly was no expert when it came to relationships.

"Thanks," Tessa said and sniffled.

They drank the bottle of wine and made some makeshift nachos with leftover chili, cheddar and a half bag of tortilla chips that were on the verge of stale. But it worked somehow, and the chips crisped up in the oven. By the time they went to bed, Tessa was in a better mood and Sophie hoped that she'd be able to work things out with Cody.

It was almost two weeks before she heard from Emily again and they set up a time on Tuesday for her to come into the office.

This time, she showed up as agreed and apologized again for canceling.

"I didn't want to get into it on the phone, but Jim's mother had been rushed to the hospital with a heart attack. We didn't know anything more than that at that point. It turned out she had some major blockages and needed a quadruple bypass. She came through the surgery well and is recuperating at home. It was scary though. We couldn't focus on anything else as you can imagine."

Sophie nodded. "I'm so glad she's doing well now."

They went into one of the smaller conference rooms and Sophie offered Emily a cup of the fluffy coffee and she was intrigued. Sophie quickly made one for each of them and, as they sipped their coffee, she jotted down notes about what Emily was ideally looking for.

"We want this to be our forever property. The one we are in is lovely, but it only has three bedrooms and one of those is used as an office. So, the children have to share, and we just desperately need more space. I'd love five or six bedrooms if possible because we need that home office and I'd love a guest room for when his parents or mine come to visit. And we might have one or possibly two more kids. The thought of moving again, is too exhausting to consider," she said dramatically, and Sophie smiled.

"Moving is awful," she agreed. "What about location? You mentioned you like the area by the Met ideally?"

Emily nodded. "Yes, somewhere along Fifth Avenue, walking distance to the Met. That's what we have now, and we love it. We just need more space."

"And you mentioned a range ideally of the mid to upper teens? But possibly you could go to twenty if something was really perfect?"

"Yes. Obviously, we'd prefer not to go to twenty if we don't have to. But we could. Jim was made a partner a few years ago and that changed our income significantly. We'll be paying cash, as well."

Sophie swallowed at that. She couldn't fathom having twenty million sitting in a bank account readily available for apartment buying. But she knew how lucrative the hedge fund industry was and how Jim's yearly salary now that he was a partner could be well in excess of ten million.

"Excellent. Well, I pulled a few ideas together and based on what you are looking for, we have five properties that you might want to consider. One of them is a new listing that just came in this week. They are all impressive properties. I would recommend seeing all of them and then you can let me know what you think and if we need to refine the search."

Emily took a quick look at the listings and agreed to see all but one, which was the smallest and least expensive.

"They all look intriguing. I have to admit, I'm especially curious to see the newest one, I've been in that building and it's stunning." She was talking about Caroline's new listing and Sophie had to agree. It was special.

"Great, I'll see about setting up some showings. What days and times work best?"

Emily thought for a moment. "I'm available the rest of the week any day before noon and on Saturday, Jim could come with me. I'd like to see them all this week if at all possible."

"I'll make some calls and let you know as soon as I hear from the sellers." Sophie tried to keep the excitement out of her voice. She wanted to project confidence, and the illusion that she dealt with properties of this caliber regularly.

She walked Emily out and they passed Tessa and Caroline in the hallway. Sophie noticed that both of her roommates' eyes were drawn to Emily's elegant outfit. She was wearing a gorgeous, ivory-colored, long wool coat, her hair was pulled back into an elegant low ponytail and her lipstick was a vibrant red that made her pale skin look pink and rosy. And she wore a black quilted Louis Vuitton crossbody bag that contrasted perfectly with the coat.

"Thanks for coming in, Emily," Sophie said.

Emily smiled. "I really appreciate that you rescheduled. I look forward to seeing these homes and any other new ones that might come in."

Sophie went back to the bullpen and walked over to Caroline's and Tessa's desks which were next to each other. They both looked up and Tessa spoke first.

"Was that a new buyer? What range is she looking in?"

Sophie smiled. "She's ideally targeting mid to high teens but could go to twenty for something amazing."

Caroline's jaw dropped. "Where did you find her?"

"She's in my training class for volunteers at the Met." She told them about Emily and her hedge fund husband. "She's really nice and they just need a bigger place."

Caroline's eyes lit up. "My new listing might be perfect."

"I told her about both of your listings, and she wants to set up showings."

"I can't believe you might have a buyer for my listing." Tessa really seemed shocked. She snapped out of it fast though. "I'll call them now."

CHAPTER THIRTY

Sophie booked showings for Emily every day for the rest of the week, with the last two on Saturday. The ones they saw during the week were all on the lower end of her range, around fifteen and sixteen million. They were impressive homes and Emily took lots of pictures as they walked through and seemed to like all of them.

"I'm anxious to get this done as soon as possible. Now that I've decided I'm ready, I don't want to wait any longer than necessary. It's driving me crazy how small our place is," Emily said.

Sophie nodded sympathetically. Emily's idea of small was spacious for New York standards, but she understood. And she was more than happy to help.

Each day, she asked Emily for feedback and, although it was all mostly positive, by the end of the day on Friday, Emily had decided that all but one of the properties they'd seen were too small.

"I'm hopeful for tomorrow and glad that Jim will be

joining us. I think maybe we've saved the best for last," Emily said.

"Those two are the biggest properties available in that area," Sophie confirmed. She too, hoped that they would love one of them enough to make an offer. But she knew that often the higher-priced sales took longer as the buyers were pickier and might want to hold out for the perfect property. Though she knew Emily didn't want to wait around. And both were what Sophie would consider spectacular. She hoped that Emily and Jim would agree.

Tessa's and Caroline's listings were a block apart. Sophie met Emily and Jim at Tessa's listing first and when they finished, they could go right onto Caroline's as the property was empty and there were no other showings scheduled that day.

Sophie arrived ten minutes early and a few minutes later, Emily and her husband walked up. Emily looked excited as she introduced Jim.

"Sophie, this is my husband. Jim, meet Sophie."

Jim smiled and held out his hand. His handshake was firm and businesslike, but his eyes were warm and as they walked around the unit, it was clear to Sophie that Jim adored his wife.

"Oh, this kitchen is incredible," Emily said. There was a huge, honed marble island with six chairs along one side and several smoky blown glass hanging lights above it. The kitchen cabinets were pale gray, with brushed aluminum appliances and a charcoal gray tile backsplash. The kitchen looked as though it was rarely used as there was nothing on the counters and the cupboards were mostly empty.

"It is beautiful," Jim agreed. "But marble stains and with two little ones and possibly more on the way, I'm not sure how practical it is."

Emily looked disappointed. "You might be right," she agreed.

Jim put his hands on his wife's shoulder and smiled down at her. "If you really want marble, we can make it work."

She returned his smile. "We'll see. Let's keep going."

The unit was beautifully decorated with dark burgundy and hunter green silk drapes on the enormous windows that overlooked Fifth Avenue and Central Park. The owner was a fifty-something bachelor, a businessman, and this was one of several homes. The overall feel was luxurious and somewhat masculine. The bath in the primary bedroom had sleek black marble and although it was beautiful, it seemed a little cold, Sophie thought.

Jim loved the library though, which he would use as an office. It was a dark room with lots of black leather and polished mahogany wood. There was a massive desk surrounded by custom-built bookcases along both walls. He walked over to a shelf of leather-bound books and took a closer look. Emily joined him and smiled.

"I could totally see you working here," she said.

He nodded. "It's a great room. Love the high ceilings."

As they walked out, Sophie casually asked, "So what do you think?"

Emily and Jim exchanged glances and Emily smiled. "It's an amazing apartment. I don't love some of the colors, but I think so far it is at the top of the list. It has everything we are looking for."

Sophie wondered how Caroline's unit would compare. It had a very different feel to it. That property was just a block away, and Emily seemed excited about seeing it.

"This one is the closest so far to the Met," Emily said and glanced at Jim. He took her hand and smiled. It was a gorgeous day to be out walking. It was cold but clear. As they walked, the wind seemed to pick up and Sophie pulled her long coat around her a bit tighter.

The building was just ahead, and the unit was on the sixth floor. They took the elevator up and Sophie opened the door and stepped back so they could enter the unit first. She smiled to herself as she heard Emily's quick intake of breath.

"Wow. Jim, look at this entrance, it's so impressive and welcoming at the same time." The foyer had champagne-colored marble floors and a soaring twelve-foot-high ceiling. They walked through to the living room, which was a huge, open area with a wall of oversized windows that overlooked Central Park and the Met.

There was an elegant cream-colored fireplace with custom moldings and French doors that led into a dining room on one side and on the other went into an office. The primary bedroom was spacious and had a walk-in-closet with a small island in the middle. It looked like something a movie star would have and Sophie saw the love in Emily's eyes.

"This is such a glamorous space. I might want to just hang out in this closet," Emily said. There was a comfy pink suede chair by a white desk with three-way mirrors. She could sit there and put her makeup on and check the fit of her clothes.

Jim was more impressed by the bathroom which had both a clawfoot tub and a standing shower encased in glass. It had all-white marble and seafoam green glass subway tiles in the shower that gave it a peaceful, spa-like feeling.

The kitchen was a little smaller than the one they'd just looked at, but it was cozier and to Sophie's eyes, more user-friendly. There was a half-moon-shaped island with five chairs along one side. The island was raised on the side where the chairs were and on the other side, there was a stove, so Emily or Jim, could cook while facing those seated at the island and they would also have a view to the living area as well. It would make for easy entertaining or keeping an eye on the kids. And the counter material looked like marble but was a more durable quartz.

"I love this," Emily breathed. She glanced around the apartment and back at Jim. "I love all of it. I can see us living here. What do you think?"

He nodded. "I like it. If you think this is the one, let's do it."

"Are there any other offers on it yet?" Emily asked. "Or offers coming?"

"None yet. But I think there is another open house scheduled for tomorrow. They might cancel that if you present a compelling offer today," Sophie said.

"I think we'll head home and discuss this. We'll call you shortly once we've decided on the offer amount."

"Perfect. Once you do that, I'll get the paperwork over to you for signatures."

"And we'll get our documents together that you'll need for the co-op board to review," Jim said. Most co-op boards required a number of documents including financial statements, even for an all-cash purchase. The potential buyers still had to provide bank statements showing that they had three to four times the monthly fees in their account for the next few years.

When Sophie walked into her apartment Tessa and Caroline were waiting eagerly for news. Sophie took a deep breath. She knew how desperately Tessa needed a buyer for her property. The clock was ticking, and she only had two weeks left and no serious interest yet. Sophie wasn't looking forward to delivering the feedback.

"They liked both units," she began. "They saw Tessa's first and their feedback was really positive. But then they fell in love with Caroline's. It seemed like a better fit for them with the colors and overall layout. They were going home to discuss and hopefully will be calling this afternoon to make an offer."

Caroline looked thrilled but also sympathetic toward Tessa. "I'm sorry, Tessa," she said. "Hopefully you'll have someone good come to your open house tomorrow."

Tessa stood from the chair at the island. Her disappointment was evident. "I'm not going to hold my breath on that. Everything right now is falling apart for me. I think I'm going to go for a run." She was dressed for it, as if she'd been anticipating this news. She grabbed her phone. "I'll catch up with you two later."

As soon as the door closed behind her, the energy in the room changed and felt lighter.

"I wanted to scream but didn't want to rub it in Tessa's

face. I really do hope she finds someone soon or she's going to be miserable to live with," Caroline said.

"I hope so too," Sophie agreed. "Her listing is a gorgeous unit. It just felt more masculine color-wise. Yours is more their style and it's the closest to the Met. It's perfect, really."

The call came twenty minutes later from Emily.

"We're ready to make an offer. Jim wants to offer seventeen five, do you think they will take it?" She sounded nervous.

"Let's find out. I'll have Caroline run it by the seller."

When she ended the call, Caroline already had her phone out and was looking up her client's number. "Do you think they might take that? Or are they firm on eighteen?" Sophie asked.

"I don't know that they'll come down that much, but they might flex a little, hopefully."

Sophie made herself a coffee while Caroline spoke to her client. She could only hear Caroline's side of the conversation and held her breath for a moment when Caroline asked the question.

"We have an interested buyer, and they are putting an offer together. I should have the details shortly. They wanted to know if you are flexible at all on the price."

Caroline was quiet and Sophie paced around the room, sipped her coffee and waited.

"They mentioned seventeen five." There was a long silence as Caroline was silent and her seller was talking, quite loudly actually. But not loud enough that Sophie could make out the words. "Right, I agree, that is too much of a cut. Okay, I'll let them know." She ended the call and turned to Sophie. "He won't come down that much. But we can tell your buyers that if they can come up to seventeen eight, that might get it done."

Sophie was glad the seller was flexible, but she wished the seller would commit to a price.

"So does that mean they will still have you do an open house tomorrow?" It made Sophie nervous that someone else could swoop in who would make a full-asking-price offer.

Caroline nodded. "Yes. It's still a new listing and sellers can be hesitant when an offer comes quickly but it's not the asking price. They may want to hold off and see if there might be a better offer out there."

"So, what should I advise my clients?" Sophie asked. Caroline knew how to handle negotiations like this.

"If it were my buyer, I would tell them that if they come up to the asking price, the seller will accept and cancel the open house. If they come up to seventeen eight it's possible that they will still have the open house and another buyer could come from that or from another realtor. The seller will not take less than that."

"Okay. Calling now."

Sophie called Emily back and relayed the information exactly as Caroline told her. Emily was quiet for a long moment. "I don't want to lose this place. Let me go talk to Jim and I'll call you right back."

It was more than an hour before Emily called back. Both Sophie and Caroline had been anxiously awaiting the call. Both wanted to go out and run errands, but neither wanted to leave until they knew what the offer would be. Sophie was surprised too, that Tessa wasn't back yet from her run. She wasn't usually gone this long.

The call finally came, and Emily sounded excited as she shared the offer details. "Jim and I want to offer the full asking price. We really think it's the perfect place for us and we don't want to risk losing it. We don't want the open house to happen tomorrow." Emily sounded nervous about the idea of someone walking in off the street and falling in love with it. It wasn't likely, but it was possible, so Sophie was thrilled about the offer.

"I think that's a good thing. I'll make the official offer as soon as you sign the paperwork. Will send along in a few minutes."

"Thanks so much, Sophie! We're both so excited."

"Stay tuned. I'll call as soon as it's officially accepted."

Two hours later, all the paperwork had been signed and emailed and Caroline's seller accepted the full price offer. Emily was thrilled when Sophie gave her the news that it was a done deal.

"I wish we could move in now. I am so ready to go, but I know this is just the first step. I'm not worried about the co-op board approving us. We have the funds and one of Jim's colleagues lives in the building and is on the board. They get along great, and I like his wife, too."

"That's great news," Sophie said.

"Three months from now, we'll be in, and you'll have to come and visit. I really can't thank you enough for finding this place for us. Jim was impressed too. We'd like to give you the listing for this apartment if you'd like it."

Sophie was shocked. She hadn't expected that they would give her the listing. She hadn't really thought about it because she knew they were cash buyers and didn't have to sell their place to buy the new one. She supposed it should have occurred to her though.

"I'd be honored."

"Do you want to come around Monday or Tuesday afternoon to see the place? We have a listing price in mind, but I'd like to hear your opinion first and see what the comps say."

"Of course. I could do Monday around two or three, if that works?"

"Let's do three. See you then, Sophie."

Sophie ended the call and Caroline laughed. She and Tessa were sitting at the kitchen island and had overheard most of the conversation. "So, not only did you sell my eighteen million dollar co-op, they also just gave you a listing?"

Sophie nodded. "I really can't believe it."

Tessa laughed, somewhat bitterly. "I can. Everything you touch right now is going your way. Enjoy it while it lasts." She grabbed her jacket and purse. It was almost six by now and Tessa had showered and changed into a black cocktail dress. It was a gorgeous and dramatic look with her reddish-brown long hair and green eyes.

"Where are you off to?" Caroline asked.

"Cody is taking me to dinner. He wants to talk, so I figured we might as well go to a place I've been dying to try."

"Oh, that's great. I hope it goes well," Caroline said.

"Yes, I hope you are able to work things out," Sophie said.

Tessa sighed. "I'm not sure anything has really

changed. But we'll see. You two should go out and celebrate your big sale." There was a hint of jealousy to her voice. Once she was gone, Caroline shook her head.

"I really do hope she works things out with Cody. He seems like such a solid guy." She made a face. "And he puts up with her. When things aren't going her way with the real estate, she can be so moody." Caroline glanced at the clock.

"We should go out and celebrate. Let's go have a fabulous dinner somewhere. Unless you have other plans?" Caroline's boyfriend was away for the weekend with a few of his college friends.

Sophie laughed. "No plans. That sounds great to me."

CHAPTER THIRTY-ONE

They went to a new restaurant that Rick had mentioned the day before. He'd raved about the place, which had just recently opened. It was right around the corner from the office, as well, so Sophie suspected it might become one of Rick's favorite places to wine and dine clients.

Inspired by Tessa's outfit, Sophie and Caroline decided to dress up more than they usually would. Sophie had bought a deep pink dress at a sample sale recently and welcomed an excuse to wear it. The dress was sleeveless with a boat neck and was fitted all the way to just below her knees. It had a bit of a retro look to it, like something Audrey Hepburn would have worn. Sophie loved the way it made her waist look smaller.

Caroline wore a black cocktail dress with a halter top and floaty skirt. She paired it with a double strand of pearls. They grabbed their long coats and called for an Uber as they were both wearing heels and it was too far to walk.

There was a half hour wait for a table, so they put their name in and went to the bar to get a cocktail. Sophie was glad that they'd dressed up as the vibe was sophisticated. The restaurant had soaring ceilings, deep burgundy walls and sleek black tables and countertops at the bar. As they waited for the bartender, Sophie gazed around the room. She saw a sea of suits and ties and women in mostly black.

"What do you feel like having? I'm thinking champagne," Caroline asked.

"Yes! That's perfect."

A few minutes later the bartender came over and before Caroline could speak, they heard a familiar voice behind them. It was Rick and he was grinning from ear to ear. He was with Troy from the office, who was one of his best friends.

"Carl, I've got this," he said to the bartender. "We'll take a bottle of Veuve for the girls and two Macallans on ice."

Sophie had emailed Rick earlier that afternoon once the deal was finalized. It was a Saturday, so she didn't get a reply back and didn't expect one. But he'd obviously seen the email.

Once they all had their drinks, and thanked Rick, he raised his glass in a toast.

"Congrats! You ladies are killing it!"

They sipped their champagne and Sophie laughed as Rick told them about one of his recent crazy clients, a buyer that was prepared to spend up to fifty million.

"I've been working with him for over a year now. I was all excited at first. Who wouldn't be, right?" Sophie and Caroline nodded. Rick talked fast and he was always animated and high energy. "So, I think I've shown him over twenty properties now. A few every month. He's in no rush, and I was starting to wonder if he was just playing around and had no intention to buy. I'd just about written him off, when I took him to that new project where there were two units side by side. If he didn't like one of those two, I was out of ideas." He paused and took a sip of his scotch. "Well, he sure surprised me. He loved them and is buying both units. He's going to knock down the wall and make one huge penthouse apartment. It will be pretty incredible."

Sophie couldn't even fathom spending that kind of money. "Congrats! What does he do?"

Rick grinned. "I have no idea. His main residence is in Dubai. I think maybe something in finance. Oh, and it's a cash sale. Came to one hundred and eighteen million more than twice what he told me he wanted to spend."

Sophie and Caroline exchanged glances and were struck speechless.

Troy laughed. "That's crazy." He looked at Sophie and Caroline. "This is the best job in the world."

"How long have you been doing it?" Sophie asked. She guessed that Troy was close to Rick's age, around forty.

"A little over ten years now. Been with Fulton for the last five. I started at one of the big shops. Lots of turnover, but I learned the business. Did a few deals with Rick and liked his energy. When he said he was going on his own, I jumped." He grinned. "Haven't regretted it yet."

Rick nodded. "Those big shops are okay for learning, but they're too corporate and stuffy. We like to be nimble and stay on the cutting edge with social media and marketing." He looked at Sophie, "Have you started on TikTok yet? Great way to showcase your listings and if you post regularly, people get to know you."

Sophie hadn't thought much about TikTok. It had been mentioned along with all the social media and she started where she was already established, on Instagram and Facebook, mostly. She went on TikTok occasionally, but mostly for book recommendations and she was oddly fascinated with the makeup videos, even though she didn't wear much of it herself.

"I haven't, but I will look into it," she said.

"I got on it recently," Caroline said. "And I think it helps. I put my listings everywhere."

Troy changed the subject and they chatted about Broadway shows they'd all seen. Rick had just seen Sweeney Todd starring Josh Groban the weekend before with his girlfriend, Julia and raved about it.

"What is Julia up to tonight?" Caroline asked.

Rick's smiled faded. He took another sip of scotch. "She was supposed to be here. We broke up this morning, actually. Please keep it to yourselves though. I'm not saying anything at the office just yet."

"Oh, I'm so sorry, Rick," Caroline clearly regretted asking the question.

Sophie just nodded. She had never met Julia. Rick didn't seem overly upset, though.

Rick sighed. "We just wanted different things. It's all good." He glanced at Troy. "I called Troy to see if he wanted to join me tonight instead, since I knew his wife was away. We have a VIP table reserved in the kitchen. The chef will come talk to us and we can watch them do their thing. I did it once before here and have gotten to know Eric, the chef. It's pretty cool."

"That sounds fun," Sophie said. She'd never heard of a VIP table like that.

"Are you two meeting anyone here?" Rick asked.

"No. It's just us. We wanted to get out and celebrate our big deal," Caroline said.

He smiled. "Why don't you join us for dinner? The table seats four. It will be fun."

It sounded intriguing to Sophie. She glanced at Caroline, and she smiled.

"We'd love to," Caroline said.

A few minutes later, the hostess texted Rick that their table was ready. He led the way into the kitchen and to the half-moon shaped table that faced the line where the cooks were rushing around. Sophie and Caroline sat in the middle and Rick sat to Sophie's right.

Their server came right over and told them what the chef had planned.

"It will be a tasting menu, seven courses with accompanying wines. First up is the amuse bouche." He set what looked like a giant spoon in front of each of them. It held a tasting of a pale, frothy soup with some kind of seafood.

"Dungeness crab bisque," he said, then added, "The chef will be out soon to say hello."

Sophie lifted the spoon and took a small sip—then closed her eyes and swooned. Sweet crab mixed with a creamy buttery broth that had hints of vanilla. It was beyond delicious.

"Not too bad, right?" Rick said. His eyes twinkled.

The rest of the evening was so fun, and the food was decadent. It was easily the best dinner Sophie had ever had. Rick and Troy had them laughing all night as they tried each new course. The conversation always turned back to real estate and then wandered off again. Sophie learned that Rick had only been dating Julia for six months and they broke up because she was pushing for more of a commitment.

"She's on a timeline and wants to get engaged by the time she's thirty-three which is in three months. I was upfront with her from the beginning that I'm not in any hurry to get married. I liked her a lot, she was a great girl. But I wasn't convinced that she was the one. Maybe I would have gotten there at some point, but I kind of doubt it," he said. They were on dessert and a lot of wine had been drunk by everyone.

As they chatted, Sophie learned that Troy was a true romantic and had been married for three years. His eyes lit up when he mentioned his wife.

"I knew on our first date. I had this strong feeling that Nicole was the one for me. She was pretty smitten too, thankfully. I proposed three months later, and she moved in," Troy said.

"I think Ed might be the one for me. We've been dating for a year and a half, but I'm not in a rush. I'm happy with where things are right now," Caroline said.

Rick nodded appreciably. "See that's so smart. Why not just enjoy the present and let the future take care of itself?" He turned to Sophie. "What's your story? Are you almost engaged, too?"

Sophie laughed. "Not even close. I would need a

boyfriend for that, and I'm not dating anyone at the moment."

Rick looked at her and smiled. "Key words, at the moment. I'm sure it won't be long."

The chef, Eric, came by the table again. He'd stopped by earlier and Rick had introduced him to everyone.

"Thanks for coming in. I hope you enjoyed everything?" He asked.

"It was so amazing," Sophie said. The others rushed in saying the same. Eric looked pleased to hear it. When the bill came, Rick grabbed it, didn't even look at it, and threw a black American Express card on the tray.

"Thank you so much," Sophie and Caroline said at the same time, echoed a moment later by Troy.

"It's my pleasure," Rick said. And it was clear that he meant it. He enjoyed treating everyone. "It's also a write-off." He winked. "As we did talk business."

They all laughed. Sophie reached for a sip of their final wine. It was a tawny port, smooth and sweet and syrupy. She felt content, full and relaxed and maybe a little sleepy from all the rich food and wine. She glanced at Rick, and he was looking her way. He smiled and she noticed that he had specks of gold in his dark brown eyes. And how defined and square his jaw was. Rick was a handsome man.

Sophie knew he wouldn't be single for long once word got out that he was available. He was a catch, extremely good-looking, charming, successful and a millionaire many times over. And she knew there would be no shortage of women who would find his determination to stay single a challenge. They would want to be the one who would tame him and win the ultimate prize —marriage.

"We'll have to do this again," Rick said. It wasn't clear if he was talking to the whole table or just to Sophie. He must have meant everyone. Sophie nodded and noticed that Caroline and Troy were deep in conversation and hadn't heard Rick's comment. Still, she was sure he meant it for the table. Caroline looked over and glanced at Rick and Sophie for a long moment before turning her attention back to Troy.

Once the bill was paid, they made their way out of the restaurant. There was a chill in the air. The temperature had dropped considerably while they were inside. Sophie pulled her coat around her tightly. Rick flagged a cab for Caroline and Sophie as they were heading in the opposite direction.

"See you two on Monday," he said as they climbed into the cab.

Once they were on their way, Caroline turned to Sophie. "Well, that was an interesting night, wasn't it?"

"It was amazing. We're so lucky we ran into them. I've never had an experience like that. I could get used to it," Sophie said and laughed.

"It was incredible." Caroline looked thoughtful. "I thought I picked up a vibe between you and Rick. He will be hard to resist if he is interested. Be careful as he meant what he said. He's not looking for anything serious."

"Oh, I don't think he's interested in me that way," Sophie said. But she had sensed something, too. And she wasn't sure how she felt about it.

CHAPTER THIRTY-TWO

Tessa was in a surprisingly good mood the next day, considering that she and Cody did not get back together. She told them all about it at lunch. They'd all slept in and just made sandwiches. It was a laze around and do laundry kind of day for Sophie and Caroline as it was a rare Sunday that neither had to rush to an open house. Tessa had one at two that afternoon for her big listing.

"We had a nice dinner. Cody thought we were getting back together. I considered it but nothing has changed, for either of us, so there's no point to it."

"You seem to be pretty good with it," Caroline commented.

Tessa nodded. "I was upset last week. I'm over it now. Well, mostly over it. Time to meet someone new."

Sophie couldn't imagine bouncing back so quickly from a breakup. Not if she was really in love. Tessa's feelings for Cody must not have been as strong as she'd thought. Yet she'd wanted to marry him. Maybe she was just putting on a brave face. Sophie still couldn't read Tessa very well. It was hard to know what she was really thinking.

"What about you Sophie? Any progress yet with our hot neighbor?" Tessa asked.

Sophie felt herself blush. "I'm not after him. I don't think he's ready to date yet."

"Hmmm. Well, if you don't want to go after him, maybe I will. It doesn't seem like you're all that interested?"

Sophie was stunned. Tessa was interested in Max? She couldn't lay claim to him as there was nothing but friendship between them.

"Max and I are good friends," she said.

Tessa nodded. "That's what I thought. Okay, I'm off. Wish me luck. I need a buyer asap!"

She whirled out of the room and Caroline raised her eyebrows at Sophie.

"Why didn't you tell her to back off? It's obvious to me that you're interested in more than friendship with Max."

"She took me by surprise. And I'm not sure she's serious. I think Tessa just likes to say things for shock value. I also have no idea how Max feels, so it doesn't seem fair to say back off if there's nothing other than friendship there."

"Hmmm. I don't know what to think about Tessa sometimes. She's not the most patient person and she can sometimes seem entitled. Her parents used to be rich. She grew up in a wealthy suburb and is an only child. She got everything she wanted. But her senior year of high school, her father had a few investments go belly up and they lost everything. I think it has been hard for her to go from having it all to struggling for years. She'd doing fine now, of course. But I think she has a hard time when she sees other people doing better than she is—especially if she's been doing it longer."

Sophie nodded. "Yeah, I sensed that. She's made a few comments like how everything seems to be going my way."

"Real estate is like that. You can do everything right and still have all your deals blow up in your face. Other times everything you touch will happen. There's no rhyme or reason to it," Caroline said.

"Rick stressed that, too. How important it is to keep going and have lots of possible deals pending." Something occurred to her. "Why didn't you mention to Tessa that Rick and Julia broke up?"

Caroline sighed. "Two reasons. First, he asked us to keep it quiet for now. But also, if she gets the idea that Rick is interested in you, that will drive her crazy. And I'm not ready yet to see her go after him. Can you imagine?"

Sophie could see Tessa strutting around the office if she and Rick became an item. "I don't think that would last very long, once she realizes that Rick is even more marriage averse than Cody," she said.

"That's very true."

Sophie's cell phone rang. It was her mother. They'd been talking more often, usually talked briefly on Sundays.

"So, I just wanted to tell you the plan for Thursday," her mother began. "Everyone is coming around one. We'll have our usual cocktails and snacks and then sit down to eat around two. It looks like there will be ten of us." Sophie's mother usually hosted and her father's two sisters, husbands and their kids who were about Sophie's age always came. Sophie liked her aunts and cousins and always looked forward to it.

"Great, I'm taking the two o'clock train on Wednesday so I should be in Hudson around four."

"That's perfect. I'll have your father pick you up at the station. We'll get most of our peeling and chopping done Wednesday night, and the pies and stuffing."

"I'll bring some wine. We had a pinot noir a few weeks ago that might be good with the turkey." Sophie usually took peeling and chopping duty while her mother made the stuffing and pie pastry. She couldn't believe it was already Thanksgiving. The months in New York had gone by so fast.

"All right honey, I'll see you on Thursday."

"Bye mom." It would be nice to get home for a few days. She'd stay Wednesday and Thursday night and take the train home on Friday.

Tessa was in a fantastic mood that evening as the open house had gone very well.

"I had two buyers come through that seemed pretty interested. And they aren't working with anyone else. I'm not counting on anything, of course, but maybe one of them might turn into something, even if it's not a sale on this property."

They decided to get pizza for dinner and Sophie texted Max to see if he wanted to join them.

"Sure. I had a great writing session and I'm starving now. I'll be over in ten."

Sophie placed their usual order and when Max

arrived, he handed her a bottle of red wine. She opened it and poured them all a glass. Caroline had set out a bowl of nuts to snack on until the pizza arrived.

When Max asked how their week went, Caroline and Sophie hesitated. They both felt bad talking about their big sale when Sophie's buyer decided against Tessa's listing.

Tessa answered the question though. "Caroline and Sophie made a huge sale this week. I haven't sold mine yet, but my open house went well, so fingers crossed."

Their pizzas arrived soon after and they all helped themselves and settled in the living room to watch the latest episode of *Murders*. When it was over, Sophie and Max went back for another slice of pizza and Tessa opened a new bottle of wine and topped off their glasses. They sat around and chatted for the next hour and it was a fun, relaxing evening. Tessa had them laughing as she told them about a super picky buyer that she'd shown a listing to earlier that week.

"It was perfect. Everything she said she was looking for. She couldn't find one thing wrong with it, but still wants to 'see what else comes up'. I am starting to think she's not serious. And she's wasting my time!"

"You never know though," Caroline said. "I've had a few like that and when I haven't given up and keep showing them new listings, eventually they have bought. I think it's more a timing thing with whatever might be going on in their lives."

"Hmmm. Maybe. I guess I won't kick her to the curb just yet."

"Sophie, are you here Wednesday night?" Max asked.

"A buddy of mine gave me tickets to see a comedy show. I thought it looked pretty good."

Sophie felt a pang of regret. "No, I wish I could go. I'm heading home Wednesday afternoon."

"I could go," Tessa said. "I love a good comedy show. And I'm not going home until Thursday morning."

Max looked surprised but quickly recovered and smiled. "Sure, let's do it."

Caroline stood and glanced at Tessa with a cold look. "I'm tired and am going to head to bed. Good night, all."

Max took his last sip of wine and stood too. "I should head out too. Sophie if I don't see you before you go, have a great Thanksgiving. Tessa, I'll swing by around six on Wednesday."

Tessa glanced Sophie's way and a slow smile spread across her face. "Great. Looking forward to it."

Once he left, Sophie dumped the rest of her wine out in the sink and rinsed it out. Tessa was still sprawled on the sofa sipping her wine.

"I'm off to bed too," Sophie said shortly. She didn't feel like trying to make conversation with Tessa. She was too annoyed that she'd jumped to go to the comedy show with Max. And she knew that had bothered Caroline, too.

CHAPTER THIRTY-THREE

After the morning meeting on Monday, Rick emailed and asked Sophie to pop into his office for a minute. The meeting had run a little longer than usual as several people had new listings and updates to share. Both Sophie and Caroline had rung the bell, and everyone had clapped, even Tessa, though hers was more like a golf clap, not overly enthusiastic.

Sophie grabbed her iPad and headed to his office. The bullpen was buzzing. Just about everyone was on the phone talking to clients. The energy was high, and Sophie found it inspiring and motivating. When she reached Rick's office, he waved her inside and gestured for her to sit across from him.

"What does your day look like today?" He asked. "Are you free around eleven or twelve to go with me to see a new client?"

"I could do either time. I don't have any appointments until this afternoon."

He smiled. "Fantastic, we'll leave here at eleven. We're

off to see one of my very first clients. I'll fill you in along the way. I have to jump into a zoom meeting now."

Sophie stood. Apparently the meeting was over. "Okay, sounds good."

She headed back to her desk and Caroline raised an eyebrow as she sat down.

"What was that about?" Caroline asked softly.

Sophie shrugged. "I'm really not sure yet. Rick wants me to go with him to see an old client about a new listing."

Caroline smiled. "Oh, I don't want to jinx anything, but that might be very good for you."

"Good how?" Sophie pressed for more info.

"I don't want to get your hopes up. He might just be taking you along for the experience. Keep me posted when you get back."

Sophie swung around and dove into her email. She had a busy morning with several scheduled calls, and she needed to book some showings. And she was meeting with Emily at three to see her current apartment and take pictures. She was very excited about that listing. Her preliminary research based on the size and recent sales of similar properties in that area gave her a range of five to six million depending on the layout and condition. Given that price, she wasn't sure how quickly it would sell, though it was a highly desired location.

A few minutes before eleven, Sophie closed her laptop and headed to Rick's office. Most of the other agents were already out of the office. Rick already had his coat on. He led the way to his car which was parked right out front.

Evan, his morning driver, smiled. "Where to, boss?"

Rick gave him the address and pulled up a picture of the apartment on his iPad.

"I sold this to Lillian and Frank Sussman twelve years ago. She reached out on Friday. She let me know that Frank passed a few years ago and she's ready to sell and move closer to her daughter, in Florida. She's a nice lady, I think you'll like her."

Sophie nodded. She still wasn't sure why Rick wanted her to go along, but she was happy to see a new listing.

They reached the address ten minutes later. Rick led the way into an older building on the Upper East Side with about twelve floors. There was a doorman, which was always a selling point. They went to the sixth floor and when Rick knocked on the door it was immediately opened by a tiny woman who wasn't quite five feet tall. She had short bouncy white curls that framed a sweet face with blue gray eyes and a big smile. She was wearing a soft baby blue cardigan, gray wool pants and a string of freshwater pearls. Rick held out his arms and she went into them, and they hugged each other tightly.

"It's so good to see you. I'm so glad you remembered me," Lillian said.

"Of course, I did! You were one of my first clients, Lillian." He flashed her one of his most charming smiles, "And one of my favorites."

Lillian laughed delightedly. "Charming as ever I see."

"This is Sophie, one of my newer associates. She'll be working with me on this to make sure we give your property the highest priority," Rick said.

"How nice. It's lovely to meet you, dear." Lillian smiled her way.

"You as well," Sophie said.

"Come in, come in. Would either of you like a hot cup of tea or coffee?" Lillian offered.

Rick and Sophie both declined. Lillian showed them around the apartment. It was spotless, with high ceilings, a small but well laid out kitchen, two bedrooms, a full bathroom in the primary bedroom and a half bath off the living room. There was also an alcove off the living room that was set up as a library. All four walls had bookcases full of books. Most of it was fiction and more than half was romance. There was also an overstuffed chair by a window that let in a lot of light.

"That's my favorite spot in the apartment," Lillian said, glancing at the chair. "I'll make myself a cup of tea and spend an afternoon there reading. I love a good romance and sometimes a mystery, just to mix things up."

Rick nodded. "I enjoy the occasional mystery. I'm a big fan of Lee Child. Have you read him?"

"I have. I'm more of a cozy mystery reader. I like Jana Deleon. Her books make me laugh out loud."

"That sounds fun," Sophie said. "I mostly read romance, but I might have to check out those books, too."

They ended in the dining area of the living room and sat at a cozy clear-glass table.

"So, Lillian, you're sure you want to leave this marvelous apartment?" Rick asked. It was clear that she loved it there.

She nodded slowly and looked determined. "I'm ready. As much as I love it here, it's just not the same since I lost my Frank. There are too many memories here. And my daughter and grandchildren are in Florida. There's a lovely independent living community a few miles from where she lives."

Rick nodded. "It will be nice to be near your family. Have you thought about what you'd like to price your home at?"

"I'm really not sure. I would hope at least a million, maybe a bit more? What do you think?"

He grinned. "I think we can do quite a bit better than that. When we decide on a price, we always look at recent sales of similar homes in the area. I think we should ask 1.75 million. What do you think about that?"

Lillian's eyes widened. "Are you sure? That seems like an awful lot. More than I expected."

"I think that is a fair price and there is quite a bit of demand for that price point. I don't think it should take too long to find a buyer."

"Well, isn't that something?" She looked a bit dazed by it all.

"As I mentioned earlier, Sophie will be working with me on this. So please reach out to her anytime if you have any questions. We can set up an open house for next weekend if you like? I would suggest this weekend, but with the holiday there may be a lot of people out of town."

"I will be one of them. I'm flying to Florida tomorrow and back on Sunday. So, the following weekend would be just fine for an open house."

"Good. We'll plan on Sunday afternoon maybe from 1-2, if that would work for you?" Rick asked.

"Yes, I'll go visit a friend or do some shopping. Let me give you a key." She got up and went to the kitchen, opened a drawer and pulled out a single key.

"Here you go." She set it on the table.

Rick picked it up and put it in his blazer pocket. "Perfect. We'll get started on this right away for you. I just need your signature on our listing agreement." Rick slid a stack of papers to Lillian. She glanced at them quickly, then signed and pushed them back to him.

"Fantastic." Rick pulled out a form and ran through a series of questions about the unit. All the information they would need for the listing. When he finished, he took out his phone.

"I'd like to get a few pictures. It's a good thing it's a sunny day, the light coming in here is wonderful." He walked around the apartment, snapping pictures of all the rooms, from different angles. He'd told Sophie when she first started that it was a good idea to take more pictures than you think you'd need. Multiple shots of every room and to try and use the light to showcase each room at its best. They could go through all the shots back at the office and choose the best ones for the listing and online brochures.

Sophie snapped a few as well in the library, where the sun was streaming through the windows.

"Your home is really beautiful," she said to Lillian who stood nearby, watching them.

She looked pleased to hear it. "Thank you, dear. I really have loved living here. I'm sure I will miss it, but I will have the fondest memories. And I won't miss the cold winters!"

Sophie smiled. "I'm sure. And this is a great time to move down there and enjoy the warm weather."

When Rick finished taking pictures, he pulled Lillian in for another hug.

"It was so great seeing you again, Lillian. We're going to get started on this right now. Either myself or Sophie will be in touch about the open house and to schedule any showings."

Lillian walked them to the door and thanked them both for coming.

"It was lovely to meet you dear. I look forward to hearing from you both."

Once they were in the car and heading back to the office, Rick explained how Sophie would be involved.

"So, I occasionally refer listings to one of my agents. I do it to reward initiative and good work and you've demonstrated that with your recent sales and listing activity."

"You're giving me a listing?" Sophie was shocked. She'd heard Tessa complain about it, but she didn't realize how Rick actually did it.

He nodded. "Technically it's a house listing. It's still mine, but you'll be working it as if it was yours. You'll handle any open houses and showings. It helps me to better leverage my time." He grinned. "And I'll still get my usual broker share if you sell it, so it's all good. I also thought you'd work well with Lillian. She's a sweet lady and I want to make sure she's taken care of."

"Thank you so much. I'll do my best." Sophie was beyond excited to have another listing of her own. And she really liked Lillian.

"Good." His phone rang and he glanced at the caller ID and then took the call. Sophie glanced out the window while Rick talked to his client. He ended the call as they pulled up to the office.

As Sophie was about to get out of the car, Rick spoke.

"Oh, one other thing. Are you free tomorrow night? I almost forgot about this charity event at the Met. I RSVP'd months ago. And now I have an extra ticket." Because Julia was no longer going, Sophie realized. She hesitated for a moment unsure if this was a work event or a date.

Rick flashed his persuasive smile. "Think of it as a fun networking thing. Great food, and a chance for you to meet a lot of influential people. I'll make the introductions. I remembered that you said you were doing some volunteer work there."

Sophie was impressed that he remembered. She relaxed a little since it was clearly a work thing. And a good opportunity to meet potential clients.

"I'd love to."

"Great. I'll swing by your place a little before six and we can walk over, if that works for you?"

Sophie nodded. "Sure, sounds good."

They headed inside. Rick disappeared into his office and immediately got on the phone. A few of the agents were back in the office, eating lunch at their desks. Caroline looked up as Sophie walked in and sat down.

"So....? How did it go?"

Sophie told her about the listing.

"I knew it! I didn't want to get your hopes up in case he didn't actually give it to you. You deserve it. Though I don't imagine Tessa will be pleased once she finds out," Caroline said.

"Ugh. You really think it will bother her?"

"She always whines that it's not fair when anyone is handed a listing. Unless of course it's her turn. And then it's totally deserved."

Sophie laughed. "I am starting to see that side of her."

"Don't let it bother you. Just focus on doing your job and making money."

"There's something else," Sophie began. "Rick also invited me to go with him to a charity event at the Met tomorrow. I'm sure I'm taking Julia's ticket. I was a little hesitant, but he said it should be a good networking opportunity. And I did make my last sale to someone I met through the Met."

"Oh, you have to go!" Caroline looked deep in thought for a moment. "Do you have a dress in mind to wear? If not, I have a gorgeous silky black dress you're welcome to borrow. I got it for a similar event last year. I think we're about the same size."

"I would love to try it on. I don't think I have anything dressy enough. If it doesn't fit, I'll have to find something fast tomorrow," Sophie said.

"I bet it will look great on you," Caroline said.

Sophie finished inputting all the information about Lillian's property into the computer to generate a listing. She had to run out as soon as she was done to get to Emily's apartment for their meeting.

When she arrived, Emily let her in, and Sophie was surprised at how quiet it was.

Emily laughed. "It's a rare moment of peace, trust me. Jim's at the office and the kids are both napping. I figure we have twenty minutes or so before it gets very loud.

She showed Sophie around. The unit was lovely but less than half the size of the one they were moving into. It had three bedrooms, one of which Jim was using as an office, a small galley kitchen, and a living and dining area. And of course the location was prime, near the Met and in a well maintained building with a doorman, high ceilings and custom moldings everywhere.

Sophie asked Emily what she and Jim were hoping to get for a price.

"We'd like to be over four, ideally closer to five, but we're really not sure. What do you think?"

"I think that is definitely the range." Sophie showed her the comps that she had printed out of recent sales. "I think four point five might be a good starting point. That will be competitively priced for this area with three bedrooms. You could go a little higher, but I wouldn't advise it."

Emily nodded. "Okay, four point five it is. And I'm sure you'll want to do an open house?"

Sophie nodded. "I think it would be a good idea. We could wait until the weekend after next, or I'm happy to do one this weekend. I'll be back in town on Friday."

Emily thought for a moment. "If you don't mind doing one this week, that might be great actually as we'll be away until Sunday evening."

"We should probably plan on the following Sunday too," Sophie said. "As I don't know what to expect for traffic as this is a big weekend for going out of town."

"That's true. Let's do both, then. We'll make sure we're out of the way that day."

Emily handed her a key, signed the paperwork and answered all of Sophie's questions about the property and co-op process.

"The condo board here can be tough. I should let you know that. They'll want to see a bigger than usual down payment and they can be snooty about what people do for work. It can't be a celebrity. A few have tried and they are always shot down."

"Good to know." Sophie had heard that about other buildings as well.

Sophie walked around and took pictures of all the rooms. When they got to the primary bedroom, she noticed a stunning dusty pink dress hanging by the door, wrapped in dry cleaner plastic.

Emily walked over to it. "I'll put it in the closet so it's out of the way. I just picked it up this morning."

"It's beautiful. Are you planning to wear it soon?" The color flattered Emily's hair and skin tone.

"Tomorrow actually. That's why I rushed to pick it up earlier. There's an event at the Met. Jim and some his colleagues are going, and the Met is one of the charities we donate to."

"I'm going as well. I just found out today. My boss had an extra ticket."

Emily's eyes lit up. "You are? That's wonderful! It will be nice to see a familiar face there. I never know anyone other than Jim's co-workers. Look for me when you arrive."

"I will." Sophie was a little less intimidated about the event now that she knew Emily would be there, too.

She headed to her apartment and worked from home the rest of the day. She had the place to herself for a few hours and got a lot done. Caroline was the first to come home and once she was settled she excitedly went and got the dress from her bedroom.

It was gorgeous, a shimmery black satin with spaghetti straps and a slim silhouette that flared a little at the knees, giving it an elegant and flirty look. Sophie tried it on, and it fit well. She turned to see the back of the dress, which dipped to her mid back and had a soft black bow. It was perfect. She paired it with diamond solitaire earrings she got from her parents when she turned twenty-one and a delicate pendant necklace that had once been her grand-mother's engagement ring. She'd left it to Sophie, and she had it turned into a pretty necklace so she could wear it often. A pair of simple black heels and a small silver clutch and she would be ready to go. She walked out to show Caroline the complete look, and she squealed. "It's perfect!"

Sophie smiled and stepped out of her heels. They were comfortable but she didn't want to wear them a moment longer than she had to.

"Thanks so much. It really is perfect. I would have been rushing around in a mad panic tomorrow to find something."

"Happy to help. See if you can get someone to take pictures. I want to live vicariously through you."

Sophie laughed. "I definitely will. I'm starting to look forward to it."

CHAPTER THIRTY-FOUR

The next day, Sophie made sure she was home in plenty of time to get ready for the event at the Met. She curled her long brown hair so that it fell in soft spirals to her shoulders. And she took extra care with her makeup, adding some shimmery brown eyeshadow, smoky liner and ruby red lipstick. Normally she stuck to minimal makeup and paler lips, but her long black dress needed something more dramatic, and it was the Met after all. A blue-toned red seemed perfect.

At five of six she was ready and walked into the living room. Caroline was eating a bowl of pasta at the island, and Tessa was sipping a glass of red wine and spreading goat cheese on a cracker. They both looked up and their expressions were so different that Sophie almost laughed. Tessa's brows furrowed and she looked confused while Caroline jumped up and ran over to get a closer look.

"You look amazing. I love what you did with your hair."

"Thanks. It takes a while, so I don't usually bother, but for special occasions I like to add some waves."

"Where are you off to?" Tessa asked.

"I'm going to a charity event at the Met."

Sophie's phone rang and she recognized the number, it was Walter, the building's doorman.

"Hi Walter."

"Sophie, I have a Rick Fulton here. He says you are expecting him?"

"Thanks, Walter. Please send him up."

Sophie almost laughed at the expression on Tessa's face. She was dying of curiosity. Before Tessa could ask who it was, Sophie heard footsteps coming down the hall and a knock at the door. She opened it and Rick stood there looking sharp in a well-tailored black suit and a festive burgundy tie. He smiled when he saw her.

"Sophie, you look gorgeous." He glanced around the apartment. "So, this is your aunt's place. It's pretty sweet. Want to give me a quick tour?"

"Sure, come on in."

Rick saw Caroline and Tessa in the kitchen and waved hello.

"You look great, Rick. Love the suit," Caroline said. She looked as though she was enjoying this all immensely. Meanwhile Tessa looked completely perplexed.

Rick nodded appreciatively. "Thanks. Just got this one a few weeks ago. Breaking it in for the first time tonight."

Sophie walked him around the apartment and he was suitably impressed. "It's really a great place. You could get a lot of money for it if you ever wanted to sell. Then buy yourself something smaller and put a nice chunk of money in the bank."

Sophie laughed. "You sound like my mother. That's exactly what she thinks I should do, too."

"It's just one option. As long as you can afford to stay here and you love it, why not stay put? You won't lose money by staying. This location is always in high demand."

"I really do love it here. And having roommates takes a little of the pressure off."

"If you keep going the way you've started out, you won't have to worry about that—even without roommates," he said.

They said goodbye to Caroline and Tessa and headed out.

The temperature had dropped a bit, and small flakes of snow began to swirl around them as they walked. The snowflakes looked so pretty in the glow of the street lamps. Sophie felt happy and full of the holiday spirit as she walked along with Rick to the Met. They arrived about ten minutes later and followed the crowd that was streaming in.

The event was held in a huge room with incredible art on the walls. It was so beautiful that it felt surreal to Sophie, like she was living someone else's life by being there.

But then she saw two familiar faces, as Emily and Jim walked in and it suddenly felt more normal, more real. They hung their coats up and Rick led the way to one of several bars set up around the room. "What would you like to drink?" he asked.

Sophie thought for a moment. "Cabernet, please."

Rick handed Sophie her wine a minute later. He was drinking scotch on the rocks.

He immediately saw someone he knew and led Sophie over to say hello and introduced her. Mr. and Mrs. Thurman did something in finance and Rick recently sold one of their homes. Over the next hour, Sophie met so many people that it was hard to keep all their names straight. Most were former clients of Rick's, but he also knew a lot of people personally as well just from living in the city for so many years. And after chatting with an older couple, Claudia and Stan Ashton, Sophie learned that they knew her aunt.

"I volunteer at the Met and met your aunt years ago. She was a lovely woman. I was sorry to hear of her passing," Claudia said.

"Thank you. I still miss her. I'm actually in the volunteer training program. I'm looking forward to following in her footsteps there," Sophie said.

Claudia smiled. "How wonderful. Perhaps I will see you there."

"Do you mind if I run off for a minute? There's someone I've been trying to catch, and he just arrived," Rick said.

"No, of course I don't mind." Sophie looked around after Rick walked off and spotted Emily across the room. She was standing by Jim, who was chatting with a group of men and Emily looked bored to tears. When she saw Sophie looking her way, she waved her over.

"Thank god you're here," Emily said softly once Sophie reached her. "I started drifting once these guys mention derivatives. What do you think? Are you having fun?"

"It is fun, so far. I just met Claire Ashton who also volunteers here. Rick knows her and her husband."

"I don't know her, but I know of her," Emily said. "I think he's actually a billionaire. They live on Fifth Avenue too, in one of the few actual mansions. There are some that go back to the Gilded Age."

"I never would have guessed," Sophie said. "She was so friendly and down to earth."

Emily nodded. "The very richest people often are. They don't have to impress anyone. Jim told me that Warren Buffett who has all the money in the world, still lives in a modest home in the suburbs and drives an old pickup truck."

Sophie smiled. "I love that. I do like Fifth Avenue though."

Emily laughed. "I do too. Oh, those crab cakes look good."

A tuxedo clad waiter glided over and held out a silver platter with delicious looking bite-sized crab cakes. Emily and Sophie both took one. And it was as good as it looked.

"You should sit with us for the dinner," Emily said. "We have two open seats at our table."

"I'd love to. I'm not sure what Rick will want to do though. He may have plans to sit with prospective clients."

"Tell him that our table might be good for him, too. These guys are buying and selling properties every few years, it seems."

Sophie sipped her wine and gazed around the room. She'd never seen so many beautifully dressed people in one place. She and Emily people-watched for a bit, commenting on some of the gorgeous dresses. Emily looked stunning too, in a sleek pale pink satin slip dress that flattered her collar length blonde bob.

"There you are." Rick walked up to them, and Sophie introduced him to Emily.

"I was just telling Sophie, that the two of you should join us at our table for dinner," Emily said.

Rick smiled and glanced at the group of men nearby—Jim and his colleagues.

"That's so nice of you. I wish I could, but I already promised two of the guys at my assigned table that we'd discuss a little business over dinner." He glanced at Sophie. "Sophie you should stay though. It will be more fun for you."

Sophie hesitated. "Are you sure?" She wanted to stay with Emily but felt bad leaving Rick.

He flashed his most charming grin. "Of course. We can catch up again after dinner." He turned and wandered off and Emily laughed.

"Well, that settles that, doesn't it?" Let's go sit, it looks like they want to start serving soon.

Emily led Sophie to their table. It was a big round one that sat about ten people. Jim and his group followed. There were five men total and three wives, including Emily. They all introduced themselves and the man on the other side of Sophie laughed when he spoke.

"I'm Dave, the fill in. Harry's wife couldn't make it tonight, so he's stuck with me."

Sophie guessed that Dave was in his late thirties or maybe even early forties. He had one of those baby faces, smooth shaven with a small, upturned nose , deep dimples and a ready smile that gave him a mischievous look. He was easy to talk to and explained that he'd worked with the firm for over ten years.

"It's a great group of guys. No one ever leaves, so I was lucky they made room for me," he said modestly.

"He's being humble," Jim said. "Dave is a brilliant analyst and built us a computer program that, well, I don't know how we lived without it."

"You enjoy your work," Sophie said.

Dave grinned. "I suppose you could say I'm mildly obsessed. What about you? What do you do?"

"I work in real estate sales. I'm with Fulton. I'm fairly new, but I really love it so far," Sophie said passionately.

"Sophie found us our new home, and we couldn't be happier about it," Emily said.

Paul, the man sitting next to Dave, looked intrigued when he heard that. He had an air about him that made Sophie guess that he might be the head of the firm. He was maybe late fifties with thick black hair that was lightly tinged with gray and cool brown eyes that seemed to take everything in.

"And now you have the listing for their current home? Jim mentioned just yesterday that he was going to use someone new."

Sophie nodded. "Yes, we're doing our first open house this weekend."

Paul raised an eyebrow. "You're not going out of town for the holiday weekend?"

"Oh, I am. I'm heading out Wednesday afternoon. But I'll be back for the weekend. I'm looking forward to it."

"Sophie is doing one the following weekend, too,"

Emily said. "In case traffic is slow this weekend. As you said, people might be out of town."

He nodded. "Good. Last realtor we used was just awful. No sense of urgency about anything." He looked around the table. "As you can imagine, that didn't go over well." He turned back to Sophie and smiled. "Good luck with your open houses."

Their food arrived a moment later, a simple salad with a truffle vinaigrette followed by poached lobster on a lemon mousse topped with caviar. It was decadent and Sophie savored every bite. Dessert was baked Alaska, something Sophie had read about in old novels and never tried before. The filling was vanilla ice cream and passion-fruit sorbet, surrounded by a yellow sponge cake and smothered with fluffy meringue. It was baked just long enough for the meringue tips to toast golden brown.

Emily and Sophie ate just about everything. They sipped coffee with their dessert and Emily laughed.

"I'm so full, can I confess all I want to do now is go home and get into my sweats and curl up on the sofa. These heels are killing me."

"Mine are too. I don't wear them often enough," Sophie said.

"The dancing will start soon," Emily said. "Once the band starts, the dance floor will fill up. I figure we'll stay for a few songs and then we can sneak home."

That sounded good to Sophie too. She had to fight back a yawn. It was after nine and she usually headed to bed by ten. She looked over at the table where Rick was seated. His dessert sat in front of him, mostly untouched and he was deep in conversation with the man next to him.

"I need to move around. Let's go dance," Emily said. Jim was in the middle of telling a work story and it didn't look like he would be joining them on the dance floor anytime soon. Sophie followed Emily and they joined the crowd of people already dancing to a lively song that everyone knew. Rick caught her eye and gave her the thumbs up, and Sophie laughed.

"I wasn't sure what this event would be like," she admitted too Emily. "It's definitely a work thing for Rick. He's networking up a storm."

Emily laughed. "Well, for what these tickets cost, he should be."

They danced two more songs and just as they were about to go and sit, Rick joined them on the dance floor, and they all danced. The music was fun, and everyone seemed to be having a good time. When the song ended, the next song was a slow one and Sophie started to follow Emily to the table, but Rick took her hand.

"One more dance?" He held her gaze and smiled.

Sophie nodded and let him pull her toward him. She wrapped her arms around his neck, and he put his lightly on her waist. They swayed to the music.

"Are you having fun?" he asked.

"Yes, it's been a great night. Thanks for bringing me." It had been fun, sitting with Emily and taking it all in.

"I thought you might enjoy it. And living where you do, I thought you might meet some of your neighbors and other people it would be good to know. You never know when someone might need a realtor."

"You were deep in conversation. Are you working on something?" Sophie asked.

"Yes, sort of. I knew one of the guys at my table was thinking about selling his unit. I'm on the board of my co-op and that's who was at my table, a few of the other board members. He's not quite ready to put it on the market, but he's almost there and had a lot of questions. So, we'll see what happens."

"Oh, good luck."

"Thanks. It would be a sweet listing. He has the top two floors of our building, it's probably high thirties maybe even a forty million dollar listing. His unit is spectacular."

The numbers that Sophie often heard made her head spin. "What does he do that he can afford something like that?"

Rick laughed. "Family money. He's never had a real job. Just manages his family trusts and to his credit, they've tripled under his watch. He makes millions yearly just on the interest."

"Wow."

"Yeah, not a bad gig. But this can be incredible too. I hit eight figures in personal income this year. That could be you someday, too, Sophie if you stay with it."

Sophie couldn't imagine hitting seven figures let alone eight. She just nodded.

When the song ended, she had to fight back another yawn. It was after ten on a Tuesday and she was suddenly exhausted. She glanced over at the table where Emily was sitting and saw that they were standing by the table and Jim was helping her with her long coat. Sophie and Rick walked over to them.

"We were just about to head out. This was a fun night,

though," Emily said. "Sophie, have a great Thanksgiving, and I'll talk to you soon."

"We could head out too, if you're ready?" Rick suggested.

"Sure, I'll just get my coat."

Five minutes later, they were walking outside. The wind had picked up and the snow was coming down fast and furious. The ground was starting to get slippery, and Sophie walked carefully. Rick chatted as they walked, telling her all about the people at his table and some of the other clients he'd run into.

"I try never to miss this event. It's the best networking in the city. Where else can you find this many powerful people in one place?"

When they reached Sophie's building, Rick pulled her in for a quick hug. "Thanks for coming with tonight, Sophie. See you in the morning?"

"Thank you. And yes, see you tomorrow."

Sophie smiled as she walked into the building and said hello to Walter, the night doorman. It had been an interesting evening and she was relieved that Rick's interest in her seemed to just be professional. She found him attractive, but really didn't think of him romantically and she knew that dating her boss could be very messy. Things were going so well now, that she didn't want anything to ruin that.

CHAPTER THIRTY-FIVE

Caroline and Tessa were still up when Sophie got home. They were both in their pajamas, watching Netflix and Caroline was yawning. She usually went to bed earlier than this.

"I was just about to give up on you and head to bed," Caroline teased. "How did it go?"

Sophie shrugged her coat off and hung it on the wrought iron rack by the door. When she kicked off her heels her feet instantly felt relief.

"It was really fun. Emily was there, so it was nice to see a familiar face. Rick knew so many people."

"Did he introduce you to everyone?" Tessa asked. Her expression was difficult to read.

Sophie nodded. "Yes, to so many that I won't possibly be able to remember all of their names."

"How was the food and the outfits? Did you see a lot of gorgeous gowns?" Caroline asked. The question made Sophie smile.

"Yes, and the food was great. We had lobster, caviar and baked Alaska."

"Yum! Baked Alaska, that sounds like something my grandmother would have served," Caroline said.

"I know! I thought the same. It was really good, though. Better than I expected."

"So, are you and Rick dating now?" Tessa asked. There was an edge to her voice almost as if Sophie had done something wrong.

"No. This was just a work event. He'd bought a ticket for Julia but at the last minute she couldn't go," Sophie said.

"He gave you a new listing too, didn't he?" The accusatory tone was still there.

Caroline shot her a disapproving look, which Tessa ignored.

Sophie took a breath. "He did give me a listing to work with him. He said it was because I've been working so hard, and he wanted to reward that."

Tessa laughed bitterly. "Right. Okay." She stood. "I'm off to bed." She left without another word and shut her bedroom door behind her.

Sophie glanced at Caroline, who shrugged. "She's been in a weird mood all night. Don't let it bother you. I told her that too, that Julia just couldn't go. It's a white lie. I'm glad you had a good time. I'm off to bed too. See you in the morning."

"Goodnight." Sophie took off her dress carefully and climbed into her favorite soft pajamas. She fell asleep a few minutes after her head hit the pillow. She was too tired to worry about Tessa and her moods. She had to be up early as she was only working a half day before heading home for Thanksgiving. She was looking forward to it. It would be a nice break for a few days.

Sophie felt caught up in the holiday spirit as she walked toward the train Wednesday afternoon. The streets were crowded with others leaving early and heading out for the holiday weekend. The air was cold, and she could see her breath as she walked. Tiny snowflakes began to fall just as Sophie reached the entrance to the train station. She got a window seat and watched the snow fall and the intensity grow over the next two hours.

It had mostly stopped though by the time the train pulled into the Hudson station and her father was there to pick her up. He was waiting by his tan Volvo station wagon, wearing his favorite flannel shirt and his thick winter jacket. He pulled her in for a tight hug when she reached him.

"Hope you're hungry, your mother is making meatballs and sauce," he said as they climbed into the car. Sophie expected that—it was their traditional night before Thanksgiving meal. And her mother made the best tomato sauce. She'd showed Sophie several times how she did it and Sophie attempted to make it once, but she overdid the oregano and it just tasted wrong. It was much easier to buy a jar of Rao's sauce.

Her father disappeared into the den to watch TV when they got inside and after giving her mother a welcome hug, Sophie asked what she could do to help.

"Right now, everything is done. The sauce is simmering. I just took the meatballs out of the oven and they're soaking in the sauce now. The pasta should be ready in a few minutes. You could open this bottle of wine. I'm ready for a glass."

She handed Sophie a bottle of Josh Cabernet. Sophie smiled, as she'd brought a bottle of Josh too. She and her mother shared similar tastes in wine. She also brought a bottle of Flowers, the Pinor Noir that had been Aunt Penny's favorite and that she'd tasted when Max brought it over that first night. It seemed like ages ago.

Thinking about Max also reminded her that he was taking Tessa to the comedy club tonight. She wondered how that was going to go. Tessa had never seemed interested in Max before. But she was also single now. Sophie poured herself a generous glass of wine and one for her mother as well. She took a sip and tried not to think about Max with Tessa.

"So, what's new and exciting with you, Mom?"

"Let's see, your Aunt Paula needs a knee replacement. Oh, and your father and I booked a cruise. We're going on a Viking Mississipi River cruise next month with Ginny and Tom." Ginny and Tom lived a few doors down and Ginny was her mother's best friend.

"That sounds fun!"

"Why don't you go call your father. I just need to drain the pasta, and we can eat."

Over dinner, Sophie's father asked how the job was going.

"Really well actually. I've made a couple of sales now. One of them was a huge sale, with my roommate Caroline. It was her listing, my client. And it went so well that

Emily gave me the listing to sell her condo. So, I've been busy."

"That's great, honey!" Her father said. He seemed pleased for her.

Her mother still seemed somewhat skeptical about it all. "You haven't closed yet on these sales though? They could still fall apart?"

Sophie reached for her glass of wine and took a sip. "They could. Hopefully they won't."

"Well, congratulations. That will be good news, as long as they pan out," her mother said.

"Right. Oh, I went to a gala last night at the Met. It was so incredible."

Her mother looked surprised. "You went to an event at the Met? Who did you go with?"

"My boss had an extra ticket last minute so I went with him."

Her father frowned. "You're not dating your boss?"

"No! It was just a work thing. Really good networking. My client, Emily and her husband Jim were there, and I met some of his co-workers."

"Were any of them single?" Her mother asked.

Sophie shook her head. "I don't think so. They were with their wives mostly."

The conversation turned to what they had left to prepare for Thanksgiving dinner.

"When we finish dinner and clean up, we can start getting ready. I picked up a new peeler today, so that should help with the potatoes and squash. You could leave the peels on the apples, just chop them up nice and small."

The rest of the night went smoothly and was relaxing.

Sophie peeled and sliced and chopped and slowly sipped a second glass of wine. Her mother chatted as they worked, and she filled her in on all the neighborhood gossip—people Sophie hadn't seen in ages. It was fun though to hear what they were all up to. When they finished, they joined her father in the living room and Sophie watched TV for a bit with them before heading to bed. It had been a long day of traveling and she knew they'd be up early to finish getting everything ready.

Thanksgiving was mostly a great day. Sophie's aunts, uncles and cousins arrived around one and it was good to see them. Sophie's mother was an only child, but her father had two sisters. Aunt Paula was moving slowly because of her bad knee, but her Aunt Chrissy was as animated and energetic as ever. She was the tiny one in the family and was still a runner, which kept her lean. They brought appetizers and more wine, and they all stood around the kitchen nibbling on the big charcuterie board that her cousin Sarah and Aunt Paula put together. Aunt Chrissy brought the wine and her daughters, Sophie's cousins, Jillian and Kerry, made desserts—creme brûlée cheesecake and lemon cupcakes.

Her cousins were all about the same age as Sophie, within a year or two and they were all settled in their lives with serious boyfriends and great jobs in finance.

Sophie helped her mother put all the side dishes on the counter so everyone could help themselves, buffet style. They sat around the living room table eating and laughing and the mood was light and fun. Until Aunt Paula asked Sophie about her job.

"So, tell us all about this new job of yours? You're living on Fifth Avenue now and selling real estate. It all sounds very fancy!" Aunt Paula said.

Sophie laughed. "It's not quite as glamorous as it sounds. Well, sometimes it is. There are some incredible homes for sale. I've made my first two sales, which is exciting. But it can be a little scary too," she admitted. "As it is all commission and sometimes things fall apart at the last minute for all different reasons."

Aunt Paula looked somewhat concerned. "Well, that sounds stressful. You like it though?"

"I love it. I temped for a while in a few different industries and when I started at the real estate firm, I found it all fascinating."

"And your aunt left you an apartment on Fifth Avenue! That sounds glamorous, do you love living there?" Sarah asked.

"I really do. I have two roommates, which helps with the monthly fees," Sophie said.

"I'm surprised you don't sell it, get something smaller and put the rest in savings," Aunt Paula said.

"Thank you!" Sophie's mother said triumphantly. "That's what I strongly suggested that she do. She has no restrictions and could sell immediately."

Sophie smiled "I don't want to sell though. I love it here. And Tessa and Caroline signed year-long leases."

"You could still sell. The new owner could assume the leases," her mother persisted.

"That would limit who would want to buy it," Sophie said practically.

"I just worry that you could lose it, Sophie. What if your deals fall through? You already had that happen once. And what if you get hit with a big assessment? There's not a lot left in Aunt Penny's account, as you know."

"I know. I've already been hit with an assessment," she admitted.

"See, that's what I was afraid of. Maybe your roommates will understand if you decide to put it on the market," her mother insisted.

Sophie sighed. "I'm not going to do that. Not yet. If even one of these deals close, that will give me a bit of a cushion. And I have two new listings, both are great properties and could go quickly, hopefully."

"So, what else is new with everyone?" Sophie's father asked in an attempt to shift the conversation. Sophie smiled at him appreciatively.

"I'm getting knee surgery in two weeks," Aunt Paula began. Sophie listened as she told them in great detail what that involved. It was far from fascinating but much better than being grilled about her apartment. As much as she loved her family, they were best enjoyed in small doses. And Sophie was looking forward to heading back to the city the next day. She was glad that she had the excuse of an open house over the weekend.

CHAPTER THIRTY-SIX

Sophie's train arrived at Grand Central the next afternoon and she enjoyed the walk to her apartment. It was a warm day for late November and the air was calm with no wind. The temperature fell a bit as she walked and by the time she reached her building, it started to snow. Just a small flurry of tiny flakes that danced and twirled in the air and immediately disappeared when they hit the ground. It was the kind of snow Sophie liked best, pretty to watch and no mess.

She made herself a cup of cinnamon tea and settled at the breakfast table in the kitchen nook that overlooked Fifth Avenue. She watched the snow fall outside as she sipped her warm tea and thought about what to do that day. She had the apartment to herself all weekend as both Caroline and Tessa weren't due home until late Sunday afternoon. Neither of them had scheduled open houses.

She thought about heading out to the shops to explore the Black Friday deals and immediately dismissed the thought. She didn't like crowds and knew the stores would be mobbed. So, instead she decided to have a lazy day, reading and watching movies and doing laundry. But before she did that, she spent several hours online researching and building a new list of local residents that she could mail postcards to introducing herself. That way she felt as though she'd been somewhat productive before lounging on the sofa for the rest of the day and into the night.

Sophie slept late the next morning and worked on her list for a few more hours before heading out to window shop for a bit. She knew the stores wouldn't be as crowded as the day before and she was curious to see if the Christmas displays were up everywhere.

They were and she also stumbled onto a huge Christmas market at Bryant Park between Fifth and Sixth Avenue. There was even a skating rink! It was so festive and fun to browse the many stalls with all kinds of gifts, many of them homemade by local artists. Sophie picked up several cute ornaments that she knew her mother and aunts would like as well as a festive red silk tie for her father that had tiny green reindeer embroidered on it.

When she was shopped out, Sophie stopped at Maman on Lexington Ave and went inside to warm up a bit and enjoy a honey lavender latte, which was her favorite treat. She ordered it with almond milk and loved how they made a pretty design in the foam. The flavor was amazing.

She thought maybe Max would be home by now, but the building was eerily quiet when she returned. She realized he was probably returning tomorrow, like the others.

She spent her afternoon grocery shopping and then reading for a bit. By the time dinner rolled around, she was feeling stir-crazy. She had plenty of food she could cook for dinner, but she felt like getting out of the house. She decided to follow in her aunt's footsteps and head out to dinner on her own.

She wore an oversized black cashmere turtleneck sweater over dressy jeans and black leather boots. She thought about bringing a book along with her but thought it might be better to read on her phone instead. The only restaurant she felt comfortable going to by herself was the Italian restaurant where everyone was so friendly.

Richard and Tony welcomed her warmly and didn't bat an eye when she said she was there alone and was going to head to the bar.

"Of course. Patrick will take good care of you," Tony said.

The bar was u-shaped and had about a dozen or so seats. There were several open and she chose the one against the wall, where she could easily watch people coming and going. Patrick came right over and handed her a menu. She ordered a glass of red wine, an Italian Super Tuscan, and sipped on it while she looked over the menu. It was early still, not quite six, so the restaurant wasn't too busy yet. She knew it would be soon, though.

She decided on eggplant parmesan with a single meatball on the side. Patrick returned a moment later with a basket of warm Italian bread, seasoned olive oil for dipping and softened butter. She tore off a piece of bread, buttered it and dipped it in the spicy oil. She sipped her wine and watched people coming and going. An older couple two seats down, paid their check and left and another couple took their place. A few minutes later, a single guy who looked to be a little older than Sophie, sat next to her. He glanced her way and nodded as Patrick came over to help him.

He looked vaguely familiar, but Sophie couldn't figure out where she'd seen him before.

After he placed his order and had a glass of red wine set in front him, he took a sip, then glanced at Sophie and smiled. "This is going to sound like the cheesiest pick-up line ever, but you look so familiar."

Sophie laughed. "I was actually thinking the same thing. I work at a real estate office, have you been in there by any chance? I'm fairly new here so am not sure where else I would have seen you."

"Fulton?"

She nodded.

"That's it then. I was in a month ago and met with an agent, Tessa. My lease is up soon, and I was looking to find a new place. My name is Sean."

Now Sophie remembered. She and Caroline had been making coffee in the kitchen when Sean walked in. He had the kind of looks that made you stop and take notice. Sandy blonde hair, hazel eyes, pillowy lips and a strong jaw. They'd walked by him in the lobby and chatted with him for a minute, asking if he was all set, as the receptionist had disappeared for a minute. They'd asked Tessa about him later, asking if he was single.

"No such luck. He was looking to move into a new rental with his girlfriend and told me he was planning to propose soon. Obviously, that was disappointing. He was gorgeous."

Sophie smiled. "I remember now. Did she find something great for you?"

Sean's smile faded. "No, she showed me a bunch of places, but none were what we were looking for. I don't think she really understood what we wanted."

"Oh, I'm sorry to hear that."

"Yeah. I have a little time, so I put the search on hold. I need to start it up again soon. I just can't waste my time again, though. It's time consuming to look at places."

Sophie nodded sympathetically. "It is." She wondered what he was looking for that was so difficult to find. Maybe his budget was too low. Manhattan rentals were expensive and there weren't many great options unless you were willing to spend for them.

A few minutes later, Patrick delivered Sophie's eggplant. It was so hot she could see the steam coming off it, so she gave it a few minutes to cool off. As she took her first bite, Sean's dinner was served—a big bowl of spaghetti and meatballs. His looked just as hot but he didn't hesitate and dove right in.

"I love the food here," he said. "My girlfriend is still away at her parents for the holiday weekend, so I decided to come in. Didn't feel like cooking."

Sophie smiled. "Same here. My roommates aren't due home until tomorrow. My aunt used to live nearby, and this was her favorite neighborhood restaurant."

"This is the area my girlfriend and I are hoping to find something in. But there haven't been many new rentals lately it seems. I check online every few days."

Sophie felt a rush as she mentally ran through their newest rental listings. She checked them every morning and they'd just added a new one Wednesday before everyone left. It was one of the more senior agent's listings, Sue Evans. And it was a stunning unit.

"What are you looking for?"

"Three bedrooms ideally as we both work from home. Washer and dryer in unit, elevator and doorman. We also want to be on or near Fifth Avenue and walking distance to the Met. I guess it is a lot."

"You may want to give Tessa a call on Monday. We had something new come in Wednesday and it's an incredible unit. Right on Fifth. It's at 1025, which is a lovely, doorman building and it's literally right across from the Met. It's a two bedroom, but the living room is massive. You could easily convert part of it to a third bedroom or office. I'm not sure if it will work for your budget, but it's worth talking to Tessa about. I think it will probably go fast."

Sean had put his fork down and was listening intently. When Sophie finished telling him about the rental he immediately said, "That sounds perfect. And our budget is fairly open as we'll be splitting the cost. Can you show it to me?"

Sophie hesitated. Sean wasn't her client, he was Tessa's and she'd just been trying to help. She shook her head and smiled. "You've already been working with Tessa. She can show it to you. I'm sure she'd love to."

He nodded. "I get it. You don't want to step on any toes. I'll call her first thing Monday."

Sophie breathed a sigh of relief. The last thing she wanted to deal with was more conflict with Tessa, especially work related. She finished eating, packed the leftovers up to take home and took her last sip of wine. It had been nice to get out of the house and now she could head home, climb into her sweats and have a little ice cream for dessert while watching a Hallmark Christmas movie marathon.

CHAPTER THIRTY-SEVEN

Sophie did her cookie trick again the next day. She made a batch of chocolate chip cookies and only baked a dozen of them. She froze the rest in balls that she could pop onto a cookie sheet and bake in Emily's oven just before the open house started. She'd designed and printed out a small sign that stated there was an open house from 1-2 and listed Emily's unit number. She wasn't sure if the doorman in that building would allow the sign to be displayed but she figured it didn't hurt to ask nicely.

She put the warm cookies in a clear plastic bag and tied it with a red ribbon. When she arrived at Emily's building, she walked up to the doorman who looked to be in his early forties. He was balding, and had a bit of a pot belly, but also a friendly smile. Emily had introduced her when she'd taken the listing and he recognized her.

Sophie held out the bag of cookies and his eyes lit up. "Hi Billy, I'm Sophie Lawton with Fulton Real Estate, and I'm holding an open house for Emily today. I always bake cookies for my open houses and thought you might enjoy a few." She handed him the bag and he took it eagerly.

"Nice to see you again."

Sophie smiled "I appreciate your help sending people up to the unit. I made this little sign. I'm not sure if it's possible to display it here, so people coming into the building might see it?"

Billy opened the bag and took out a cookie. "They're still warm." He took a bite and closed his eyes for a moment. "Delicious. Thank you."

He took the sign from her outstretched hand and set it on the desk in front of him.

"I'll have people sign in here with their ID before sending them up to you. That's our policy."

Sophie nodded. "Perfect. Thanks so much, Billy."

She headed up to the unit and once she was inside, she turned on the oven and put the dough balls on the cookie sheet she'd brought with her. She baked two batches and put them on a cheery red platter on the table in the entry foyer. The open house was only for an hour, and she had no idea what to expect. She didn't think it would be overly busy given that it was the holiday weekend, but she hoped that at least a few people might come.

Sophie waited and ate three cookies as she nervously wondered if she might have an open house where no one showed up. Finally, at one thirty, there was a knock on the door that she'd left slightly ajar. She welcomed an older couple, Florence and Stuart Smith. She had them sign in and was initially excited that they didn't seem to be working with a realtor. But a moment later, Florence also let her know that they really weren't looking.

"I hate to get your hopes up dear, but we already live in the building. We were just curious to see inside this unit," Florence admitted.

Sophie smiled. "Oh, no problem at all. I'd be curious too. Please wander around and help yourself to a cookie."

They each took one and left to explore the unit. A few minutes later, two fashionably dressed women in their late thirties walked in together and signed the book. They introduced themselves.

"I'm Marcia and this is Sunny. We're both brokers. We thought we'd have a look around so we're familiar with the unit as we may possibly have clients we can call for it."

"Great, thanks for coming. Please look around and let me know if you have any questions. And be sure to take a cookie." Marcia glanced at the plate of cookies longingly.

"I'm doing keto at the moment so no sugar for me. They look amazing though." Sunny didn't take one either. They wandered off and Sophie felt a little better At least there were people looking at the unit and maybe Marcia or Sunny might have a buyer for her.

No one else came in until five of two. A tall and very skinny man with wiry gray hair and a Mr. Rogers style cardigan stepped through the door. He wasn't wearing a coat and it was cold outside, so Sophie guessed he was another neighbor.

"Hi there. I'm Carl Givens. I saw the sign in the lobby and thought I'd walk down the hall and take a peek. I hope you don't mind. I'm not actually in the market myself."

Sophie smiled. "Of course, I don't mind. Come on in, and please grab a few cookies."

"Oh, don't mind if I do." He picked up two cookies,

took a bite of one and set off to explore the unit. A few minutes later, he was back.

Sophie had a stack of brochures that had information about the unit next to the sign in book. Carl signed in and took one. She encouraged him to take a few more cookies, too. "I can't eat them all."

"You don't have to ask me twice. Thank you."

He left and Sophie checked the time on her watch. It was five past two. Time to shut the open house down. She piled the leftover cookies into an extra bag she'd brought with her. She grabbed the cookie sheet and headed downstairs.

Billy smiled when he saw her. She noticed that his bag of cookies was half gone. "How'd it go?" He asked.

"Good. It was a little quiet but that's expected for this weekend, I think."

He nodded. "A few people noticed the sign and asked me about it. A few residents, too. Maybe they will spread the word for you?"

"That would be nice. I'll be back next weekend. Hopefully it will be busier. Thanks so much, Billy."

"Of course. Will you be bringing more cookies next weekend?"

Sophie laughed. "Yes, I will. Let me add a few more to your bag though. I have tons left over." She poured half of her bag into his and he looked like he'd won the lottery.

"Thank you. These won't go to waste."

"See you next weekend, Billy." Sophie headed home. There were still plenty of leftover cookies for her and Caroline to enjoy later. She'd offer them to Tessa, but she usually passed on sweets and liked to say that sugar was evil. That was probably how she stayed so thin. It didn't seem like a fun way to live if one couldn't enjoy a home-made chocolate chip cookie or two now and then.

CHAPTER THIRTY-EIGHT

"*Murders* tonight?" The text message from Max came a little after four that afternoon. Caroline had just gotten home, and she and Sophie were catching up over a cup of vanilla tea.

"Do you mind if I invite Max over? He wants to watch *Murders* with us?" Sophie asked.

"Of course. I wonder how things went with him and Tessa at the comedy show? I texted her to wish her a Happy Thanksgiving and she didn't mention it," Caroline said.

"I don't see the two of them dating," Sophie said. "But, you never know. Tessa is gorgeous. Maybe she is his type."

"He asked you to go first," Caroline reminded her. "I don't see it either. I'm not sure who would be her type, actually."

Sophie texted Max back. "Sure. Caroline's back. Want to come here to watch, say around seven?"

He texted back immediately. "See you then. I'll grab the pizza this time."

. . .

At a few minutes past seven, Max arrived with the pizzas. Sophie grabbed paper plates and napkins while Caroline poured them all a glass of wine. They sat around the kitchen table and talked about their Thanksgivings.

"It was good to see my family, but then of course my mother started in on how I should sell this place and get something smaller. She's convinced that I won't be able to support myself. She actually suggested that I kick you and Tessa out." Sophie sighed. "Of course, I told her I wasn't doing any such thing. I know she means well. She's just worried that my deals won't close."

"If people haven't worked on commission like we do, it's hard for them to understand. It just seems terrifying," Caroline said and laughed. "In a way it is scary, but you do get used to it after a while."

"I hope yours was calmer," Sophie said.

"Yes! My parents are used to it now. We had a nice relaxing time. Tons of food of course. Ed came over Thanksgiving night and had desert with us."

"Oh, I didn't realize he lived near you?" Sophie said.

"He's about an hour and a half away. It was nice that he made the trip in. He stayed over that night and headed home in the morning. My mother and I hit the shops for Black Friday and he wanted no part of that."

"What about you, Max?" Caroline asked.

"I flew to Palm Beach and my mother and I went to Flagler Steakhouse at the Breakers hotel. It's our usual thing. She doesn't cook. I spent the rest of the weekend visiting with her and getting some writing done. It was a good break."

They ate more pizza and had a bit more wine before Sophie asked, "So how was the comedy show? Did you and Tessa have fun?"

"It was pretty good. I love a good comedy show. We grabbed a burger at a pub nearby first." He answered very matter-of-factly so it was hard for Sophie to get a read on how he actually enjoyed spending time with Tessa.

Max met her eyes, and she couldn't read them at all.

"I heard you had a hot date the night before," he said. "How was your evening at the Met?"

She put her pizza down. His tone was teasing, but she couldn't help but wonder what Tessa had said to him.

"It wasn't a date. Just a networking thing with my boss. It was pretty fun though."

He smiled and reached for another slice of pizza. "Glad you had a good time. I didn't think you were actually dating your boss by the way. I thought Tessa might be joking."

"That's Tessa, always joking," Caroline said.

"I'm surprised she's not back yet," Sophie said.

Caroline's phone dinged with a text message, and she glanced at it.

"That was Tessa. She said she won't be home until late tonight." Sophie felt a sense of relief. She wasn't ready to deal with Tessa and her moodiness just yet.

"Let's go into the living room and watch *Murders*. If you guys are ready."

Max swallowed his last bite of pizza. "Let's do it."

. . .

Sophie headed into the office early Monday morning. She wanted to get in and ready for the week ahead. She grabbed her notebook with her list of contacts she'd put together over the weekend. She intended to get a mailing out that day introducing herself and highlighting a few of her local listings. It might not do anything, but it was possible that it could generate a referral that might turn into a buyer or a seller.

After the sales meeting, Sophie went back to her desk intending to get started on the mailing but had a few messages she had to return first. A half hour later, she opened up her notebook and started inputting the information into the database so she could send the mailing out. An hour later, she was just about ready to click send to generate the labels for the letter she was mailing, when her phone rang. She didn't recognize the number on the caller id.

"This is Sophie Lawton."

"Sophie, it's Sean Prescott. From the restaurant the other night. We talked about a rental." Tessa's Sean.

"Hi Sean. Tessa is here this morning, I can transfer you over to her," she offered.

"I already talked to Tessa. I called her first thing. And she said nothing new had come in. I asked if she was sure? And she asked if I was still looking for three bedrooms. I told her I could flex for two if there was a bigger room that could be partitioned off. She still said there was nothing. So, here I am. Is that rental you mentioned still available?"

Sophie quickly pulled up the rentals list on her laptop. "Yes, it's a new listing. It's still available."

"Okay, I'd like to see it ASAP. Can we go today?"

Sophie took a deep breath. She wasn't sure what she could or should do. "Sean, let me find out. Can I call you right back?"

"Sure thing."

Sophie hung up the phone and glanced toward Rick's office. He was off the phone and staring intently at this computer, reading an email. She stood and walked to his office and stood in the doorway. He looked up, and waved her in.

"What's up Sophie?"

Sophie told him about Sean, and her conversation with him at the restaurant. "He told me at the restaurant that he wanted me to show him the rental, but I insisted that he call Tessa since they were already working together. He agreed and I thought that was the end of it. But he just called now and said he did call her this morning, and she said she didn't have anything to show him."

Rick frowned. He picked up the phone and punched an extension. "Tessa, can you pop into my office for a second?"

She walked in a moment later and looked confused to see Sophie there as well.

"Tessa, did you talk to a Sean Prescott this morning about a rental?"

"Yes, I've been keeping an eye out for him."

"What did you tell him today?"

"Just that I'd let him know if we get any three bedrooms in."

"What about the unit at 1025?" Rick asked.

"That's not a three bedroom."

"No, but it has a huge living room that could be made into an office or third bedroom."

"I suppose so. I just thought of it as a two bedroom and that's not what he said he wanted." She glanced at Sophie. "Why is she here?"

Rick explained that Sophie had met Sean and immediately thought of the unit. "She told him to call you, Tessa. Since he did that, and you didn't tell him about this rental, he wants to work with Sophie. We just wanted to be upfront with you on that. I'm sure you understand."

Tessa shot a cold glare Sophie's way. "Sure, no problem." She turned and walked out of the room.

Rick grinned. "There you go. Go ahead and show him the rental."

Sophie still felt uncomfortable about it. "Are you sure? Maybe I could split it with Tessa if he rents it."

Rick shook his head. "No, you won't split it. If he rents this apartment it won't be because of anything Tessa did. She said there was nothing to show him. You thought of it and saw the possibility of turning the two bedroom into three." He looked at the computer for a moment and then added, "He was just an ad call that Tessa picked up over a month ago. You developed more of a relationship with him in one night. Relationships are everything. That's why he called you. Take him there and see what he thinks."

"Okay, I will."

Sophie walked back to her desk and had to walk by Tessa, and she turned in her chair so her back was facing Sophie. The air felt decidedly frosty. Caroline could sense it too.

THE FIFTH AVENUE APARTMENT

"What was that all about? I saw the two of you in Rick's office."

Sophie told her and Caroline looked sympathetic. "That's a tricky one. I see why Rick wanted you to run with it. Tessa dropped the ball. She does as little with rentals as possible."

"Rick said he was an ad call," Sophie said.

"That makes sense. I wouldn't worry about it. Remember the saying, it's not personal, it's just business. Tessa wouldn't hesitate to do the same if it was the other way around."

Sophie smiled. "Okay. I'm sure you're right about that."

"I am. Good luck with it!"

Sophie checked with Sue, who had the rental listing and she said that it was empty so they could go anytime. She called Sean and agreed to meet him and his girlfriend at the apartment at noon.

She got there ten minutes early and they were both already waiting outside the building. Sean introduced her to his girlfriend, Grace, who had short curly brown hair, black rimmed glasses and a big smile.

"I was so excited when Sean said you mentioned an apartment by the Met. This location is ideal," Grace said.

Sophie smiled. "I love this building. I think it's so elegant inside and it's quiet too." She led them inside past the smiling doorman, through the long, marble lined foyer to the security desk.

"I'm showing the Emerson's unit on 10," said. The man behind the security desk nodded and Sophie continued on. When they reached the apartment on the tenth floor, she opened the door and stepped back to let them walk in first. The unit had an impressive entrance, a small foyer that led into an oversized living room and nook area that could easily be turned into an office with a partition.

One of the two bedrooms had already been turned into a library/office and both Sean and Grace stopped short when they saw it. The room was a book lovers dream with two walls of bookshelves filled completely with books. There was a cozy sofa that faced a fireplace and a television and by the window there was an oversized desk.

"We might be fighting over this room," Sean said with a laugh. "This gives us ideas for how to set our own stuff up".

"I can see how we can turn that area by the window into an office," Grace said. "And in this room, we can put our pull-out sofa, so it can be a guest room, too."

"That window in the makeshift office will have the best view, too. It looks directly at the Met," Sean said.

"It does. I think I might prefer that spot actually," Grace said.

They looked at the kitchen, which was small but had a nice layout and a little side area with several stools that turned it into a dining nook. It was really a lovely and very cozy apartment with high ceilings and elegant finishing touches like crown moldings.

After they'd had a chance to see the whole apartment, Sophie asked them what they thought of it. She knew it was still an expensive rental.

Sean smiled at Grace, who nodded and pulled a checkbook out of her purse.

"Can we give you a deposit today? We want this apartment. It's pretty much perfect."

Sophie could tell they liked it, but she was surprised that they wanted to move that fast.

"Of course. I'll email you the rental application and we should know in a day or two. They just need to do a quick background check."

"I'll send it right back," Sean said.

"We don't want anyone else to offer on it," Grace said.

"I'll call Sue, the listing broker to let her know. I'll email you very shortly," Sophie said.

"Great. Thanks for thinking of this place for us, Sophie. I'm glad we ran into each other at the Italian restaurant." He smiled at Grace. "Maybe we'll be regulars there. We'll be able to walk over once we move in."

When they left Sean and Grace went in the opposite direction and Sophie walked to her apartment and was home in about ten minutes. She called Sue to let her know she had a deposit.

"Fantastic," Sue said. "It's a great place, but I didn't think it would go so fast. Most people don't want to spend that much on a rental. As soon as you get the application to me, I'll submit it and we should be all set in a day or two."

Sophie settled at the kitchen island and opened her laptop. She emailed the rental application to Sean and checked her emails and returned several calls. She smiled when she saw the return email from Sean a half hour later with the completed application. She clicked it open to make sure it was filled out completely before forwarding it to Sue.

She glanced at the financial section and saw that both Grace and Sean earned mid-six figure salaries. Together they were just shy of a million. So, it made sense that they could afford to pay more for a rental. She forwarded the email to Sue. Hopefully in a day or two they would be approved. And Sophie would have another commission coming her way. She still felt a little badly though that it meant Tessa lost out. She hoped that Tessa wouldn't be too upset about it.

CHAPTER THIRTY-NINE

Tessa was decidedly cool toward Sophie for the rest of the week, and she only saw her in passing, as Tessa went out with friends every night. Sophie and Caroline sat in the living room every night in their sweats and watched Tessa head out. They were both sound asleep when she came home. Sophie didn't know how she managed it as Tessa still made it to work on time every morning.

That Thursday night, while Caroline and Sophie were in the kitchen discussing whether to order Thai takeout or Indian for dinner, Tessa strolled out of her bedroom looking gorgeous in a sleek black strapless dress and very high heels. Her long blonde hair was curled and fluffed, and her makeup was flawless, with a hint of gray shadow that made her blue eyes pop and a slick of nude lipstick that looked elegant and sophisticated.

"Where are you off to? That looks like a date outfit," Caroline said.

Tessa grinned. "It is. My date should be here any minute." She glanced Sophie's way when there was a knock at the door. Tessa swung it open, and Max stood there looking more handsome than Sophie had ever seen him. He had a hint of a shadow along his jaw and his dark hair was combed back as his wayward waves were a hint too long. But Sophie thought he looked great. He was wearing dress pants, a white shirt, blue gray tie and a charcoal gray blazer. He smiled when he saw them.

"Where are you two off to?" Sophie asked.

"Tessa's taking me to see a show. We're going to see Josh Groban in Sweeney Todd."

"And we're going to dinner first. To Rao's. I've always wanted to go there." Tessa seemed excited and Sophie couldn't blame her. It was near impossible to get a table at Rao's. The famous tiny Italian restaurant only had nine tables and all of them were owned by long-standing customers.

"How did you get in there?" Caroline asked in awe.

"My mother and her best friend, Shirley share a table," Max said. "They have a slot once a month. Neither one of them could go tonight so my mother asked if I wanted to go."

"Sounds like fun," Sophie said. She forced a smile. It sounded like a dream date. She hadn't realized Tessa was that interested in Max. She hadn't mentioned him all week, or that they had plans. When they left and the door shut behind them, Caroline turned to Sophie. "What was that? Has she said anything at all to you about going out with Max again? She hasn't mentioned him at all to me since they last went out."

Sophie shook her head. "No, I had no idea. Max didn't mention it either. I was surprised to see the two of them together."

Sophie and Caroline were still up and watching the news when Tessa waltzed through the door a little after eleven. That was early for her. Sophie felt a slight sense of satisfaction that they'd come right home after the show.

"How was it?" Caroline asked.

Tessa shrugged off her coat and flopped in one of the club chairs adjacent to the sofa where Sophie and Caroline were sitting. "It was incredible. Such a great night. The food at Rao's is as good as they say. And the whole place has the coolest vibe. And Frank, the owner, knows Max! He came right over and asked after his mother. The show was great too. I wanted to go dancing after, but Max said he needed to be up early." She smiled big and glanced at Sophie. "Still, it was a very romantic date. Max is a catch. I could possibly fall for him." Sophie felt a pit in her stomach. Could Max be as interested in Tessa?

"Sounds like fun. Do you have plans to go out again?" Caroline asked.

"Not yet, but I'm sure we will. I'll make sure of it!" She stood. "I am actually pretty tired. I'm going to head to bed and get out of this dress. Night!"

Tessa disappeared down the hall and Caroline and Sophie exchanged glances.

"What do you think of that?" Sophie asked.

"I'm not sure. I don't really see them as a couple, but

Tessa seems pretty determined. I'm not sure Max knows what he's getting into," Caroline said.

Sophie agreed. She hated the thought of Tessa chasing after Max—especially if Max was flattered by the attention and decided to give it a go.

CHAPTER FORTY

"Sophie, there's a Russ Winston on line one. He's called the main number and said he was willing to talk to either you or Tessa, whoever was available as you both sent him a postcard. He's a potential buyer. After you talk to him, come see me if you get a chance. I noticed something the other day that seemed a little weird."

"Thanks, Ava, will do."

Sophie clicked over and took the call. Russ Winston had received her postcard and was the first person that responded. "Your timing was perfect as I'm ready to start a search," he began. "I'm looking to downsize. My wife passed recently and frankly, it's too sad to stay here."

"I'm so sorry for your loss," Sophie said.

"Thank you, dear. It has been just over a year and I'm ready now. I'd like to be in the same area, possibly even the same building, but a smaller unit. One bedroom is all I need. And I don't have to sell this place first. I don't want the pressure of having to coordinate that. I want to move into a new place, then clear out this unit, maybe have you stage it, or refer me to someone that can do that, and see if we can sell it for top dollar."

"Well, I can certainly help you with that." Sophie spent another half hour with him. She didn't want to rush him. He'd told her that he was eighty-one and she enjoyed talking to him. She made a plan to call him back that afternoon to go over a few properties and set up some showings. When she finished the call, she did a quick search of available homes in his area and there were quite a few. She narrowed it down to her top five and called to set up showings for the next day and Monday. She set up three for Saturday and two for Monday and called Russ to let him know. And then she walked to the front reception desk to chat with Ava.

Ava had been in the role for a little over a month and was doing a great job. She was in her mid-twenties and was a college student going to school for her MFA degree in the evenings. She looked up from her computer when she heard Sophie approach.

"So, I thought this was a little strange the other day, but I didn't say anything. I still don't really know how you all do things here. But I thought it was a little odd that you and Tessa sent out a mailing on the same day, to the exact same list. When that last caller said he received mail from both of you, it reminded me, and I thought you should know since you gave me your mailing first. Maybe it's not a big deal, though?" Ava seemed a little worried that maybe she shouldn't have said anything.

Sophie took a breath. It was disconcerting to say the least that Tessa did that. "Thanks for letting me know, Ava.

I'm still fairly new here, but it does seem a little confusing. I'll talk to Tessa about it."

Ava nodded. "Okay. If anyone calls in like he did and says he heard from both of you, I'll forward the call to you. But some people might call your cells directly."

And Sophie wouldn't be surprised if Tessa's mailing only had her cell phone on it. Sophie had listed her cell, email and the main office line. She went back to her desk, thinking about what Tessa had done and she realized two things—if the list was identical as Ava had said, then Tessa saw Sophie's list. And Sophie had left her notebook in the living room, wide open as she'd been adding names to it over the weekend. Tessa could have easily snapped a few pictures.

The second thing was that Tessa had done that before the incident with Sean and the rental. It was troubling that Tessa helped herself to Sophie's list that she'd spent hours compiling and didn't think anything of it. Sophie would be less surprised it if it had happened after she'd lost Sean as a client.

She didn't want to make a big fuss over it as it was already done, and it wasn't like any of those contacts were already Sophie's clients. They were just prospects, and no one owned them. Still, it was disappointing. And it was a lesson learned. From now on, she would be careful what she shared with Tessa, and she wouldn't leave any valuable info literally lying around.

Sophie passed Rick in the hallway on the way back to her desk. He stopped and asked how her day was going.

"Good. I just landed a new potential buyer from my neighborhood mailing."

Rick grinned and high-fived her. "Fantastic! We should celebrate with an after-work drink. It's almost five, want to go for a quick one?"

It was Friday afternoon and there was only one other agent left. Sue was the on-call agent that day. Rick called back to her. "Drinks in five? You, me and Sophie, you in?"

"I'm in! I'm ready," Sue said with a laugh.

"Meet me by the reception desk in five and we'll head out," Rick said.

Sophie nodded. His enthusiasm was contagious. She was also interested in chatting more with Sue, as she knew that she'd been with the firm since it started.

"See you in five," she confirmed.

"Cheers to a great week!" Rick lifted his glass of bourbon and Sue and Sophie tapped their martini glasses against his. Sue got a traditional vodka martini with a twist while Sophie splurged for a salted caramel martini, made with caramel vodka, Bailey's Irish cream and Kahlua. The glass was rimmed with gooey caramel dusted with flaky sea salt. It tasted like dessert and Sophie loved it. It was so rich and sweet that she could only have one though. It was perfect for sipping slowly.

They were at the new restaurant around the corner that Rick had quickly become a regular at. They sat in the bar at a round cocktail table that gave them a good view of the afterwork crowd streaming in. Rick recognized many of them and several people stopped by the table to say hello and chat for a minute.

"You're like the mayor here." Sue chuckled as another

person waved at Rick and headed their way. "I don't go out as much as I used to," she admitted to Sophie. I remarried a few years ago, and now I head home at a reasonable hour so we can have dinner together." She took a sip of her drink and looked at Sophie curiously.

"I gather that you are roommates now with Caroline and Tessa. How is that working out?"

"Really well, so far. Caroline is so easy to get along with and a lot of fun. Both she and Tessa had boyfriends until recently, so I often had the place to myself on weekends. It's just Tessa that no longer has a boyfriend," she clarified.

"What about you? Are you dating anyone?" Sue asked.

"Not at the moment, no."

"Did you say Tessa and her boyfriend broke up?" Rick asked. "I didn't know that. I thought they were pretty serious." He seemed surprised and Sophie realized that Tessa hadn't told anyone at work.

"Yeah, they were together for almost two years. Tessa wanted to get engaged."

"He wasn't ready?" Sue asked.

"Not yet. He was happy the way things were, but Tessa didn't want to wait, so she ended it."

Rick nodded. "That sounds similar to my situation with Julia. I haven't told many people at work yet, either. I haven't wanted to talk about it."

Sue and Rick ordered another round of drinks and they decided to get a platter of nachos to split. Sophie still had more than half of her drink left. When the nachos came, they all helped themselves. They were loaded with guacamole, shredded chicken, refried beans, and cheese and were very good.

While they ate, Sue told them about a new listing she was getting. "It's a one bedroom at 1025 Fifth Avenue, a real gem. I sold it to a young couple almost ten years ago and they're expecting a baby and need a bigger place."

"Where do they want to move to?" Sophie asked.

"They love their building. That's why they waited this long to move because they hate to leave. If they could ever find a nice two bedroom there, that would be their first choice. But they know that's a long shot, so they will look in the general area."

Sophie smiled and leaned forward, feeling excited. "So, I don't have the listing yet, but I just got a new buyer. He lives in that building and is looking to downsize to a one bedroom. He wasn't going to list his place until after he moves, but maybe he'd be open to having them look—if he likes their unit."

Sue laughed. "I love it. That would be beyond perfect, Sophie. I like how you think. We'll have to see what he thinks and go from there. That would be wild if it works out."

Rick looked pleased. "I knew you had potential, Sophie. Being able to make those connections and move fast will always give you an edge."

"Thank you." Sophie turned her attention back to Sue. "When will you officially have the listing? I have some showings lined up for my buyer tomorrow and Monday, would love to add that one too, if possible."

"I'm seeing them tomorrow at ten. I can let you know after that if they'd be open to showings as soon as Monday, if that works?"

Sophie nodded. "That's fine. We're seeing two others

that day, so that would be perfect if we could squeeze one more in."

They stayed for another hour, finishing their drinks and food, and laughing about the funny things that happened in the real estate business. Rick and Sue had plenty of stories.

"How did you get into real estate sales?" Sophie asked Sue.

"Once my kids were in middle school, I wanted to get back to work, but I'd been out of my field for so long and I wanted to try something different. I liked the flexibility of real estate, being able to still pick up the kids if they needed a ride or make sure I saw their games and I'd always been fascinated by the industry. I also liked the idea of commission sales and being paid based on results."

"Sue was my first hire," Rick said proudly.

Sue nodded. "We'd worked together at a huge corporate firm. When Rick said he was going to start up his own office, I liked the idea of a less stuffy, faster paced environment. I never regretted it."

"I don't think I would like a more corporate environment. I had enough of that working at law firms." Sophie smiled. "This is so much better."

"Uh oh, trouble at two o'clock," Rick said softly.

Sophie turned to see where he was looking and saw an attractive, very thin woman with a razor sharp dark brown bob coming their way. When she reached the table, her eyes swept over Rick and Sue and lingered on Sophie for a long moment before going back to Rick.

"So, this is your new hangout?" The woman said shortly.

Rick flashed his extra charming smile, "Hi Julia. You know Sue, and this is our newest hire, Sophie. Sophie this is…"

"His ex-girlfriend." Julia narrowed her eyes a bit. "Are you the one that took my spot at the Met event?"

Sophie nodded while Rick started to look annoyed. "You said you didn't want to go."

"Right. I didn't want to go, with you." She glanced at the front door, where several people had just walked in. "I have to go my date is here." She turned and walked toward the front door where a gray suited man with dark glasses and a briefcase stood looking around the room. He smiled when he saw Julia.

Rick let out a heavy sigh. "Sorry about that. I think she was a little jealous that I took someone in her place. But she didn't want to go. And I wasn't going to waste those tickets."

"She seems mad that you replaced her so quickly. Maybe she has the wrong idea about Sophie," Sue said.

"Possibly," Rick agreed. "But it seems hypocritical for her to get mad since she's here with a date. Sophie noticed that a muscle twitched in his jaw as he watched Julia walk off with her date.

"It's never easy seeing an ex with someone else," Sue said.

Or someone you're interested in. Sophie thought of Max and Tessa as they headed out the other night. That had been painful. Even if there was nothing there romantically, it was still hard to see it and wonder if there might be sparks brewing. And she had no idea how the night went from Max's perspective.

"Are you guys ready to call it a night?" Rick signed the credit card slip and took his last sip of bourbon. Sophie and Sue stood, and they walked out, thanking Rick as they went. They'd both offered to chip in, but he wouldn't hear of it, said it was on the company. "It was my pleasure. Like I said, we had a great week."

When Sophie got home, the apartment was quiet. She knew that Caroline was at her boyfriends for the night, and she assumed that Tessa was out clubbing. She didn't expect her to be home until very late. She changed into her comfy pajamas and curled up on the sofa to watch tv for a while. She clicked through the channels and landed on an old episode of Friends that was just starting. It fit her mood perfectly. An episode or two of Friends and she'd be relaxed and ready for bed.

A few minutes later, her phone dinged with a text message. She sat up when she saw that it was from Max.

Happy Friday. I'm going to pick out a tree tomorrow. Do you want to come along and get one for your place, too? I have a truck we can haul them home in.

Sophie had a few showings in the morning with her new buyer and was free after that.

"Would love to. What time were you thinking?"

"How's three?"

"Perfect."

And just like that, her mood lifted a little. Surely, if he'd had a wonderful night with Tessa, he wouldn't be texting to go tree shopping with her. Or would he? That was something friends would do. Still, Sophie felt optimistic and was looking forward to it.

CHAPTER FORTY-ONE

Sophie met Russ Winston at his apartment the next day at ten thirty. Their first showing was at eleven around the corner, but Russ wanted her to see his place first, and she was eager to see it. It was a lovely unit with two big bedrooms, two bathrooms, and a big living room and dining room area with a bay window that looked out over the park and museum.

Russ looked around his apartment proudly. It was well decorated with custom made window treatments. "My wife picked all that out. I'm not sure if I should leave them here or take them with me."

"It might depend on where you go. If you have similar size windows," Sophie said gently. She knew he was really wondering if it would be too painful to take them or if he'd want to hold on to those memories. Only he could decide.

"Yes, you're right. We can worry about that later. What do you think of the place?"

"It's wonderful. A truly lovely home. Your wife did a beautiful job decorating."

He looked down for a moment and when he glanced her way again, his eyes were shiny. He smiled. "She was a special lady. I think she would approve of this, of the move. So, shall we head out then?"

They saw three units over the next two hours. Russ seemed to like all of them, and Sophie felt optimistic that she'd be able to find him something that would work.

"What do you think? Do you have a favorite from the ones we saw today?" She asked when they left the last apartment.

Russ thought for a moment. "I think I'd rule out the first one. It seemed a little dark, not enough light coming through the windows. But the other two were nice enough. I am looking forward to seeing the others, especially the one in this building. I think I'll know more then."

"Of course." Sophie had set it up for Monday at noon. It would be the third one that day. She'd set it up that way on purpose, hopefully saving the best for last, since she knew how much he loved the building.

At a few minutes before three, Sophie's phone buzzed with a text message from Max,

Meet me out front, am about two minutes away.

Sophie pulled on a jacket, grabbed her purse, and headed downstairs and onto the sidewalk. There was no sign of Max. The wind whipped her hair across her face and made her shiver and zip her coat as high as it could go. The air was cold and raw with dampness. Snow flurries were expected later that afternoon.

She had no idea what Max's truck looked like, so she

was surprised when a huge, shiny blue Ford 150 truck pulled up in front of her. Max waved to her from the driver's side. She ran over and hopped in.

"Is this yours? I was surprised when you said you had a truck in the city," Sophie said, as Max pulled into traffic.

"It's mine. My mother doesn't keep a car here anymore, so I took over her space. I like having it in case I want to go away for the weekend. My dad has a cabin in Vermont, and I like to get away now and then and do a little hiking and fishing and sometimes even write. It's good for when I get stuck. Something about walking around in the woods seems to shake the ideas loose."

Sophie laughed. "Who said ideas don't grow on trees? That sounds relaxing." She wasn't much into fishing, but she did like walking and hiking in the country.

"It's a great location, too, not far from Killington. Do you ski?" Max asked.

"Very poorly. I like to go occasionally though. I have to admit I enjoy the after skiing more—having a hot beverage with friends and watching the snow fall."

"Apres skiing." Max grinned. "That's more my speed, too. I have friends that ski circles around me. I never went often enough to get good at it."

"Do you see your dad much?" Sophie didn't remember Max mentioning him before.

"A few times a year. Usually around the holidays and during the summer I get up there once or twice. We're not super close. My parents divorced when I was twelve and let's just say that it wasn't amicable. He remarried and has mellowed out some. His new wife is much younger, but she's nice enough."

"You and your mom are close, though?" He talked about her often.

Max smiled "We are. She's great. She never remarried but she's had the same boyfriend for close to fifteen years. She says she has no interest in marrying again, but it wouldn't surprise me if they make it official someday."

"Do you like him?"

He nodded. "Roger is a good guy. He's from Tampa. That's why she spends so much time in Florida. They pretty much live together now even though she has a condo nearby. I told her she should just rent hers out and stay with Roger all the time, but she likes having her independence and a place to call her own. And of course, she knows she can come here whenever she wants. I left her bedroom as is when I took the place over."

"That was nice of you."

Max shrugged. "It wasn't a big deal really. The bedrooms are about the same size. And she likes to come back to the city. She makes it here every few months, usually for a long weekend. She sees her friends and if I'm lucky I get her for dinner one night."

Sophie smiled. "It's nice that you are so close. I love my parents, but my mother isn't always easy to be around. I just have to remind myself that she is just wants to make sure I'm all right."

"When you get your first big commission check, you should take a picture and email it to her," Max joked.

"That's actually not a bad idea!" Sophie said.

A few minutes later, Max pulled up to the tree lot just as another truck was leaving and he slid into the empty space.

"Okay, let's go tree shopping."

They walked onto the lot that had row after row of Christmas trees. All different shapes and sizes.

"What kind of tree are you looking for?" Sophie asked.

"I get the same thing every year, a three or four foot tall mini-tree. I put it in my library, so I can see it all day. You should get a big one though. You have that great space by your bay window that looks out over the street. And the ceilings are high, at lease eleven or twelve feet. You have a lot of room to work with."

"My aunt used to get a huge tree," Sophie said. It made her a little sad, thinking of it.

But it made Max smile. "I know she did. Guess who helped her pick out her tree for the past few years?"

Sophie laughed. "So, you know exactly what will look good. You can help me find the perfect one. I have all of Aunt Penny's ornaments, lights, and garlands."

They walked up and down the aisles until Max saw what he was looking for. He grabbed a little tree, between three and four feet tall. Then kept walking until he stopped by a stunning, very tall and plush tree. "What do you think?"

It looked perfect to Sophie. "I love it!"

Sophie picked up the small tree and Max grabbed the big one and carried it to the makeshift counter where two men wearing sweatshirts that said Falcon and Son construction were ringing people up and helping them with their trees. Sophie guessed based on their ages and similar looks that they were father and son.

"Hey Tom," Max nodded at the older man behind the register. "And John."

The older man smiled big when her recognized Max. "Hey Max, nice to see you." He glanced at Sophie and then back at Max. "I'm sorry about miss Penny. I read about it in the paper."

"We miss her," Max said. "This is her great niece, Sophie. She's living here now and wanted to get a tree like Penny used to get."

Tom nodded his approval of their chosen tree. "Well, that's a real beauty. You need some help getting it to the truck?" He offered. There was a line behind them now and it was starting to flurry a bit.

Max shook his head. "No, we can manage. Thanks, though."

Sophie handed Tom money for her tree and Max paid for his. His tree was so much smaller than Sophie's that it was easy to carry it to his truck. Max made it look like Sophie's tree was light as a feather, but she knew it was heavy.

When they climbed back in the truck to head home, as soon as they pulled into the traffic, she thanked him. "I really appreciate this. I hadn't even thought about getting a tree yet."

"Happy to help. I'm used to doing this every year. I really do miss your aunt. She was a sweet lady." They were both quiet for a moment. Sophie had been thinking about her aunt more lately. She always saw her around the holidays and usually spent a long weekend with her a few weeks before Christmas. Aunt Penny would have her tree up and all decorated and they'd go Christmas shopping and out to tea at the Plaza hotel. Her aunt had loved afternoon tea at the Plaza, and it was a real treat. Sophie sighed, remembering their many visits there.

"I'm glad you are here now though," Max added and smiled. He glanced her way and Sophie's pulse raced faster for a second.

"I'm so glad too," she said.

When they pulled up to the apartment, Max put his hazard lights on. "Okay we have to move fast."

Sophie jumped out and took Max's tree and headed for the stairs. He followed close behind with her enormous tree. They squeezed into the elevator and laughed at the trail of pine needles the trees left.

"I'll clean that up once we get the trees inside," Sophie said.

"I'm not worried about it. Thank you, though."

They went into her apartment first and Max leaned her tree against the wall by the big bay window. He picked up his smaller tree. "I have to head out and move my truck, but I'll be back soon to help you get that into the tree stand."

"Thank you. I need to find her stand. I'm sure it's with the other Christmas stuff."

Max left and Sophie gazed at the huge tree. She couldn't wait to see how it would look all decorated. She needed to find that tree stand first. Fortunately, it was where she'd hoped it would be, in a closet with two other bags of Christmas decorations.

She brought everything to the living room and organized it, putting all the garlands in one pile, the lights in another and the tree stand ready for the tree. She still had the apartment to herself, as Caroline had stayed at her boyfriends the night before. Sophie had no idea where Tessa was. She thought she might be staying at a friend's house. She didn't mind. It was more peaceful when Tessa was elsewhere.

The snow was coming down more heavily now. Sophie stood by the bay window for a moment and watched it fall furiously. It was already getting dark out now too and it wasn't quite five o'clock. It definitely felt like winter. She shivered and decided to make herself a cup of hot chocolate.

The microwave beeped that her hot chocolate was ready, and a moment later there was a knock on the door. Max was back. She opened the door and he stood there looking adorable with snowflakes in his hair. He stamped his shoes on the rug outside the apartment before stepping inside.

"Do you want some hot chocolate? I just made some."

"Sure. That sounds really good actually. It's freezing out there, now."

"Whipped cream?" Sophie offered.

Max laughed. "But of course."

She got the can out of the fridge and piled a generous amount of whipped cream on top of his hot chocolate and handed him the mug. She made herself one and added a similar amount of whipped cream.

They took a few sips and got to work. Max helped her to settle the tree into the stand and tightened the side screws to lock it into place. Sophie put on some Christmas music, Michael Buble's Holiday hits and they started decorating the tree. Max picked up a ceramic ornament with a photo of a young girl of about four. It looked homemade.

Sophie smiled when she saw it. She'd made that ornament in pre-school and her aunt had kept it on her tree all these years.

Max grinned when he saw it. "You were cute back then, too." His eyes held hers for a moment and they were full of warmth. Sophie felt something in the air between them. It was the first time she'd felt the hint of a vibe, of possible interest from Max.

She laughed. "Can you tell I made that? It was my first art project, and I gave it to her as a Christmas gift. She said she loved it."

"I'm sure she did. She kept it all these years," Max said.

The mood was festive as they finished decorating the tree. When it was just about done, Sophie picked up the glittery gold star that connected to the tree lights. She handed it to Max, and he had to climb on a chair to reach the top of the tree and plug it into the lights. The final step was a shimmery silver garland. Sophie wrapped it around the tree a few times and then handed the last bit to Max to place it higher near the top. He leaned over her as he reached up high and when he had the garland in place, he turned and was just a few inches away from Sophie. They gazed at each other, and she felt the vibe again, even more strongly. Max smiled and she leaned in a little in anticipation of a kiss. Max's lips were almost on hers when the apartment door opened suddenly, and they both jumped.

Caroline walked in, holding two shopping bags and an overnight tote. She stopped short when she saw Sophie and Max by the tree. She dropped everything and ran over for a closer look.

"This tree is amazing! I love it."

Sophie smiled. "Thanks. Max picked it out and helped me get it set up."

Max leaned over and plugged the lights in, and they all took a step back to admire the tree. It looked beautiful all lit up.

"Do you want us to help with yours?" Sophie asked him.

Max shook his head. "Mine will take two seconds. Thank you, though. I actually have to run. I'm meeting up with one of my college roommates tonight for our quarterly poker get-together."

"That sounds fun," Sophie said. "Are you a card shark?" she teased him.

He laughed. "Hardly. It's just for fun. We sit around and drink bourbon and eat greasy takeout and catch up on what's going on with our lives."

"Tomorrow night then for *Murders*?" Caroline invited him.

"Definitely." He glanced at Sophie. "Good luck with your open house tomorrow."

"Thanks." Sophie watched him go and when the door shut behind him, Caroline smiled. "Did I sense a little something there? Maybe my timing wasn't so good?"

Sophie smiled. "Your timing was fine. I really don't know. I thought maybe I sensed something, but the moment passed. Maybe I imagined it." She didn't want to get her hopes up.

"I think there's something there. And I don't think he's into Tessa."

"Hopefully not." Sophie didn't think so, either.

"So, are you still up for dinner at the Italian place? Ed

is out with his buddies tonight, so I am all yours," Caroline said.

The door opened and Tessa strolled in, wearing her gym clothes. She glanced over at Caroline and Sophie and then saw the tree. "Looks good."

"What are you up to tonight?" Caroline asked. "Sophie and I are going out to dinner. You're welcome to join us."

"Thanks, but I have plans with April and Joy. We're going to a new club that opened in midtown."

"Okay, have fun." Caroline paused for a moment and then asked, "So, how are things going with Max?"

Tessa made a face. "They're not. He hasn't suggested going out again. And over dinner at Rao's he actually kept talking about Sophie. It was annoying. And on that note, I'm jumping in the shower and then heading out. See ya."

Sophie watched her go and felt a sense of hope if Max had been talking about her at dinner. It meant she was on his mind. Or maybe it just meant that Sophie was the only thing that Max and Tessa had in common.

CHAPTER FORTY-TWO

Sophie had a much better turnout at her second open house for Emily's unit. She baked cookies again as she loved the homey scent when people walked through the door. And almost everyone took at least one cookie. She had a total of two dozen people come through and while all of them were working with realtors, a few of them seemed interested.

Sue from the office also came with the young couple that gave her the new listing at 1025 Fifth Avenue. She introduced them to Sophie.

"We're excited for your buyer to see their property on Monday. I told Dan and Paula about this open house and thought it might be good for them to see as it's in the neighborhood and is bigger." They were in their early thirties and Paula mentioned that she was almost eight months pregnant. She was tall and slender and looked like she had a basketball in her stomach. Sophie wondered about the timing for them. Once her baby came it seemed like it might be a hectic time to move. Sophie didn't ask the question, but Dan saw her look at Paula's baby bump and smiled.

"We know it takes on average about three months for a co-op and we were thinking that Paula might feel more up to the move then," Dan said.

"I think it would be too difficult to do it sooner, and we don't want to wait too long," Paula explained.

Sue encouraged them to look around, and stayed in the kitchen with Sophie, so they could wander around on their own. She helped herself to a cookie.

"Do you think this could work for them?" Sophie was surprised. She'd thought they were looking for a two bedroom and Emily's unit had three, which meant it was quite a bit more expensive.

"They say they are flexible, but I think seeing this unit and its price tag will help them to have more realistic expectations for what they can afford."

Sophie nodded. "That makes sense. It helps to look and really understand what's available in this area."

Sophie answered questions that came up as people walked around and once the last person left at a few minutes after two, she packed everything up and headed out. The feedback she heard was positive overall and she felt confident that the unit should sell fairly quickly, hopefully.

When she got home, Caroline was doing laundry and Christmas carols were playing. She'd also picked up several red pillar candles and set them around the living room and kitchen. The color gave the room a cheery feel and Sophie could faintly smell the candle's scent of apple and cinnamon. She set the bag of leftover chocolate chip cookies on the kitchen counter and Caroline came right over and took one.

"I was hoping you'd bring some home. I could make a meal out of these cookies."

Sophie laughed. "You have. Didn't you eat a few for breakfast last weekend?"

"Hmmm, I guess I did."

The apartment felt calm and quiet and festive. Caroline had plugged in the Christmas tree lights, so it glowed merrily by the window. Sophie had picked up some more mini-lights and Christmas garlands on her way home to decorate the mantel. Aunt Penny had three heavy silver reindeer that held the Christmas stockings. There was one for Aunt Penny, Uncle Joe, and Sophie. It felt bittersweet to Sophie as she took them out of their boxes. She'd loved those long weekends here before Christmas and she missed both Uncle Joe and Aunt Penny. She knew Aunt Penny would approve of the decorating though and she set about making the mantel look festive. The final touch was to place the reindeer at the edge of the mantel. She would add the stockings later. She had her old one, but wanted to pick two more up, for Caroline and Tessa.

When she was finished, Caroline admired her handiwork. "It looks so pretty."

She wandered back to the kitchen and opened the refrigerator and then the freezer before turning to Sophie. "I'm sick of pizza. What if we just make some appetizers? We have some frozen chicken wings we can heat up and I can make taco dip. We have all the ingredients except for tortilla chips. But I can run out and grab those and maybe some avocado for guac on the side. What you think?"

"That sounds good to me. I'll run out and get the chips and avocado and you can show me how you make the dip?"

"Perfect. It's super simple. I'll take wings out now so they defrost some."

Sophie went out to the corner store a few hours later and picked up what they needed. She also grabbed a container of homemade blue cheese dressing to have with the chicken wings as a dipping sauce.

When she returned, Caroline had the wings lined up on a cookie sheet and was brushing barbecue sauce onto them. "I won't put these in the oven until a half hour before Max comes, so they are nice and hot," she said.

"What can I do to help?" Sophie asked.

Caroline thought for a minute. "Do you want to make the guac? It only gets better when it sits, so we can make that ahead."

"Sure. I can handle that." Sophie got a mixing bowl and sliced the three ripe avocados, took out the big pit and scooped them into the bowl. The avocados were perfectly soft and buttery. She added a little diced onion, garlic, jalapeño, chopped cilantro and juice from half a lemon. She mixed it all up, tasted and added a pinch of salt and pepper. Then she scooped some onto a chip and handed it to Caroline to taste.

"Oh, that's good. Maybe just add a splash of salsa?"

Sophie did as suggested and took another taste. The tablespoon of fresh salsa balanced the guac perfectly. She wrapped it up, pressing on the plastic so the film touched the avocado so it wouldn't brown. She put it in the refrigerator and then watched as Caroline made the taco dip.

"This is so easy. You just brown a pound of ground beef, or turkey, it's good both ways. Once it's browned, I add two tablespoons of taco seasoning and a quarter cup of water, then a big squirt of Sriracha hot sauce. Maybe a tablespoon or so, just for a little kick. Then I dump in a can of refried beans and mix until it's well blended."

Sophie could smell the hot sauce and seasonings and her stomach rumbled in anticipation.

"Last step is the cheese. You can use a cup of shredded cheddar, but I like to use half a carton of cheddar pub cheese." She pulled the carton from the fridge and scooped the leftover creamy cheese into the pan. Once it was all blended, she poured the mix into a square casserole dish and sprinkled a handful of shredded cheddar across the top. "Now we'll just pop this in the oven when the wings have ten minutes to go and they'll be ready at the same time," she said.

"I'm suddenly starving," Sophie admitted.

"Me too. Let's open the wine and pour a glass while we wait."

Sophie opened a bottle of Josh cabernet and poured two glasses. She also filled a small bowl with mixed nuts to take the edge off her hunger.

"Have you heard from Tessa?" Sophie asked. She hadn't seen her all day and guessed she'd slept at her friend April's house the night before.

Caroline nodded. "She said they are going to a party at one of April's friends tonight and she'll probably just stay over again and head into work from there."

Sophie was secretly relieved that Tessa wouldn't make an appearance while they were hanging out with Max. She knew Max would be fine with it, but Tessa always seemed to bring tension with her and Sophie was looking forward to a relaxing time with Caroline and Max.

Sophie had texted Max that they were doing appetizers instead of pizza and he arrived at seven sharp with a bottle of Caymus cabernet. Sophie knew nothing about it, but Caroline's eyes widened when she saw the label.

"Yum. I'll open that now so it can breathe. This is nice splurge, thank you."

Max shrugged. "It's my mother's favorite and I bought a case of it the last time she was here."

Sophie was curious. "I've never had it. Am looking forward to trying it."

"It's so good," Caroline said. "But for me it would be a special occasion wine. I don't usually spend much more than twenty dollars on a bottle of wine."

Sophie nodded. "Same here. Though I did splurge recently on Austin Hope and Flowers, that pinot noir Aunt Penny loved."

Max grinned. "I don't mind spending on wine now and then. It's all about the experience for me. And it is delicious. That said, I've been known to enjoy cheap wine from a box, too. I am not a wine snob."

Sophie laughed. "It's fun discovering a good, cheap wine. This is a treat though." Sophie poured Max a glass of the Josh to start.

"Okay, everything's ready." Caroline put the hot wings on a platter with the blue cheese dressing on the side for dipping. She carried the bubbling taco dip to the table while Sophie got the guac out of the refrigerator.

They sat around the table and inhaled the taco dip and wings. The chicken wings were good, but the taco dip was addictive, especially with the guacamole on the side. It was almost like nachos.

"This dip is crazy good," Max said as he scooped a pile of dip on a chip.

"Thanks. It's my mother's recipe. She makes it for every Super Bowl and tailgate parties," Caroline said.

Max glanced at Sophie. "How did your open house go today?"

"I think it was pretty good. A lot of people came through and everyone seemed to like it. It's hard to know for sure. Hopefully, I'll hear from at least one or two realtors next week. Everyone that came through was already working with someone," Sophie.

"What do you think of the job so far? Is it what you hoped it would be?" Caroline asked. She reached for her wine and took a sip.

"I actually really love it," Sophie said. "It sounds silly, but on most days, I feel like this is exactly what I'm supposed to be doing. I get excited about new listings that come in and I try to be familiar with all of them, so that I'll automatically think of them when I'm talking with people. I do have my mother's voice whispering in my head sometimes though, nervous about working on all commission and knowing a deal can still fall apart at the last minute. I've already had that happen."

Caroline nodded. "There are ups and downs, for sure. Tessa is going through a down period where everything is falling apart for her. And you've been in a lucky streak. It happens to all of us."

Sophie smiled. "When I have those moments of doubt, I just remind myself of what Rick said, how I just need to always be moving forward and generating new activity, so that if a deal does fall apart, something else will take its place."

She sipped her wine and glanced at Max. "What about you? Do you love what you do? Could you ever imagine yourself doing something else?"

Max laughed. "No. I don't know what else I would do. I mean I suppose if my books stop selling I could always go back to bartending. I didn't hate that, and the money was pretty good." He reached for his wine. "What you said though about how real estate makes you excited and feels like what you are meant to do, that's how it is for me with the writing. I look forward to going to work and dreaming up stories. And I feel incredibly lucky that I get to do that for a living. And that people actually read my stuff."

"Lots of people," Caroline said with a smile.

"What about you, Caroline? How did you get into real estate? And do you love it?" Sophie asked.

"I kind of fell into it. My family has a real estate business, and I grew up working there in the summer. After I graduated college, I worked in Human Resources at a tech company, but I got bored with it after a few years. I worked at my parent's real estate firm again over the summer and realized it's what I wanted to do. But I wanted to be in the city."

When they were done eating, they put the leftovers in the fridge. They'd finished the bottle of Josh, so Max filled their glasses with Caymus and they settled in the living room. Caroline sat in one of the big club chairs and Max and Sophie sat on the sofa. They were close enough that she was aware of him next to her. He looked her way and smiled as Caroline clicked on the TV and found the recording of *Murders*.

"What do you think of the wine?" He asked.

Sophie took a sip and closed her eyes, savoring the rich flavor. "It's so good. Amazing."

"I thought you might like it," he said softly. He smiled and she noticed how warm his eyes looked and how there were the tiniest little lines around the corners. It gave his face some character and only made him more handsome.

The show came on and they were quiet for the next hour, sipping the delicious wine and relaxing. When the show ended, Caroline stood and stretched and yawned.

Sophie immediately yawned as well, and a moment later Max followed.

"I should probably head home. You two have to be up early." He stood and Caroline yawned again and they all laughed. "I'm so sorry. It must be the wine, and all that food," she said.

"Are you guys around next weekend? Or are you taking time off for the holiday?" Max asked. There was only one more weekend left before Christmas the following Friday.

"I'm here. I'll be finishing up my Christmas shopping," Caroline said.

"Me too. I was thinking about going ice skating maybe on Saturday. I saw the rink when I was doing some shopping last weekend. Would either of you be up for that?" Sophie asked.

"Not me. I don't skate. And I'm way behind on my shopping," Caroline said.

"It's been a while for me, but I'd be up for going. I think we can rent skates there. Might be fun," Max said.

Sophie was thrilled. She hadn't expected that Max would be up for it and had thought Caroline might be. "Great. I'm open anytime that afternoon."

Max smiled. "I'll text you and we'll pick a time. Maybe we'll get a bite to eat after?"

"Sure, sounds good." It sounded more than good. It sounded like an actual date, and Sophie was already looking forward to it.

CHAPTER FORTY-THREE

Sophie and Caroline headed out to the office early Monday morning. Both wanted to get in and get a head start on their week. The weekly sales meeting started at eight and they arrived a little after seven thirty. Just enough time to settle in at their desks, check email and grab a cup of coffee before heading into the conference room.

As usual, they went around the room and everyone gave updates and talked about new listings and upcoming open houses.

"Tessa, what's the latest on our big one? Any prospects? The clock is ticking hard. How much time do you have left?" Rick asked.

Tessa made a face. "A little over a week, and I've still got nothing. I've done several open houses this month but low traffic. There was interest, but so far, no offers. I'm still doing everything I can to generate a buyer. Please keep it in mind if you talk to anyone new."

"Will do," Rick said.

"Sophie, what do you have going on?" Sophie gave updates on her listings and mentioned her new buyer. "I think that's the closest thing to an offer. I showed him three listings on Saturday and we're looking at three today. I think he'll make a decision, and I suspect he's leaning toward Sue's listing as it is in the same building. If that closes, then he'll give me his unit to sell."

Rick nodded. "Good luck with that. He's the buyer you got off a mailing I think?"

"He is," Sophie confirmed.

Rick looked around the room. "Those mailings can really be worth doing. Sophie put the time in to build a list of local homes and I am always happy to pay for the mailing itself. Keep it in mind to keep your pipelines full." He grinned. "Okay, have a great week everyone!"

They all filed out of the room and went back to their desks. Ten minutes later, Sue walked over wearing a big smile and leaned against Sophie's desk. "Good news. Dan just called and he and Paula want to put an offer in on your listing."

Sophie was truly surprised. "Really? Wow. I didn't expect that."

"You and me both. But a few things they said gave me the sense that they were flexible. And once they saw that unit, they fell in love and didn't want to consider anything smaller. They will likely have a second child and this way they won't have to worry about moving again."

"Well, that's great news for a Monday morning," Sophie said.

"Do you have any other offers yet?" Sue asked.

"No, not yet. A few people seemed interested, but I haven't heard from their realtors yet."

"Okay, they are prepared to offer full asking price. They really want it and don't want to lose out. I think they were a little spooked by all the traffic at your open house. Dan's going to drop a check by this morning and sign the offer paperwork."

Sophie smiled. "That's awesome. If all goes well, it wouldn't surprise me if Russ wants to offer on their unit, too. He really doesn't want to leave the building if he doesn't have to."

"I thought his unit would be the one they would go for, I really did. But they don't even want to consider it now. Emily's unit is in a great location too, so they are pretty excited about it. I'll text you as soon as I have his deposit check and will email the signed offer letter over ASAP."

Caroline turned around and gave Sophie a high-five. "That's an awesome way to start your week!"

Tessa was also looking her way and had clearly overhead everything, but instead of commenting she turned back and got on the phone. Sophie almost felt a little guilty that things seemed to be going her way while Tessa was still struggling and if she didn't find a buyer very soon, she was likely going to lose her big listing.

Sophie finished up replying to emails and was about to head out for her first showing when a woman holding a big box stormed past the reception desk and into the main room where all the agents sat. Sophie's desk faced that direction so she saw her coming but couldn't see her face as it was blocked by the box she was holding. Evidently the woman could see her though as she stopped by Sophie's desk and then dropped the box onto it. It was Julia, Rick's ex.

"Sophie, right?" Julia said.

Sophie nodded wondering what she could possibly want from her.

"Here you go. He's your problem now. I don't care what you do with this stuff, but I wanted it out of my house." She spun around and walked off.

Sophie peeked into the box. It was filled with Rick's belongings, a few suits, toothbrush, shirts, ties and sweatpants. She glanced at Rick's office, and he was looking at her in horror. The bullpen was suddenly silent, and all eyes were on Sophie, and she didn't know what to say. Rick walked over and picked up the box.

"I'm so sorry, Sophie." He glanced around the room. "I apologize for the interruption. I haven't announced it but a few of you know that Julia and I recently broke up. Sophie last minute agreed to go with me to a charity networking event that Julia was going to attend until we ended things. She somehow got the idea that Sophie and I are dating, and I can assure you that we are not." He took the box into his office and stuck it in a corner, then sat at his desk and stared at his computer. After a moment, everyone resumed what they were doing.

"Well, that was certainly dramatic," Caroline said.

This time Tessa spoke up. "And very interesting. I didn't realize that they'd broken up either. I thought you'd just said she was out of town?" Her eyes were accusatory as if Sophie had deliberately misled her. Which in a way, she had.

"I'm sorry. Rick wanted to keep quiet about the

breakup. Maybe he thought they'd get back together, I don't know."

"I wouldn't say that looks very likely now," Tessa said.

And Sophie agreed. "No, it sure doesn't."

Sophie met Russ at the first listing address. The three properties were in the same area, both were on side streets off Fifth Avenue. Russ liked them both, they were perfectly fine one bedroom units. But she knew he was most interested in seeing the one in his building.

And when they walked in, a big smile spread slowly across his face. It was a sunny day, and the apartment had a huge window that faced Fifth Avenue and the Met and sunlight poured in, lighting up the whole room. It was about eleven hundred square feet with an all-white kitchen, that was small but efficient, a spacious living room with a dining nook. Russ walked all around the unit from the entry foyer to the bedroom and when he came back to the table by the window, his smile was even bigger.

"This is it. It's perfect. I love that I'll just be moving down a few floors. This unit has everything I need. And I'll be able to sock a little money away in the bank."

"Yes, you should be able to. I would guess around four hundred thousand at least," Sophie said.

Russ looked pleased by the number. He nodded. "That's about what I suspected. I've been looking at the recent sales data. So, I'd like to make them a good offer. And hopefully you can sell mine, too and we'll all be happy!" Russ was in a fantastic mood and Sophie was thrilled for him. He wrote out a check for the deposit and promised to read over the paperback and send it back by email right away.

"Are there any offers on it yet?" He asked somewhat nervously.

Sophie had asked Sue the same question earlier. "No, not yet. But there's a lot of interest and an open house scheduled for this coming weekend."

Russ frowned. "I don't want that to happen. How can I stop it?"

"If you were to offer asking price, they would most likely accept and cancel the open house. If you offer a bit less, there's a chance they will accept, but they might also want to hold off and see how it goes at the open house."

Russ thought for a minute. "Okay, I don't want to play any games. I'll give them what they want. The price seems fair based on similar recent sales."

Sophie agreed. She also knew the lower price points were the ones that were more in demand and more likely to have multiple bid situations. "It is. That is what I would recommend, Russ."

"Okay, here you go then." He handed her a check.

"I'm heading back to the office now and I'll get the offer paperwork over to you shortly," Sophie said.

When they stepped out of the apartment into the hall, Russ turned to head to the elevator and go up to his unit on the ninth floor. He'd said his goodbyes but after taking a few steps, he turned back, an anxious look on his face.

"Do I have anything to worry about? You think they will take the offer?" Sophie wanted to give him a hug and assure him that he had nothing to worry about. But she couldn't do that, and she knew that there was always the chance that a better offer might come in. But his odds were very good.

"I wouldn't worry just yet. I think your chances are excellent! We'll keep our fingers crossed for good news very soon."

CHAPTER FORTY-FOUR

Sophie called Sue on her way back to the office.

"What did he think?" Sue asked.

"He loved it and wants to make an offer. He's nervous that someone else is going to come along and get it. Does he have anything to worry about?" Sophie asked.

"Well, there is a good bit of interest, but no offers yet. It depends on how strong his offer is. If it's below asking, they will probably want to hold off and see what happens at the open house."

"That's what I told him. If he offers full asking, do you think that will get it done?" Sophie asked. She felt a bit anxious too. She wanted to make the sale, but she wanted Russ to get the home that he wanted.

"I'm pretty sure they will accept that. I'll call to let them know an offer is coming."

Five minutes later, Sue called back. "They're excited. They said if he offers their asking price, they will accept."

"Great!" Sophie finished the paperwork and emailed it off to Russ for him to review and electronically sign and return to her. Less than an hour later, she had the signed offer letter back and forwarded it to Sue.

And at a quarter to five, Sue walked in the office with a big smile. Caroline and Tessa were the only other two in the office. It was Tessa's afternoon to be the agent on duty and Caroline had just finished a showing and popped back in the office. Tessa was in Rick's office leaning against his desk and they were both laughing. It was the end of the day, and the mood was light.

"Congratulations! Russ just got his house," Sue said.

"Yay! I'll call him with the good news." Sophie made the call and Russ picked up on the first ring.

"You heard something?" He asked.

"You got it! Congratulations, Russ."

There was a long moment of silence and then a chuckle. "Well, isn't that something. Thank you, Sophie. You just made an old man's day. I'll call you next week and we can discuss having you see if you can work your magic and sell this place for me."

"I'd love that, Russ. Thank you!"

When Sophie ended the call, she looked up and saw Rick and Tessa had walked out of the office.

"I hear congratulations are in order," Rick said. "Go ring that bell. Both of you!"

Sophie laughed as she and Sue walked up to the giant bell on the wall and took turns ringing it. "I'll never get sick of that sound," Sue said.

"We should go for a quick after-dinner drink to celebrate," Caroline said. It was a Monday, and they almost never went out after work on a Monday, but it sounded like a good idea to Sophie.

"Did someone say after work drinks? Rick said. He grinned. "First round is on me. Let's go."

"Sue, can you come for a drink?" Sophie asked.

Sue quickly texted someone, and a moment later answered the question. "I'm in. Probably just for one though."

"Tessa? You coming?" Caroline asked.

Tessa glanced at Rick. "Come on Tessa, I think you're going to be next to ring that bell."

She smiled. "Sure, let's go."

They went to the closest bar, the place that Rick loved, and it was quiet. Mondays were quiet just about everywhere. They gathered around two cocktail tables in the bar and had the whole area to themselves. Sophie noticed that Tessa seemed in a better mood than usual. She was laughing and joking. She was also sitting next to Rick and Sophie also noticed a bit later, as they had a second round of drinks, that Tessa kept touching Rick's arm when she talked to him. Tessa was someone who talked with her hands, but Sophie thought her touching his arm like that was interesting. And Rick didn't seem to mind the attention. He was laughing and joking with her and the rest of them.

They stayed for a little over two hours. Sophie, Sue, and Caroline were all drinking red wine. Tessa and Rick were both drinking a good bourbon on the rocks. Sophie was starting to feel hungry but didn't want to stay for another drink. Sue checked the time and took her last sip of wine. "I have to run. Joe is waiting on dinner for me."

She opened her purse to take out some cash, but Rick waved her money away.

"Drinks are on me. Good job today, ladies."

"Thank you," Sue said. She smiled as she turned Sophie's way. "And I hope that's the first of many deals with you. Congrats to both of us!"

"Yes, hopefully the first of many," Sophie agreed. "I should probably head home too."

"I'm ready, too," Caroline said and looked at Tessa to see if she was going to join them. She still had almost a half a glass of bourbon left. Rick's glass was empty.

"I'm not in any hurry," he said. "If you want to take your time with that, I can order another."

Tessa nodded. "I'll see you guys later at home."

It was almost nine by the time Tessa got home. Sophie and Caroline were watching TV in the living room and Caroline raised her eyebrows at Tessa.

"So, is there something going on with you and Rick? I noticed some kind of vibe there."

Tessa shrugged. "Rick is always flirty like that. Not sure it means anything. Though he is a lot of fun. And I've always found him attractive," she admitted.

Caroline and Sophie exchanged glances. "Rick's a great guy, a lot of fun. Smart and successful—but he's also your boss. That might be kind of sticky. Not to mention he and his girlfriend just broke up because he didn't want to get married. I'd hate to see you expecting something that might not be possible," Caroline said gently.

"I don't want to get ahead of myself. I'm just having fun

for now and we'll see where it goes." Tessa yawned. "I'm off to bed."

"What do you think of that?" Caroline asked once Tessa was out of the room.

"I'm not sure. Maybe they'd be good for each other. Or like you said maybe it will be a hot mess."

"I guess time will tell," Caroline said. It was clear that she didn't think it was a good match, at all.

CHAPTER FORTY-FIVE

The rest of the week flew by. Sophie was so busy with new clients and showings from her existing listings. Neither Caroline or Sophie knew exactly what was going on with Tessa and Rick, but Tessa had been out late every day that week. They'd both been up when she came home the night before and she'd admitted that she'd had dinner and drinks with Rick.

"It was kind of a last-minute thing. We were both in the office and it was late. We went to an Italian restaurant that he loved, and it was really good. We split a bottle of wine and then lingered over coffee and dessert."

"Have you kissed him?" Caroline asked. Sophie loved that she was so blunt as Sophie was dying to know too but never could have asked Tessa that question.

Tessa frowned. "No, not yet. I thought it might happen last night, but it was just a romantic dinner, great conversation and then a goodbye hug. I figure he's taking it slow because we work together."

Caroline nodded. "That's probably it."

The next morning, Friday, they all headed into the office together, arriving a little before nine. Sophie settled in at her desk, opened her email and went to make herself a fluffy coffee. She had a lot of emails to go through and a few calls to make to confirm showings for that day and an open house for Sunday. She also had a call from a potential new buyer that had come in after hours the night before, and that was the first call she made. The voice message sounded like it was from an older woman. Her name was Charlotte Houston and before she placed the call, Sophie looked her up in the computer as it sounded familiar.

Sure enough Charlotte was one of the people that Sophie had emailed to introduce herself. She lived further down on Fifth Avenue. Sophie smiled as she dialed the number.

After two rings, Charlotte answered the phone and Sophie introduced herself.

"I sent a mailing out recently and had a voice message from you over the weekend. How can I help?"

"Sophie. Yes, I got your mailing and the one from your partner, Tessa. I called you first, but it went to your voice message." She must have called the main number. "Your partner Tessa's postcard said the two of you work together, so I gave her a call too, and she answered! I think she is coming to see me today at eleven. I'm looking forward to working with you both."

"Wonderful, I'll connect with Tessa. Quick question, are you looking to buy or to sell?"

"Just to sell. I'm going to be moving in with my sister in Florida."

"Perfect. Thanks so much, Charlotte."

"You're very welcome, dear. Will I see you at eleven, too?"

Sophie thought for a moment. "Yes, hopefully you will."

She ended the call and sat there fuming for a few minutes, unsure of the best way to handle a very awkward and annoying situation. Finally, she tapped Caroline on the shoulder.

Caroline spun around. "What's up?"

"Can we go talk privately for a minute?" Sophie spoke softly so that no one, especially Tessa, would overhear.

"Sure. Let's go in the front meeting room." They had several small meeting rooms near the front reception desk where they would meet with clients when they came into the office.

Sophie shut the door behind them and told Caroline about the call.

"She told the client that the two of you work together? That's so odd. Why would she do that?" Caroline asked.

Sophie had been wondering the same thing. "Maybe to cover herself in case someone said they had a mailing from both of us? That way she could still try and take the listing."

Caroline frowned. "That is so shady. She's never done anything like that before, as far as I know. I think she's feeling really desperate right now. I'm not defending the behavior at all. It's totally wrong."

"Right. So, what do I do? Do I just let it go?" Sophie felt sick to her stomach and stressed out about it.

"No. You can't let it go. That's a listing. Potentially thousands of dollars in your pocket and it came about because of your efforts putting the list together. She also called you first. You have to talk to Rick. If you just talk to Tessa, she's not going to hand that listing over."

"No, I don't imagine she will," Sophie agreed. She was not looking forward to the conversation with either Rick or Tessa. Things were already tense with Tessa, and this was only going to make it worse. Yet, it was also all Tessa's doing.

"Okay, I'll go talk to him now."

Sophie went back to her desk and looked in the computer again. They had a database where everything was documented. So, there was a time stamp when a contact was entered, and then any further activity was also date and time stamped. Charlotte was entered into the system by Sophie. And was then sent a mailing on the same day by Sophie and a few hours later, by Tessa. It seemed cut and dry to Sophie.

She took a deep breath and walked by Tessa's desk on the way to Rick's office. Tessa was typing an email and didn't even look up when Sophie walked by. Rick got off a call just as Sophie reached his door and he waved her in.

"What's going on Sophie, more good news to report?"

"Well, sort of but not exactly."

Rick leaned forward and put his elbows on his desk. "Have a seat and talk to me."

Sophie did as instructed and told him about Charlotte and the fact that both she and Tessa had mailed to her.

"Tessa reached her first and set up an appointment?" Rick asked.

Sophie nodded. "Yes, she did. But she had left a message for me, too."

"Hmm, but Tessa talked to her first. Sorry, Sophie, I think this goes to Tessa. Sometimes you win, sometimes you lose. You'll get the next one." His phone dinged with a text message and he glanced at it, typed something in response and then looked up. Sophie was still sitting there, fuming.

"Rick. There's more to it than that." She sighed. "Here's the thing. I spent a good chunk of the weekend making that list and adding the contacts into the system. And then I sent a mailing out to my whole list. But Tessa did too—to the list that I created."

Rick frowned. "What's her name again? Charlene something?"

"Charlotte Howell."

Rick typed the name into the computer and then frowned again when he saw that what Sophie said was true.

"Jeez, Sophie. This is a first. You talked to her too? Charlotte?"

"Yes, she told me that she'd tried me first, but called the main number. Tessa only had her cell phone on hers I guess, and she tried her next."

"And she thinks you work as partners? So, why don't you go to the meeting at eleven." Sophie nodded but was still unsure what that meant.

"Is Tessa going to go too? Are we sharing her?"

Rick shook his head. "No, you are not. I'm not going to

allow someone else to benefit from your hard work. That new client is all yours. On your way out, can you please tell Tessa to come and see me. I'll let her know what's going on."

"Will do. Thank you."

Sophie walked out of the room and stopped at Tessa's desk. "Rick wants to see you in his office," she said flatly. She'd pretty much had it with Tessa.

Tessa narrowed her eyes. "What's going on?"

"Just go talk to him." Sophie wasn't going to get into it. She went back to her desk and filled Caroline in.

"Good. I knew he'd do the right thing."

"He almost didn't, until I showed him the date stamps in the system. And he didn't seem very happy that Tessa did this."

"Maybe that will snuff out this romance before it even gets started," Caroline said.

"Do you think there was really anything there?" Sophie had her doubts.

"I don't think he'd be that obvious about dating someone that works here. I think he's just flirty and likes to go out for drinks, to be honest. I do think that even if it did go anywhere, she'd end up miserable because I don't see Rick settling down anytime soon. Though, maybe one day someone might sweep him off his feet. I don't think it's going to be Tessa, though."

Five minutes later, Tessa came out of the office, glanced Sophie's way and sat back down at her desk. Sophie had noticed that she looked flustered, and her lips were pressed together. She wondered if Tessa would apologize to her or just ignore the situation entirely?

. . .

Later that evening, Sophie had the apartment to herself. Caroline had gone to Ed's apartment for the weekend and Tessa never came home after work. Sophie had no idea what she was up to. Sophie was comfy on the sofa, watching a Christmas movie and sipping a cup of chamomile tea.

Just as she was about to head to bed, a little before eleven, the front door opened, and Tessa walked in. She stopped short when she saw Sophie, then sighed and shut the door behind her. She put her bag down, shrugged off her coat and walked over to where Sophie was on the sofa. Tessa sat across from her in one of the big club chairs.

"Listen, I owe you an apology. It was a shitty thing to do, and I am sorry. I don't have a good excuse. I just saw your notebook here with all those leads written so carefully and I'd just had everything fall apart. I felt like I was never going to close another deal again. So, I sent out that mailing. It was dumb and I don't know what I was thinking. I've just been in a bad place. But that's not a good excuse."

"Thank you. It's okay," Sophie said. "I know it's been a rocky time, but things will turn around for you."

Tessa smiled. "Yeah, I think they will. I might have a buyer for my big listing. I have a second showing for it tomorrow. If that happens, I'll feel like my rotten streak is over."

"I hope you get it. I really do." Sophie knew she'd never be close friends with Tessa, the way that she was with

Caroline. But she genuinely hoped things would get better for her and that there would be less tension between them.

"Thanks, Sophie. I appreciate that. I'm off to bed now." She stood and Sophie yawned and did the same.

"I'm right behind you," she said.

CHAPTER FORTY-SIX

It was lightly snowing when Sophie and Max headed out Saturday afternoon to go ice-skating. It was too far to walk so they took the subway to Bryant Park, where the Christmas Market was still going strong. They made their way to the skating rink and both had to rent skates.

"When was the last time you skated?" Max asked her.

Sophie laughed. "It's been over ten years, maybe longer. I used to love to skate when I was younger though. I even took figure skating lessons for a few years."

He looked intrigued. "Really? Can you do jumps and twirls?"

"Jumps definitely not. I might be able to spin a little. We'll see. What about you? Did you skate much as a kid?"

He grinned. "Does hockey count? Yeah, I was really into it for a few years in high school. Until I got checked hard and broke my collarbone. That ended my high school hockey career."

"Ouch! Have you skated at all since?"

"A little. A few of my college buddies were really into it

and we used to go skating sometimes and get a makeshift hockey game going. It was fun. That was ages ago, though."

They laced up their skates and carefully stepped onto the ice. Sophie felt a little unsteady at first. Especially when two young boys came racing toward her and almost knocked her over. Max reached out to steady her, and she found that she just needed that minute to find her footing. Skating came right back to her as she pushed her blades forward and then turned and skated backward and zig zagged back and forth. Max kept right up with her and as they came around the corner of the rink, a new song came on. It was the lively Christmas song, Frosty the Snowman.

Sophie noticed couples all around them holding hands as they skated to the music. She glanced at Max, and he winked and held out his hand. She took it and they skated around and around. It was festive and fun. They skated for close to an hour and just as they were slowing down the song All I want for Christmas is You started to play.

"One more song?" Max asked and she nodded.

He took her hand again and pulled her toward him as they skated around, and she twirled back and forth. When the song finally ended, he pulled her in again, held her gaze and then touched his lips to hers. It was a quick kiss, but Sophie felt it all the way to her toes. When the kiss ended, Max whispered, "You have no idea how long I've wanted to do that."

"Really? What stopped you?" Sophie teased him as they stepped off the ice and went to take off their shoes.

"Well, at first I just wasn't ready. I'd just broken up with Millie and even though I always found you attractive, at that point, I was just grateful to have you as a friend and neighbor. The more we spent time together, the more I found myself thinking and wondering. But I wasn't sure how you felt. I knew you were focused on getting your job up and running. And then Tessa told me you were dating your boss, which threw me a bit. I didn't see it. But then I realized she thought she was interested in me. She's a beautiful girl, but we have absolutely nothing in common." He grinned. "Even if I had been interested. I don't think that would have lasted. Recently though, I started sensing that maybe you might possibly be interested, too?"

Sophie nodded. "Quite possibly."

"Good! So, where to now? Are you hungry? I thought maybe we could head back and have dinner at the Italian place your aunt loved so much. I happen to like it, too and it's close to home."

"I'd love that."

They walked about halfway, enjoying the Christmas lights everywhere and the softly falling snow. They took the subway the rest of the way and had a delicious dinner at the Italian restaurant. They were greeted warmly by Tony at the front desk. He sat them at a table for two by the window that looked out on Fifth Avenue. Max ordered a good bottle of Italian Amarone for them to share and Sophie got her usual eggplant parmigiana with a meatball on the side and Max got the lasagna. They shared a piece of tiramisu for dessert before walking back to the apartment.

"It's still early. Do you want to come in and watch a movie?" Max asked.

"I do. I want to see how your tree looks all decorated, too."

Max opened the door and they stepped inside. Sophie walked into his office and Max flipped the switch that turned on the Christmas lights. The tree was small, but made the room look so festive. It had mini white lights, a green tinsel garland, red plaid bows and an assortment of ornaments.

"It's adorable," she said.

Max smiled and wrapped his arms around her. "You're adorable." He kissed her again, longer this time and Sophie felt a wave a sheer happiness. For the first time in a long time, she felt truly settled. She'd finally found a job that she loved and that she could be successful at. She was living in Manhattan, which had always been a dream and made some new friends. And now there was Max, too. They'd started as friends and now they were exploring a new romance and Sophie felt like all the pieces of her life were finally fitting together the way that they should.

EPILOGUE

"So, this used to be Aunt Penny's? I'm impressed," Max said as they sat on the outside patio of the Hamptons house that overlooked the ocean. It was a beautiful day, and her father was cooking up steak tips, burgers and dogs on the grill, while her mother chatted with her aunts, who were in town for the Fourth of July weekend with their husbands.

"I think my parents have fallen in love with it. Aunt Penny was smart to make them wait a year. They've been here most weekends and are planning to spend all of July and August here. My father will just work remotely and has been muttering about selling the Hudson house and moving here full-time."

They'd arrived earlier that day, driving out in Max's truck and Sophie took the day off to get an early start and miss some of the traffic.

"There's Caroline, coming up the driveway now,"

357

Sophie said. She got up to go welcome her and Max followed. Ed parked his black BMW SUV, and as soon as the car stopped, Caroline threw the door open and ran over to Sophie. She held her hand up and Sophie screamed. The oval diamond engagement ring was beautiful.

"Congratulations! I'm so happy for you," Sophie said. She thought that Caroline and Ed were great together. "Do you have any idea when you'll do it?"

"We're thinking almost a year from now, in June. I think this fall, when our year is up, I'm going to move in with Ed, so we can save some money and hopefully buy something together not long after we get married. But I can stay longer if you need me to?"

Sophie grinned. "I'll miss having you as a roommate, but you won't be far away. And I think I feel confident now that I'll be able to cover the monthly fees from my commissions." Sophie had been over the moon when she received her first commission check just after Christmas. And she'd been saving as much as possible since then, to have an emergency fund in case she hit a slow stretch with no closings.

"Good! And Tessa's wedding will be first, on New Year's Eve," Caroline said.

The save the date cards had come earlier that week. Tessa and Cody had reunited on Christmas Eve when he invited her to dinner and proposed. She'd moved in with him immediately. Caroline had been a little horrified that she was breaking her lease, but Sophie didn't mind. She thought of the old saying, 'Two's company, three's a crowd.'

She was much closer with Caroline, and it was definitely more peaceful once Tessa moved out.

And Sophie found that she got on better with Tessa once she was gone, too. She was less stressed out now that she was back with Cody and engaged. She was out of her slump at work too, once she found a buyer for that huge listing.

"You're next," Caroline said, once they were inside and Sophie was pouring them both a glass of chardonnay.

Sophie smiled. Things were going so well with Max, and she could see it moving toward an engagement possibly, but neither one of them were in a hurry.

"Maybe someday. I'm just really happy with how things are going now. It's actually nice having him right next door. We spend a lot of time together, as you know, but I like having my own place."

"Do you think you'll ever want to sell the apartment? Maybe move in with Max?" Caroline asked.

"Maybe he'll move in with me! We haven't talked about either option yet. Whatever we do though, I don't see myself selling it. Not anytime soon. I love it there. I feel like it's where I was meant to be," Sophie said.

Caroline held up her glass of wine and clinked it against Sophie's. "Cheers to that. And to many happy times ahead in your Fifth Avenue Apartment."

Max walked up behind Sophie and pulled her in for a quick kiss. He grinned. "I heard that last bit and couldn't agree more. Best thing that happened to me was when you moved in next door."

Sophie sighed as she looked around at her friends and family. Her life had changed so much in the past year. She lifted her glass again and made a new toast. "To Aunt Penny and her fabulous Fifth Avenue Apartment. Because of her, I made a new best friend, found my dream job, and fell in love with my next-door-neighbor."

Thank you so much for reading The Fifth Avenue Apartment. I hope you enjoyed it!

Next up is Nantucket Summer House followed by The Seaside Sisters.

ABOUT THE AUTHOR

Pamela M. Kelley is a USA Today and Wall Street Journal bestselling author of women's fiction, family sagas, and suspense. Readers often describe her books as feel-good reads with people you'd want as friends.

She lives in a historic seaside town near Cape Cod and just south of Boston. She has always been an avid reader of women's fiction, romance, mysteries, thrillers and cook books. There's also a good chance you might get hungry when you read her books as she is a foodie, and occasionally shares a recipe or two.

Made in the USA
Columbia, SC
24 November 2023

26991282R00219